W9-BSG-830

Doctor Death

Doctor Death

A Madeleine Karno Mystery

Lene Kaaberbøl

TRANSLATED BY
ELISABETH DYSSEGAARD

ATRIA BOOKS

NEW YORK   LONDON   TORONTO   SYDNEY   NEW DELHI

ATRIA BOOKS
A Division of Simon & Schuster, Inc.
1230 Avenue of the Americas
New York, NY 10020

Copyright © 2015 *Doctor Death* by Lene Kaaberbøl
Originally published as *Kadaverdoktoren* in Danish in 2010 by Modtryk.
Copyright © 2015 of English translation by Elisabeth Dyssegaard

First Atria Books hardcover edition February 2015

ATRIA B O O K S and colophon are trademarks of Simon & Schuster, Inc.

For information about special discounts for bulk purchases, please contact Simon & Schuster Special Sales at 1-866-506-1949 or business@simonandschuster.com.

The Simon & Schuster Speakers Bureau can bring authors to your live event. For more information or to book an event contact the Simon & Schuster Speakers Bureau at 1-866-248-3049 or visit our website at www.simonspeakers.com.

Interior design by Kyoko Watanabe

Manufactured in the United States of America

10 9 8 7 6 5 4 3 2 1

Library of Congress Cataloging-in-Publication Data

Kaaberbøl, Lene.
  [*Kadaverdoktoren*. English]
  Doctor Death : a novel / Lene Kaaberbøl. —First Atria Books hardcover edition.
     pages   cm
  Originally published in Danish with the title *Kadaverdoktoren* (København : Modtryk, 2010).
  1. Forensic pathologists—Fiction. 2. Fathers and daughters—Fiction. 3. Homicide—Fiction. 4. France—Fiction. I. Title.
  PT8177.21.A24K3313 2015
  839.813'8—dc23   2014044129

ISBN 978-1-4767-3138-4
ISBN 978-1-4767-3141-4 (ebook)

*To my sister Eva—with love and with admiration for the work
she does and the strength it takes to do it*

Doctor Death

I

February 23–March 20, 1894

I t is snowing. The snow falls on the young girl's face, on her cheeks, mouth, and nose, and on her eyes. She does not blink it away. She lies very still in her nest of snow, slightly curled up, with a fur coat covering her like a quilt.

Around her the city is living its nightlife, the hansom cabs clatter by in the cobblestone slush on the boulevard, just a few steps away. But here in the passageway where she lies, there is no life.

Her brother is the one who finds her. He has been to the theater with some friends, and then to a dance hall, and he is happy and lighthearted when he returns home, happy and a little bit tipsy. That is why he does not understand what he is seeing, not at first.

"Hello?" he says when he notices that someone or something is lying at the entrance to his family's home. Then he recognizes the coat, which is unusual: astrakhan with a collar of ocelot. "Cici?" he asks, because that is the girl's pet name. "Cici, why are you lying there?"

Only then does he discover why she does not blink and makes no move to get up.

"It is unusual," said the Commissioner to my father. "It is difficult to believe that it is a natural death, considering the circumstances, but there are no external signs of violence."

The young girl lay on a stretcher in the hospital's chapel. They had removed the fur coat, which was now hanging across the lid of the waiting coffin. Papa had turned the gas lamps all the way up in order to see as clearly as possible. The hospital had recently had its first electric lights installed, but the chapel had not yet seen such progress. Light for the living was more important than light for the dead, it was thought, and that was probably true. But it made my father's work even more difficult.

Beneath the cloak, Cecile Montaine was wearing only a light white chemise and white pantalets. Both were filthy and had been worn for a while. Her narrow feet were naked and bloodless, but there was no sign of frostbite. Someone had closed her half-open eyes, but you could still see why she was considered a beauty, with long black eyelashes, sweetly curved lips, a narrow nose, symmetrical features. Her hair was pitch-black like her eyelashes and wet with melted snow.

"Dear Lord," said the third person present in the chapel. "Oh, dear Lord." The hand holding the prayer book shook a bit, and it was clear that Father Abigore, the Montaine family priest, was in shock.

"Could the cold have killed her?" asked the Commissioner.

"It's possible. But right outside her own door?"

"No, that is not logical. Unless she died somewhere else and was later placed where her brother found her?"

"I think she died where she was found," said my father. "The clinical signs suggest as much."

They both stole a glance at the priest and refrained from discussing lividity while he was listening.

"Sickness? Poison?" asked the Commissioner.

"It is difficult to say when the family will not agree to an autopsy." My father bent over the girl and carefully examined the halfway open mouth and the nostrils. Then he straightened up. "Did she suffer from consumption?"

The Commissioner looked over at the priest, passing on the question. Father Abigore stood staring at the dead girl and did not realize at first that he was being addressed.

"Father?"

"What?" With a start, the priest focused on them. "Consumption? No, certainly not. When she left her school a few weeks ago, she was as sound and healthy as one could possibly expect of a young lady of seventeen."

"And why did she leave school?" asked the Commissioner.

"I must confess that we thought it was because of an unfortunate attachment she had made to a young man who disappeared at the same time. But now . . . Perhaps we have done her an injustice." His gaze was once again drawn to the young dead girl, as if he were unable to look anywhere else. "Consumptive? Why would you think that?"

"There is dried blood in the nasal and oral cavities," said my father. Suddenly, he leaned forward with a wordless exclamation.

"What is it?" asked the priest nervously.

But my father had no time to answer. He grabbed a pipette from his bag and quickly bent over the young girl's face again.

"What are you doing?" asked the priest indignantly and took a step closer. "You promised, nothing unseemly. Nothing undignified for the dead!"

"It is not undignified," my father cut him off. "But absolutely necessary. Move, you are blocking the light!"

My father later said that it was perhaps just as well that the family had insisted on having a priest present for the examination, because it was a miracle of God that he saw them in the poor light, and even more incredible that he managed to capture two in the glass tube of the pipette.

"What? What?" asked the Commissioner. "What have you found?"

My father shook his head. "I don't know. I have never seen anything like this before. But they look like some type of mites."

"Mites?"

"Yes." He held the pipette toward the Commissioner. "Do you see it? One is still moving."

The priest swallowed abruptly and held the hand with the prayer book in front of his mouth.

"But I thought you said she had not been dead for very long," said the Commissioner.

"Nor has she," said my father slowly, once again holding the glass up toward the light of the gas lamp in order to more clearly observe the pale minute creatures he had caught. "These are not carrion parasites. I think they lived in her while *she* lived and are leaving her now that she is dead."

Of course, I cannot know that this is precisely what occurred. I was not there. My father was reluctant to let me assist when he examined the dead. He said it could only hurt my reputation and my future—by which he meant my chances of marriage. For the most part, my father was a man of progress, absorbed by the newest ideas and the latest technology. But he was incomprehensibly old-fashioned on this particular point.

"It is bad enough that *I* engage in such activities," he had said when I tried to convince him. "But if it becomes common knowledge that I let my daughter assist . . . No, Maddie, it is out of the question. Out of the question!"

"I thought one was not supposed to let the limited horizons of others stand in the way of progress," I said. That was his standard argument when people called him Doctor Death, or accused him of desecrating the dead. Some of his living patients, especially the more well-to-do, had left him because they did not like the fact that his hands had also touched the dead. But every time the Commissioner sent for him, he went.

"The dead can no longer speak for themselves," he was in the habit of saying. "Someone needs to help them tell their story."

But this "someone" was not supposed to be me.

"This discussion is over," he said. And so I just had to wait at home with as much equanimity as I could muster until he and the Commissioner returned from Saint Bernardine in the early hours of the morning.

We lived on Carmelite Street, behind the old monastery and conveniently close to the Hospital of Saint Bernardine, where my father often worked. Ours was not a large house, in fact it was the narrowest on the whole street, but the second floor let out into the small rooftop garden my mother had created many years ago above what had then been the kitchen. Because it was so elevated, it received plenty of sun in the summer in spite of the taller buildings surrounding us. Right now all the bushes wore tall, powdered wigs of snow, and the small basin in the middle was frozen so solid that I feared all the goldfish might be dead. My toes were well on their way to joining them; I wriggled them inside my button boots to bring some life to them again, but I did not go inside. If I did, the two men in the salon would cease talking about Cecile Montaine, and I would not get to hear any more of the clinical details that I have just described.

Perhaps I now appear as cold as the snow that covered her body, but do not misunderstand me. I had all the compassion in the world for her family, and when I thought about how prematurely and inexplicably she had departed this life, tears sprang to my eyes. She was three years younger than me, and the realization that often seizes the living when they encounter death—*that might have been me*—felt more urgent than usual.

But feelings had no place here. In spite of my father's resistance, it was my plan to one day follow in his footsteps, and that meant I had to learn what I could *where* I could—including here in the rooftop garden with the door to the salon open just a crack.

"I will have to examine the mites tomorrow, in daylight," said Papa. "It is hopeless to attempt to determine what species they are now. It is not even certain that they have anything to do with the cause of death, but they did come from her nostrils, and my best guess is that she died from respiratory failure."

"She stopped breathing, you mean?" growled the Commissioner. "Is that not how we all die?"

"Most of us are lucky enough to die before we stop breathing, Monsieur le Commissaire, not the other way around. As you know perfectly well."

The Commissioner sighed and stretched his strong, robust legs.

"The family would like to have the funeral over with. And I

would like to have a cause of death before they are allowed to bury her."

"Tomorrow. Perhaps. If only I was allowed to look at her lungs . . ."

"Unfortunately that is out of the question, my dear friend. Her father will not permit it. And I cannot lawfully twist his arm, especially considering that everything until now suggests a natural, if peculiar, death."

"But that is reactionary and illogical!" my father exclaimed. "Think how much more we could learn, how many illnesses we could cure, and how many lives we could save, if only all corpses were professionally autopsied and examined. Or at least all *interesting* corpses."

The Commissioner set down his cognac glass and got up.

"That may be. But how would you feel if it was your own sweet Madeleine lying there?"

My father waved his hand dismissively. "It is not."

"But if it were?"

My father had risen as well. He was half a head taller than the Commissioner, but rangy and thin in the worn overcoat that he had not yet discarded.

"As long as the autopsy was performed by an experienced and dedicated scientist," he said with dignity, "I would allow it."

Upon which they shook hands.

Most young women would probably have run away screaming if they had heard their father declare that he would be willing to let an unknown man disembowel them for closer scientific examination. But I am not like most. I felt a small warm glow of pride out there in the cold.

In the chapel of Saint Bernardine's, Cecile Montaine lay lifeless and unmoving on her bier, as Father Abigore watched over her. He had dimmed the gaslights and had lit candles instead and was now on his knees praying next to the dead girl. In the weak light he could not see that more of the little pale white mites were crawling from her nostrils and mouth, across the white cloth that covered her, and toward the prayer book that he held in his folded hands.

It was fortunate that it was such a cold night, as the mites could not survive for long in the chill air. Most of them died quickly.

But not all.

"Clearly an arachnid," my father dictated. "With eight legs that are strongly developed in relation to the body size. The legs are eight jointed and have noticeable claws. The oral aperture is small, again relative to the size of the body and head. The abdomen appears flexible, as with ticks, which suggests a parasitic, possibly blood-sucking existence, but there is no chitin back shell, for which reason I postulate that the specimen can be classified as belonging to the soft mites . . ."

He broke off his recitation and stood up straight. There was a purposeful frustration to his movements.

"I don't know enough about parasitology," he complained. "Maddie, would you draw it? Then we might consult an expert— if we can find one."

"Of course, Papa."

I pulled my tall stool over to the microscope. For me it was immeasurably more absorbing to register bacterial life-forms and parasites than to reproduce the flower arrangements and *natures mortes* that Madame Aubrey's Academy for Young Ladies had considered appropriate subjects for the daughters of the bourgeoisie.

But the lessons in watercolor and art appreciation had given me a certain basic competence with pencil, pen, and brush—one of the few lessons from the academy that I had found useful in real life.

While I sat there in the sunlight streaming through the tall windows and drew mandibles and scaly legs with carefully measured accuracy—on a scale of 1:100 since the creature measured barely 2.4 millimeters—my father and the Commissioner conversed over the cups of coffee Papa had made with the aid of the Bunsen burner. My father had turned the former kitchen into his laboratory more than a decade ago, and we had never built a new one. It simplified our housekeeping quite a bit, for which I was grateful. Madame Vogler came in a few days a week to do laundry and housecleaning, and her daughter Elise did the rest—received guests, when any came, lit the stoves, aired the rooms, ran errands for us, and took care of the modest daily shopping we required. Beyond that we usually ate at Chez Louis, which was right around the corner.

"Mademoiselle Montaine disappeared on the third of February," said the Commissioner. "And since Emile Oblonski vanished at the same time, it was assumed that the young couple had eloped together. Which might of course be the case, but Cecile's fate places Oblonski's absence in a somewhat different light."

"Are you implying that he in some way is responsible for the death of our young lady?"

"I am implying nothing. Especially not while I still do not have a cause of death."

My father eyed the Commissioner.

"I have been denied even the permission to examine her unclothed body," he said. "How am I supposed to venture an opinion on a reasonably scientific basis?"

The Commissioner looked at the ceiling as if he could find an answer to his dilemma by deciphering its various paint flakes and soot marks. Finally he said, "Half an hour. Not a second more. No visible signs of the examination afterward and bring Madeleine with you, so that we may at least be said to have shown the proper respect, should we be discovered."

Yes! I thought triumphantly. Now he cannot continue to refuse.

My father's forefinger was tapping the table lightly with a tiny metronome-like sound. It was a sign of indecision, but this time I knew in advance what the result of his deliberations would be.

"Maddie, will you do us that small favor?"

"Of course, Papa."

The dead body is precisely that—dead. All life processes have ceased, the blood separates into its basic elements, the skin turns bluish and sallow, all secretions dry up. And still the body continues for a time to have an identity. It is a human being, not just a temporary collection of tissue, bones, and organs that have ceased to function. Cecile was still recognizably Cecile, and to undress the dead body was a strange and intimate act that disturbingly interfered with the dispassionate objectivity I was trying to maintain.

The silk of the chemise was soft and smooth except under the arms and at the back, where the salt of dried sweat had caked and stiffened the material. I folded it and the soiled pantalets carefully and set them aside, because when the examination was over, I would need to dress her again to meet the Commissioner's second demand—that after the fact there be no visible signs of what had taken place.

We don't lay the dead naked in their graves. We dress them, even if they are unlikely to need it. We see it as our duty, the last dignity we can give them, even though we know that the clothes will just rot with the body.

Cecile was naked now.

And still she appeared neither exposed nor desecrated in my eyes. Even in death there was a symmetry, a completeness to her that made it seem as if she were missing nothing except life. That absence hit me suddenly, so deeply that a tiny wordless exclamation escaped my lips.

"What is it?" asked my father. He stood together with the Commissioner just outside the half-open door and waited to be called in when I was done with the undressing.

"Nothing," I said. And then I saw something that did mar the body's symmetry. "That is . . . she has some marks on her. Some scars."

"Maddie, you are not supposed to examine her. Just to undress her."

"Yes, Papa. I have done that now."

The two men entered. I took my notebook and began to make notes while my father carefully and systematically described Cecile Montaine's corpse. Age and gender, approximate height and weight, state of nourishment (generally good but with signs of recent weight loss), hair color, eye color, and so on. Only then did he focus on the scars I had observed.

"Half-moon-shaped symmetrically opposed scars and bruises. Some quite faint and of an older date, others fresh and only newly healed. About half a dozen in all, primarily occurring in the region of the breasts, on the stomach, and on the inside of the thighs."

"They are bite marks, aren't they?" asked the Commissioner.

"Yes," said my father. "Some have been quite deep, others more superficial."

"An animal?"

My father shook his head. "I do not think so. A dog, for example, would leave a much more elongated configuration, with deeper penetrations from the canines. I think these are of human origin."

The Commissioner was not a man whose face mirrored his soul; he nonetheless raised one eyebrow.

"Are you telling me she was bitten, multiple times and over an extended period of time, by a human being?"

"Yes. That is what I have to conclude."

"Is this relevant to the cause of death?"

"Not directly. The lesions have all healed. But human bites can of course carry infection just as animal bites can, so an indirect connection cannot be ruled out."

I looked at the scars. Some were faded pale white lines now, others more garishly mauve and purple. Breasts, stomach, thighs. Not arms, shoulders, or neck. Only areas that would normally be hidden by her clothing. There was an unsettling intimacy and calculation to the damage.

"Is this something that has occurred voluntarily or . . . ?" The Commissioner did not finish his sentence.

"That is difficult to determine. But I can say this much—the pain must have been considerable."

The scars in no way solved the riddle of Cecile's death. They just raised more questions. Nevertheless, while I dressed her corpse, with some difficulty because rigor mortis had not yet dissipated, my father had no choice but to write out a death certificate that stated that her death was natural. Cecile Montaine had taken ill. She had died from her illness. And with that the case was officially closed.

On the day of Cecile Montaine's burial, the thaw set in. Heavy gray snow fell in sodden clumps from the branches of the elm trees along the wall facing Hope Avenue, and the paths were a slippery mess of slush on top of old crusts of dark ice. It was not just for show that the ladies clutched at the supporting arms of the gentlemen of the party—button boots, even with a sensible heel, were not suitable footwear under these circumstances. The sky was leaden, and showers of drizzling cold rain swept across the churchyard at regular intervals.

"For the trumpet will sound, and the dead will be raised imperishable . . ." Father Abigore did his best, but the words sounded hollow when one gazed down at the rain-filled hole into which Cecile's coffin had just been lowered. He sneezed violently and had to blow his nose into a big black-bordered handkerchief before he could continue.

Madame Montaine's moans came in surges, like the labor pains of an animal, and she seemed utterly oblivious of her son's meek attempts to console her. Every sob unleashed a chain reaction around the grave, especially from the four black-clad friends from Cecile's convent school. The largest of them, a pale blond girl whose black robe had originally been tailored to another, more slender figure, cried shrilly, on the edge of hysteria. One of the accompanying teachers placed a hand on the girl's shoulder, but that only made it worse.

Cecile's seven-year-old little sister was standing a bit closer to the grave, her eyes shiny with fright, her mouth half open; the bouquet she had been given to hold hung limply down her side like a bundle of herbs. No one seemed to notice her shocked stillness, nor did anyone think to calm or comfort her; they were all so caught up in their own sorrow or in the mother's more voluble grief.

Papa, the Commissioner, and I stood some twenty paces away

from the mourners, a space that was meant to signal respect for the feelings of the bereaved, but I feared it looked merely as if we wished to distance ourselves. However, once the graveside ceremony had been completed, Cecile's father, Adrian Montaine, approached. The rain dripping from the brim of his black chapeau made the fur collar on his long coat look like a drowned animal. His graying whiskers drooped around his broad jaw, burdened by moisture, and even in his eyebrows there were drops of icy rain.

"Gentlemen," he said, nodding briefly. "Mademoiselle."

He could not continue. His entire body leaned forward in search of an answer, but he could not pose the question.

"My condolences," said the Commissioner and held out his hand. "I am so sorry for your loss."

My father mumbled a similar sentiment. I know he meant it, but on so cruel a day it sounded as hollow as the priest's words of resurrection. Dead was dead. Cecile's body was degrading into basic elements. Physical processes were at work in it, but they were no longer life processes. The coffin suddenly appeared to be a futile barrier that prevented the juices from seeping away, merely prolonging the time it would take before the bare, white bones could rest quietly in the ground.

I might perhaps with a little effort believe that Cecile was with God. But the idea that her body would one day rise from the grave, living and eternally whole—this was more than my rational mind would allow me to accept.

Cecile's father did not look as if he had found any consolation in the ritual. His eyes were swollen, and the furrows on his face looked like wounds.

"I . . . ," he began and stumbled. He suddenly grabbed my father's arm. "I have to know . . . why."

My father cleared his throat.

"As far as we have been able to determine, your daughter died of respiratory failure."

Monsieur Montaine shook his head—not in denial but because the answer was so clearly inadequate.

"She was healthy," he said. "Then she disappeared. And when she came back to us, she was dead. Tell me how this could happen, Doctor Karno. Tell me *that!*"

Father Abigore had bid farewell to the rest of the bereaved. Madame Montaine stumbled away from the grave, supported by her son and an uncle. The four convent girls also left the graveyard as a group, accompanied by their two teachers. Through the wrought-iron fence, I caught a glimpse of a waiting coach, a black chaise with a hastily put up hood and a broad-shouldered man in the coachman's seat.

The priest came over, with his handkerchief still clutched in one hand and his prayer book in the other.

"Adrian," he said, "you have to go home now. Your wife needs your support, and so does your son."

"I cannot leave her," said Adrian Montaine. "Not yet, Father."

"You must," said Abigore with a sudden and sharp authority in his voice. "Go home and turn to your life and your loved ones. Cecile is safe with the Lord."

Cecile's father remained where he was, his mouth slack and open, his breathing troubled. His gaze wandered from my father to the priest and back again. Then he suddenly spun around in an awkward wobbling turn as if he were ill or intoxicated. With no word of farewell, he stalked away from us, past the grave and on toward the gate through which his living family had disappeared a few moments earlier.

"The poor man," said the priest. "He was here all of yesterday afternoon, watching them dig the grave. It was as if he needed to make sure they did it properly. Young Adrian Junior told me that he had not been home to sleep, just to change his clothes."

Abigore looked somewhat fatigued himself. His eyes were bloodshot and puffy, and seemed to water on their own. He dabbed at them with his handkerchief, snuffled, and sneezed again.

"My apologies," he said automatically. "I am afraid I am coming down with a cold. It is this horrific weather. Let us go inside. May I offer you a cup of tea?"

"No, thank you. We had better get home," said my father. "We just wanted to show our respect."

"Naturally. Perhaps another time?" He raised his prayer book as a gesture of parting. There was perhaps a degree of relief beneath the courteously offered invitation.

"He seems to be a good priest," said the Commissioner as we watched the stooped figure head to his residence with a not entirely dignified haste.

"At least he managed to get the father to go home," said Papa. "Those poor people. I suppose they are unlikely to receive an explanation for the girl's disappearance?"

"Not with our help, at least," said the Commissioner. "A natural death does not require further investigation."

My father shook his head. "Those poor people," he repeated. "But there you are. Nothing more we can do. Let us go home. Will you join us, Mr. Commissioner?"

"Delighted, dear friend. Delighted."

I noticed them just as we were about to leave. A scatter of tiny droplets of blood in the sunken snow. They were already losing their shape and becoming paler and fuzzier at the edges as they seeped into the collapsing crystals of the snow.

"Look," I said.

My father looked down at the crimson spots.

"Blood," he said. "Where did that come from?"

"It must be either from Monsieur Montaine or Father Abigore," I said. "It is fresh."

"Is it of any significance?" asked the Commissioner.

My father frowned. "Probably not," he said. "There is so little of it. A small scratch, perhaps?"

The gravedigger and his assistant were filling the hole that was Cecile's grave. The hiss of the spades and the wet, hollow thuds of snow and dirt hitting the coffin lid followed us all the way out into the avenue.

In the days following the funeral, spring crept hesitantly across Varbourg. The snow had melted completely, and hailstorms and bursts of brilliant sunlight alternated in confusing shifts. The daffodils that had poked their delicate green shoots up through the dirt looked as if they regretted it. One hardly knew whether to wear a straw hat or a winter cape. It was on just such a wet and fickle spring evening, six days after Cecile Montaine's burial, that Louis Mercier nearly made his life's greatest heist.

Louis Charles Napoleon Mercier was named after two kings and an emperor. His mother always told him, "Louis, stand up straight. You have nothing to be ashamed of. You are named after two kings and an emperor!" But Louis had long ago learned that this argument had no effect on the other children in his street or on Monsieur Le Baton at the factory. And certainly not on Grandmother Mercier, who took care of him.

His mother did not come home very often. Only on an occasional Sunday afternoon, and for Christmas and Easter and such.

In the past he believed her when she said it was to celebrate the Lord's holidays with him and Grandma, but now he knew that husbands stayed home with their wives on those days, which meant that there wasn't much money to be made.

Louis was not quite as proud of his mother as he had once been. But he still waited for her every Sunday on Place des Patriotes. And when he saw her get off the streetcar and straighten her skirts a bit before searching the square for him . . . in those moments, he still felt all warm inside. She was so beautiful, even when she was tired and her features a little too sharp, even on the days when it rained and the careful lines of kohl became fuzzy at the edges and made her eyes startlingly large and carnival-like.

On the street he had gradually learned to size people up. He knew who was likely to tip him if he carried a bag or held an umbrella and who would just chase him away. He also knew who would be a good mark for Mouche and his gang, and sometimes got half a sou for pointing out a potential victim, even though he still hadn't dared to stick a hand in any pocket that wasn't his own. This hard-won ability was also why he knew that his mother was not the elegant lady he had once thought she was. He could not prevent his assessing gaze from noticing the cheap quality of the fabric of her dress, the worn, crooked heels of her boots, the grayish tint to the gloves that had been washed too many times with poor-quality soap. He saw as well that her makeup could no longer completely hide the age sneaking up on her. He could not *help* seeing it, though he would have preferred not to.

That Sunday she did not come.

He had waited until long past noon to be absolutely sure. But when the 3:10 had come and gone without letting her off at the Invalides monument, he had to face the fact that he had waited in vain.

Anger and misery roiled within him. He felt a pressure building up that he did not know what to do with. He was hungry and had not eaten since breakfast, but still he could not make himself go home to Grandma, could not stand to hear her say, "So, she did not come? She probably had better things to do." Or, "Yes, she is always so busy, your mother. So *very*, very busy," as she did on all the Sundays when his mother did not come, always in the same bitter, accusing tone. She could never take the money Maman gave her without sour insinuations about where it came from, and yet her gall was even blacker when it did not appear.

In the park behind the monument, he found a half-eaten winter apple that someone had dropped or thrown away. He brushed the gravel off and ate it. The shops along Third Boulevard were closed, so there were no errands he could run. Too bad—he was good at that. He could stand up straight and look people frankly in the eye with a polite "Yes, monsieur" or "No, madame" so that they occasionally said, "You look like an honest boy" and felt confident that he would not just disappear with the money.

At last he headed in the direction of Espérance. Day-old bread and frequently also soup were distributed every Sunday behind the church, but still he did not go there very often. There was something about the way they looked at you, those old harpies from the charity. Their mixture of pity and self-satisfaction was hard to take. I was named after two kings and an emperor, he thought as he tried not to hang his head. No one is entitled to look down on me!

He could also have gone home. Sure, he could. If he had been willing to listen to Grandmother Mercier's snide remarks about his mother, in order to get a piece of bread with lard and salt and a small mug of beer. It was only when his mother was there that Sunday dinner was something special. And today, the menu would probably include a smack on the head because he was so late. It made the charity aunties' condescending self-satisfaction look almost bearable.

"Boy! Yes, you!"

The quiet but authoritative call came from a tall, broad-shouldered man who stood leaning against the churchyard fence, under one of the tall elm trees. Next to him, on a leash, sat a big rough-coated dog. Louis looked at it with a certain caution—he had occasionally found that some people thought it was entertaining to set their dogs on street children, in earnest or "for a bit of sport." In fact, he was looking more at the dog than at the man, which was probably a mistake.

"Can you tell time?"

"Yes, m'sieur." Louis stood up straight but still looked more at the dog than the man. It had pulled back its upper lip so that you could see its gums. He had a feeling it did not like children.

"Are you a man of your word?"

The gentleman's hat was pushed down onto his forehead, and a gray silk scarf hid most of his lower face so you could really see only his eyes.

"Yes, m'sieur!"

"Very well. Then I have a proposition for you." The gentleman held out two coins. One was a twenty-five centime, which was a considerable amount of money. But the other . . .

"What kind of proposition, m'sieur?" said Louis, who could not stop looking at the other coin. A round shiny franc. A whole franc!

"When the clock up there"—the gentleman pointed at the Espérance church bell tower—"when it reaches eleven fifteen, then you must knock on the green door over there and deliver this message."

"To the priest? But . . . that's so late, m'sieur. Perhaps he will have gone to bed by then."

"Then you will have to keep knocking until he gets up. Not a moment before, is that clear?"

"Eleven fifteen, yes, m'sieur."

"Here is the first part of your payment." It was the twenty-five centimes, of course. "You will get the other half when we meet here again—but that will not be until one in the morning. Can you manage that? Or do you have a mother who does not want you to be out that late?"

Grandma would carry on, scold, and maybe hit him if he did not come home before she went to bed. But it wouldn't be the first time he had stayed out all night, and there was a whole franc at stake.

"No problem, m'sieur. You can trust me."

"I am counting on that. Adieu, my friend."

He spent the twenty-five centimes on a paper cone filled with roasted potatoes and garlic sausage ends, a specialty you could buy from Dreischer & Son on Rue Marronier. Ordinarily he would not have used all the money at once like that, but there was more to come. When the church tower clock struck the first toll of the quarter hour, he knocked on the door to the priest's residence behind Espérance with the note held tightly in his left hand. It took a little while for anyone to answer, and it was not the priest himself but his housekeeper, who eventually came to the door with her hair poking out in disarray from beneath her cap and a big black shawl around her shoulders.

"What do you want?" she asked in an unfriendly tone, blinking her narrowed eyes.

"A message, madame. For the priest. I was to say it was important."

The last part he came up with himself, but it *had* to be important when someone would pay that much money to have the message delivered.

She took it and shut the door in his face, with only a quickly mumbled "Thank you." Just as well that someone else was paying him for his trouble!

He sat down with his back against the church wall, in the shelter of a large bush that provided a bit of protection from the wind as well as partly hiding him from curious passersby. A little later he saw the priest emerge, mount a bicycle, and drive away, with some hollow coughs and an irritated exclamation when one pedal slipped beneath his foot.

Louis smiled. Now all he had to do was wait for his big reward. It had been a good day after all.

Early the next morning, Arturo Udinese received a shock that gave him indigestion. "Shocking, shocking," he repeated several times to his wife while he calmed his nerves with a cognac.

Mr. Udinese was the proprietor of a modest but popular brasserie just off July the 14th Boulevard, not far from the Varbourg East railway station. His customers consisted primarily of regulars, a builder or two, a few accountants, an occasional civil servant, and three or four retired officers from the nearby Veterans' Home—all solid people who appreciated good food at reasonable prices. Mr. Udinese was therefore in the habit of buying his ingredients as cheaply as possible, which was the reason he got up this morning a bit after five, while darkness still hung heavily over the town, and made his way to the rail yard behind the station, where he was met by a track worker known to most people simply as the Shovel. The two men walked together across the tracks to a train

that had arrived from Stuttgart a bit after nine the previous evening. In the course of the evening, it had been emptied and loaded and was now ready to depart for Paris at six fifteen.

"And these are decent wares?" asked Mr. Udinese.

"First-class quality," the Shovel assured him. "The entire first car is going directly to Hôtel Grande Duchesse."

A number of bills changed hands, and the Shovel opened the sliding door—not to the Grande Duchesse's wares, but to car No. 16AZ, number three in the lineup.

Mr. Udinese climbed into the boxcar. The Shovel handed him the guttering kerosene lantern that served as their only source of illumination. The lantern light flickered across stacks of wooden crates, piles of sacks, and rows of hanging carcasses. Great blocks of sawdust-covered ice kept the temperature at a level that was several degrees lower than the outside, even now in the morning chill. At one end of the car hung the halved or quartered cadavers of several full-grown steers, some pigs, and some lambs, while the plucked and skinned bodies of smaller animals like chickens and rabbits were packed with crushed ice into large wooden crates, a dozen to each one. The rough wooden floor of the boxcar was stained by dark puddles of blood, melted ice, and wet sawdust.

"Those twelve." Mr. Udinese pointed at a box of plucked cockerels. "And a veal shank, and one of the lambs." He moved farther into the car to find what he wanted.

"You can't have all twelve," said the Shovel. "What about six cocks and six hens?"

"How do you expect me to serve breast of cockerel in thyme sauce with just six cockerels?"

"Not all twelve," insisted the Shovel. "The overseer is no more stupid than the next man."

Mr. Udinese straightened up and looked sternly at the Shovel. "Sir," he said, "there are other suppliers."

"Not at this price," said the Shovel. "Make up your mind. It will soon be light."

Mr. Udinese sighed. "Fine, then. I suppose I will have to make a fricassee instead. Six cocks, six hens."

He pushed aside a couple of quartered steers to make more room, hung the lantern on an empty meat hook, and raised the lid on a big crate that according to the label contained twelve soup hens.

It did not. The doubled-up figure of a man had been crammed into the box in a squatting position, and most of the body was covered with flakes of crushed ice. The extreme angle of the head revealed a closely shaved gray nape and two large waxlike ears, and you could see a red line where a collar had habitually rubbed against the base of the skull. The collar in question was a Catholic priest's dog collar, and it was this, more than anything else, that enabled Mr. Udinese to recognize the man in the crate. His hand moved automatically in the sign of the cross.

"Sweet Jesus," he said. "It's Father Abigore!"

About an hour later, Father Abigore's lifeless body was lying on a pallet in an unheated storeroom between the freight train yard and the railroad station. Rigor mortis had set in while the body was still in the soup-hen crate, and it had not been possible to straighten the priest's sharply bent limbs without considerable use of force. Consequently, he was lying on his side now, curled up like a fetus in its mother's womb, with his head pressed down against his chest. There were still flecks of ice in his hair.

Dawn had arrived, and in spite of the corpse's position, one could see that the temple, the cheekbone, and the left eye socket had been hammered flat with a violent blow.

"Suspicious death," the Commissioner noted. "Presumably murder. What do you think, Doctor?"

"It is hard to imagine that so considerable a lesion can have been caused by a fall or some other accidental occurrence. He was hit with an object more than twenty-five centimeters wide. My guess would be that he has been felled with a shovel or a spade, not with the edge but with the flat side of the blade—a coal shovel, perhaps? There seems to be some sooty residue in the wound. There was a great deal of power in the blow."

"So we can call it homicide?"

"Everything suggests as much."

The Commissioner nodded. "Then I will have to inform the préfecture. The chief constable will not be happy. A murder, and of a priest to boot. Can you give us a time of death? An approximation will do for now, for the purposes of the certificate, but Inspector Marot, or whoever will be in charge of the investigation, will no doubt soon be pressing you for a more precise estimate."

The Commissioner had no jurisdiction over the police investigation. His job was merely to determine and attest the cause of death, and his authority went no further than the inquest. But all of Varbourg's dead were under his jurisdiction. He was Le Commissaire des Morts—the Commissioner of the Dead.

"Rigor mortis is extensive but not complete. When was he found?" my father asked.

"A little after six. In a boxcar that was inspected at one ten last night according to the stationmaster's log book. At that point there were no corpses except those of the slaughtered animals."

"Hmmm. Then I would think that he must have died no earlier than eleven thirty last night. It would not have been possible to place him in the box if rigor mortis had already set in. On the certificate, you may write between eleven thirty and two thirty, but in my opinion death must have occurred in the hour after midnight."

The Commissioner grunted and made a note in his little black book.

"Who would smash in the head of a man of the cloth?" he said. "And this one in particular? There are much more disagreeable priests."

"He did seem both compassionate and conscientious," concurred Papa. "And why arrange the body in such a bizarre way?"

"To hide the crime, presumably. The murderer had good reason to assume that the train would depart for Paris according to plan, that is to say at six fifteen, so that the corpse would not be discovered until much later and in another city. That would have made the investigation considerably more difficult. Merely identifying the good pastor would presumably have taken several days."

"But it would have been discovered eventually. There must be more effective ways of disposing of a corpse."

The Commissioner nodded. "Normally they just throw them in the river. What do I know? Maybe it was too far to carry the body. Could the killing have occurred in the boxcar?"

"Perhaps, but unfortunately I do not know a method by which one can determine how much blood came from the animals and how much is poor Abigore's. I would have expected spatters on the surroundings, not just blood on the floor. In my opinion, the boxcar is not the scene of the murder."

The Commissioner growled, a short, unhappy sound. "Well. We will have to leave that to the police investigation."

That clearly did not suit him, and my father permitted himself a small smile.

"You prefer to be closer to a solution before you let go of a case," he said.

The Commissioner growled again. "I hate homicide," he said.

"If some poor soul has died of pneumonia, then we know the cause. He was taken ill, and he died. And if the family wishes to know why, I can ask them to direct their questions to the Almighty. With homicide, it is different. There is such an unsatisfactory distance between the *cause* of a death and the *reason* for it. To know how is not the same as to know why. If someone asks, Why did Father Abigore die? I shall have to direct them not to Our Lord but to Inspector Marot, in whom I have nowhere near the same degree of faith."

Nevertheless, he immediately thereafter sent a message to the préfecture, as his position required.

"Can we bring him to the chapel of his own church?" he asked my father.

"Why not? He might as well lie there as in the morgue at the hospital."

"Good. Then let us get him home."

It was not yet possible to maneuver the corpse into a coffin, so Father Abigore lay on his humble stretcher in the public hearse, covered by only a simple shroud.

"May we offer you a ride, Doctor?" asked the Commissioner.

My father consulted his pocket watch. "Yes, please. I can walk from Espérance to the hospital."

The hearse was no stately funeral coach; there were no up-holstered seats or other comforts. Its unadorned, boxy body was lined with lead, partly to make it easier to clean, partly to lessen the smell when it was necessary to transport what the Commissioner prosaically called "late arrivals"—corpses found in the more advanced stages of decay. Of course, the lead lining increased the wagon's weight considerably, so on this mild March morning it was pulled across the wet cobblestones by two solid Belgian draft horses. Hooves the size of buckets, muscles that made each mouse-gray rear end about a meter wide. Progress was steady, but not quick. My father might have chosen a faster hansom cab, in which case much would have been different. But he did not.

It happened right by the embankment where the new promenade had just been established in the fall. The spindly linden trees planted at regular intervals along the river were still so young that they needed the support of their wrought-iron stands. At this time of day the wide walkway was empty because no society lady worth her lavender tea had begun even to think about rising from bed, and the working women hurrying across the Arsenal Bridge toward the power looms of the textile factory had neither the time nor the inclination to go for a leisurely stroll.

A dog came running along the riverbank, a very big dog, rough coated and brindled, with pointed ears. Its tongue was lolling out of its mouth, and it was not jogging, it was flat-out racing, heading directly for the hearse and the horses.

"What—?" said the coachman, who sat on the box next to my father and the Commissioner. That was the next-to-last word he spoke in this life. The dog launched itself at the nearside Belgian in a long, rising leap and closed its jaws around the muzzle of the horse. The animal screamed and threw up its head, both horses careened to one side and reared up, jerking the coachman half out of his seat as the heavy wagon teetered and only slowly recovered its equilibrium. The dog could no longer be seen from the wagon, but from the bite marks on the flank and groin of the horse it was later determined that it had continued its attacks from below.

Belgian horses are known for their stoicism, but this was too much. With an ominous creaking of swingletree and traces, they threw themselves forward. The coachman had let go of the reins with one hand to haul himself back onto the box, but this new and more violent jerk flung him first into the air and then down between the horses and the wagon. One of the Belgians lurched into the other with such force that they both began to slide down the embankment. The wagon hit one of the trees of the promenade with a splintering crash, keeled over onto one side, and was dragged for almost fifty meters by the panicked horses. By then, both my father and the Commissioner had long since been thrown from their seats. The Commissioner rolled down the embankment's grassy slope and miraculously escaped with minor bruises. Papa was less fortunate. He was briefly caught—fortunately not under the carriage's heavy lead-lined body but under the box's somewhat lighter wooden construction. When he attempted to sit up, he noted that both the radius and ulna in his left arm were broken, and a fracture of the tibia was quickly confirmed as well. In other words, he had broken both an arm and a leg.

The coachman had the worst of it. He survived, but one of the Belgian's enormous iron-shod hooves had connected so violently with his head that he never regained the power of speech. Only one word occasionally escaped his lips, randomly and without any connection to what was being said and done around him.

That one word was "devil."

Papa flatly refused to be hospitalized at Saint Bernardine's. He ordered two of the ambulance drivers to see the injured coachman off to the hospital with great speed, then directed the third to set and splint his own fractures, after which he allowed himself to be transported back to Carmelite Street in an ordinary carriage.

His face was drawn and pale. I am deliberately avoiding the term "pale as a corpse" because there *is* a difference, but worryingly pale, all the same, and glistening with the perspiration brought on by severe pain. The hansom cab driver literally had to carry him up the stairs to the salon. Fortunately, the driver Papa had hired was quite a big man.

"What happened?" I asked, between clenched teeth.

My father did not answer. He was busy groaning. The coachman had to explain about "the accident with the carriage," and it was not until later when the Commissioner came to check on the patient that I got the whole story.

"The beast must have been crazed," he said of the dog that had attacked them. "It must have been rabid. Healthy dogs do not behave that way."

"Did they catch it?" asked my father. "Has it been put down? Can we examine it?"

"No," said the Commissioner. "It disappeared. We have three riflemen patrolling the area, and we have distributed leaflets. But so far no one has seen it."

"Get ahold of Pasteur's vaccine," said my father. "Make sure you get plenty. It is a cruel disease."

The Commissioner nodded. "We have sent word to the Institute in Paris," he said. He sat on the edge of the plush-covered mahogany armchair that he preferred. He had not relinquished his hat but sat turning it in his hands, seemingly undecided whether to stay or go.

"May we offer you some refreshment?" I asked, because I wanted him to stay. It was easier to extract details from him than from my father. "Cognac? Coffee? A glass of wine?" I knew better than to offer him tea.

"I probably should be getting on . . . ," he said.

"Presumably the search for the dog is not within your jurisdiction?" I asked.

"No, but the . . ." He interrupted himself. "No, I have to go. I will come back later."

"What is it?" asked my father, who like me had noted the Commissioner's unease. "Is it the coachman? Is he dead?"

"No," said the Commissioner. "They say he will probably live."

"What, then?"

The Commissioner got up abruptly. "I have no wish to tire you," he said.

"And you do not. You are, however, making me very impatient, and that is not good for my health. What has happened?"

The Commissioner shook his head. "It is Father Abigore. Or rather his earthly remains. They have disappeared."

"Disappeared?"

"Yes. Someone used the confusion after the accident to abscond with the body. We have not yet been able to determine who or how, to say nothing of why."

My father blinked a few times, a sign that his thoughts were racing in close succession through his head.

"There must be something," he said. And repeated it, loudly and with frustration: "There must be something!"

"What do you mean?"

"From the murderer's perspective. Can't you see that? We found the body too soon. It was not supposed to have been discovered until Paris. And now he has taken care of that by abducting the dead priest. And that means . . ." He attempted to sit up but found it difficult. "It means that there must be something about that corpse. Something I missed!"

His eyes were glistening and his breathing was labored. He had taken some laudanum drops for the pain and was not used to their effect. Even though he could appear delicate, with his naturally slender body and his slightly stooped posture, he was seldom sick and apparently was not harmed by physical exertion or the long hours he habitually worked. He took his own good health for granted and did not accept the helplessness of being a patient with good grace.

"Papa," I said. "Please be careful. Lie down."

"That corpse must be found," he said, pointing at the Commissioner with his good hand. "And as soon as you find it, you must inform me. Without delay. Do you understand?"

He would never have spoken to the Commissioner in this peremptory manner if he had been himself. I think the Commissioner understood that. He placed a calming hand on my father's bony shoulder.

"My dear friend," he said. "Of course. Now lie down and await events. I am on the case."

Out in the hall I helped the Commissioner into his coat and handed him his cane and gloves.

"Sweet Madeleine," he said. "Take care of him. He is not well."

I almost began to cry. I had not cried when the coachman arrived carrying Papa nor when I understood how badly he was injured. But now the tears burned behind my eyelashes, and I had to bow my head to hide them.

"I shall," I said, and wished right then, in a moment of weakness, that there was someone to take care of me.

Perhaps now is the time to mention my mother. We might as well get it over with. She died when I was ten years old, of cholera. There. I have said it, and we do not need to discuss it any further.

At first my father lay on the chaise longue in the salon, but it was not well suited as a sickbed, so I asked our neighbor, Monsieur Moulinard, and his strapping son to carry Papa's own bed down from his bedroom. It would have been easier to carry Papa up to a bed than the other way around, but he would not hear of it. I think he found the thought of increasing the physical distance to the laboratory unbearable, even if he was at present incapable of making the short trip from the bed through the service pantry and down the kitchen stairs.

The salon, never particularly spacious, was now decidedly cramped. One had to edge around the tea table and the book cabinet, and any touches of bourgeois elegance the room might once have had evaporated entirely under the influence of pillows, bedpans, hot-water bottles, and all the usual paraphernalia of the invalid. It felt utterly wrong to see my father bedbound like this, with the distant, sweaty, damp expression the pain and the laudanum drops gave him. It made me feel uneasy.

"Should I get another pillow?" I asked.

"No, thank you," he said.

"Do you think you could sleep a little?"

He looked at me. "It is four o'clock in the afternoon."

"Yes, but . . ."

"I have a broken leg, Madeleine. I have not lost my mind. There is a copy of *Médecine Aujourd'hui* on my bedside table. Perhaps you would care to fetch it."

I fled up the stairs.

I did not enter my father's bedroom very often. Elise made the bed and did the cleaning, and my contact with him usually did not commence until he, fully dressed, shaved, and hair neatly brushed, came down to join me for breakfast. It made me hesitate for a moment on the threshold as if I were about to invade a foreign territory.

The journal was indeed lying on the bedside table next to the photograph of my mother. At first glance one might think it a wedding picture. My mother was dressed in white and seated in an armchair, while my father stood half a step behind her and held one of her hands. Only when one looked more closely did one see that her head was supported by pillows and still drooped a little bit to the right, against my father, and that her eyes were closed. I, or a pale and very frightened ten-year-old version of me, had withdrawn as far into the background as the photographer would permit.

The day the picture had been taken was missing from my memory. I *had* been there; anyone could see that. But I could remember almost nothing. Only Aunt Desirée combing my hair with water and braiding it with decisive hands, and putting powder on my face, which I had never tried before, all the while murmuring, "Poor child, oh, my poor child."

I stared at the picture for a few seconds without touching it. Many people exhibited their mourning portraits more ostentatiously. Madame Vogler, for example, had a picture of Elise's father in his coffin proudly placed on top of the sideboard in the parlor, but I was glad this one was not in a place where I would have to see it every day. I probably ought to have brought it downstairs with me, so that my father could have it by him—it was the only photograph of Maman that we had—but I could not make myself.

People who knew my mother always say that I look like her. I have her narrow nose, her prominent, not entirely feminine eyebrows, her blue eyes. My hands are like hers, too, long and narrow, with slender fingers. Her hair was darker than mine, but ten years of sunlight had bleached and yellowed the photograph so the difference was erased, and because she had been placed sitting, you could not see the difference in height. *Une petite*, Aunt Desirée always said about her, and when my own body unexpectedly shot up so that even as a fourteen-year-old I was only ten centimeters shorter than my lanky father, her disappointment was palpable.

We never spoke of my mother. Never. But she was there on the bedside table nonetheless, and in spite of everything the photographer had done to make her look alive, what we were posing with, Papa and I, remained a corpse.

"Maddie!"

My father was calling me from the salon. I grabbed the journal, turned my back on the picture of my dead mother, and hurried down the stairs.

In spite of the laudanum drops, he slept badly that night, and I, who had settled on the chaise longue so that I could help him if necessary, slept even less.

The next morning I sent Elise Vogler to the boulangerie and made tea for both of us by the fireplace in the salon. Papa looked terrible. There were deep shadows under his eyes, deep furrows around his mouth, and his skin tone was so alarming that I feared internal bleeding.

"I am going to send for Doctor Lanier," I said, referring to his orthopedically interested colleague at Saint Bernardine. "When he hears it is you, he will no doubt come right away."

"Absolutely not," said Papa. "I feel fine. Lanier has more important things to do. Besides, you are going to Heidelberg."

"I am *what?*"

"You are going to call on August Dreyfuss. He is professor of parasitology at the Forchhammer Institute, and I am sure he will be able to identify the mites for us."

"Mites," I said. "Who can think about mites now? I can't leave you!"

"Of course you can. Elise will take care of me. We will send a telegram to Professor Dreyfuss, so he knows you are coming. You can leave this very morning."

And so it was. In his laudanum haze, my father had convinced himself that there was a connection between the brutal killing of Father Abigore and Cecile Montaine's death. He was so tormented by the notion that he had not examined Abigore with sufficient diligence that I finally agreed to his request, even though it pained me to leave him in Elise's care. She was sweet and helpful, but she would not be able to stand up to him if he should suddenly decide to get out of bed.

The Forchhammer Institute was situated close to Heidelberg University's library behind St. Peter's Church. It was a large, newly built yellow brick building with a generally plain exterior that made the classical columns along the front look oddly pasted on.

"The professor has been waiting for you," said the terrifying concierge who showed me to his office, and there was no mistaking the reproach in her tone and choice of words. She was dressed completely in black, and in spite of her relative youth—she must have been in her midthirties—one got the clear impression that she was wearing widow's weeds.

Perhaps her hostility was simply due to the fact that I was French. Even though the last shot in the Franco-Prussian War had been fired several years before I was even born, there was still a great deal of bitterness on both sides, and it was only seven years since the Schnaebelé Affair had almost ignited a new conflict between the two countries.

"I am sorry," I said with my most careful German pronunciation. "We were delayed in our departure from Strasbourg." I overcame a desire to smooth both my hair and my clothes and hoped the professor was less irritable than the Black Widow.

My German is very good—Varbourg is, after all, more or less bilingual, even though the French authorities prefer not to admit it—but I had to search a little longer for the words I needed, and right now I could have done without that handicap. As it was, I felt sufficiently hampered by my sex, my age, my not particularly elegant traveling suit, and the fact that I was here to ask the important man a favor.

"This way," said the widow and led me down a long corridor made bright and modernized by the daylight that came flooding in through an elongated cupola overhead. She stopped at the last of a series of tall, black-painted doors and knocked discreetly.

"*Avanti*," someone said cheerfully from inside, even though the professor as far as I knew was not the least bit Italian. The widow's lips tightened a bit, and I sensed that she did not approve of the lighthearted tone.

"Fräulein Karno," she said and opened the door for me. She pronounced it *Kar*no and not Kar*no*, which made my own name sound foreign to my ears.

I don't know what I expected a professor of parasitology—especially one from Heidelberg—to look like. Definitely spectacles and gray temples. Possibly also a certain bulk across the middle or perhaps an ascetic leanness like my father's.

Professor Dreyfuss had none of these. He was young in a slightly indeterminate way that covered the territory between twenty-five and thirty-five; his prominent chin was marked by a very short and extremely elegant beard with no sign of gray, and his dark hair hung down over his brow with a boyish unkemptness that did not seem to match his title. He was wearing knickers, a shirt, and a padded vest, all in bright white, and had a slender rapier in his hand. He was a bit out of breath and a little sweaty, and the large window facing the institute's atrium yard had been opened wide.

"I must beg the young lady's apology for my appearance," he said in perfect French. "I am off to the fencing club once we finish here." He had clearly used the waiting time to warm up. With an elastic flick of the wrist he threw the rapier from his right hand to his left, took my hand, and kissed it lightly in a way that was at once gallant and formal. "Welcome to Heidelberg, Mademoiselle Karno."

Had I not been wearing gloves, I would have felt his lips, I thought spontaneously, and felt a ridiculous blush rising to my cheeks.

"Thank you for seeing me, Professor," I said.

"Of course," he said. "I have read several of your father's articles. I understand that he has suffered a slight misadventure?"

"Slight? Is that what he wrote? He broke both an arm and a leg, Professor, in a terrible accident that might easily have cost him his life."

"I am so sorry. Please convey my warmest wishes for a full recovery."

"Thank you."

"And so what is this fascinating specimen that you have brought me, Mademoiselle Karno?"

"A mite." From my little chatelaine bag I brought out the microscope slide case containing one of the two mites Papa had managed to collect, along with the description and drawing of it. "We think it must belong to the soft mites, but my father has never seen anything like it."

"Hmmm. Let me see." He tossed the rapier casually in an armchair and accepted the specimen with unvarnished curiosity.

His enormous desk overflowed with a judicious mixture of books, papers, and sports equipment—I noticed among other things a tennis racquet, a pair of riding spurs, and a cap of the type that rowing crews use—but on a contrastingly tidy laboratory bench by the window there was a microscope. I could not help noticing that it was Zeiss's latest model, and it was with difficulty that I repressed a wave of envy. He placed the slide under the Zeiss lens and bent over the microscope. At that moment, everything that was flamboyant and boyish fell away and was replaced by a searching intensity, and he looked what he was—a serious scientist. It suited him.

He studied the mite for several minutes. Then he smoothed the drawing and looked at it. Then back to the microscope. Then to the drawing. He compared them perhaps half a dozen times before he straightened up.

"Interesting," he said, and stared out the window for a few more seconds. Then he suddenly turned to me with a completely different expression from the one he had worn when he bid me welcome. The humor and gallantry were gone. He observed me with more or less the same searching intensity that he had devoted to the mite. I felt myself caught in his examination, pinned and studied to such a degree that it was difficult to breathe.

"Did you execute the drawing?" he asked.

"Yes."

He nodded briefly. "Very precise. Extremely precise, in fact. You have a scientist's eye for detail, Mademoiselle Karno."

My heart swelled with pride. He could have given me no compliment that would have made a greater impression.

"Can you identify the mite, Professor?" I asked.

"Not offhand, but with certain additional studies I will probably be able to classify it. Where did you get it?"

"My father found it while examining a young deceased woman. It apparently crawled out of her nose."

"I see . . ." He looked in the microscope one more time. "May I keep it? I would like to make some comparisons with various specimens from the institute's collection."

"Of course." I thought for a moment. "But can you perhaps venture a guess at whether the mite infection could have caused the young woman's death?"

He shook his head, just one sharp jerk of his chin. "I don't yet have sufficient basis for that kind of supposition. If you want to come back in a few days, I'll be able to give you a clearer and more detailed answer."

Come back? I had not been planning to make two trips to Heidelberg within a week. Even with the railroad, it was more than six hours in each direction, and the expense was a substantial strain for a modest household like ours. I had somehow imagined that the rest could be taken care of by letter or telegram.

He sensed my hesitation.

"Well, if you can't come, I shall have to come to you," he said with a faint smile.

All at once I was very conscious of being alone with a man I didn't know. True, he had left the door open, presumably out of consideration for my reputation, but still.

"I am not sure that my father can do without me," I said, embarrassed to note that it sounded like what it was—a schoolgirl's excuse.

At that moment there were steps in the corridor outside. The professor raised his head and listened.

"You had better discuss that with your father, then," he said. "I expect to have a result in a few days."

Through the door burst a long-limbed blond young man,

also sweaty and out of breath and dressed in a luminously white fencing costume.

"What is keeping you, Gussi?" he said. "We can't manage without you! They have brought von Hahn, and Grawitch is about to shit his pants from fear ..." He came to a sharp halt when he noticed me. "Aha!" he said. "The cause of the delay. I must ask the Fräulein to excuse me. I did not realize that there was a lady present."

"I was just leaving," I said quickly. "Professor, my father is deeply grateful for your help. We look forward to learning the results of your studies."

"Let me show you out," said the professor.

"I have delayed you long enough," I protested. "Goodbye."

I left before he could offer any further objections and walked away with rapid steps that resounded between the corridor's shiny walls. That there was an element of flight in my retreat, I knew only too well.

"What did he say?" my father shouted as soon as he could hear me in the hallway. "Did he know what it was?"

"He wanted to study it more closely," I answered awkwardly, with one of my hatpins between my teeth. "It will be a couple of days before we know more. How have things been? Are you feeling better?"

"I am completely fine," he growled.

But when I came into the salon, I saw that his facial color was still awful and his breathing heavy from laudanum drops. He was not well.

"I am sending Elise for Doctor Lanier," I said, and this time I ignored his protests. They were not as vigorous as before, I noted, which further increased my concern.

"Has the Commissioner been here?" I asked.

"Yes. At noon. They still have not found Father Abigore's body."

"And the dog?"

"No, not that, either."

Two days later, the Commissioner was once again seated in the mahogany armchair. It was his habit to drop by at lunchtime, and there was usually an evident relief in the way his solid, square figure sank into the chair. The Commissioner had neither wife nor children, and at the age of fifty-two it seemed unlikely that this would change. He lived in a rooming house nearby and in many ways probably led a lonely existence. He was a presentable man with a good position in life, and although his income was not princely, it was still quite reputable. He was perhaps not the type to set young girls' hearts aflutter, but why not a calm, good-natured widow with a bit of sense? Did the dead scare them off, or did he? If you did not know him, he might seem severe and inaccessible.

In any case, the house on Carmelite Street was the closest he came to a home during this time. He stopped by most days of the week, sometimes even twice a day if he thought a case provided him with sufficient excuse.

"How are you feeling, dear friend?" he asked.

"Fine," answered my father, and then, with an acknowledgment that it had been more serious than he would previously have admitted, "better."

It was true. My father was much improved. Doctor Lanier had

placed a plaster cast both on his arm and the broken leg according to Antonius Mathijsen's method, instead of the primitive splints that the medics had used. It was clear that this immobilization led to a dramatic easing of the pain. He now used the laudanum drops only to fall asleep at night and in much smaller doses. This had restored his pallor and his breathing to levels considerably more normal, and he had regained his customary sharp wits.

"Have they found Father Abigore?" he asked.

"No." The Commissioner sighed. "Marot apparently does not consider that part of the investigation important."

Police Inspector Marot's investigation of the circumstances of Father Abigore's death proceeded slowly, the Commissioner told us. His housekeeper, an elderly widow from the parish, had explained that someone had knocked on the door a little past eleven on the night in question, just as she and the priest were going to bed—a little earlier than usual because Father Abigore was still ill from the cold weather at Cecile's burial. When the housekeeper opened the door, she found an errand boy who delivered a message and disappeared into the darkness again before she had adjusted her spectacles properly. "No proper description" it said in the report, which made the Commissioner grumble crankily.

"No proper *report*," he corrected. "The woman must have said something, no matter how imprecise. Fat, thin, tall, little? They have given up in advance on finding him, in spite of the fact that he may have spoken with the murderer! And she used the note to light the stove."

But what was clear in spite of everything was that the note had said that a railroad worker had been hurt so badly that last rites were required. Ignoring his own illness, the priest immediately grabbed the bag that always stood ready for precisely this kind of emergency and rushed off on his bicycle. They found the bicycle later, propped against a gable at the Varbourg East railway station, but the bag had not resurfaced, and there was still no sign of the missing corpse.

"Marot's theory is that the body has simply been stolen and sold by an opportunistic street gang. My dear friend, is it possible for you to ask around? One might tell things to a colleague one doesn't feel like admitting to the police—or to me."

My father raised an eyebrow. "Who is it you think I should ask?"

"You probably know better than I," rebuked the Commissioner. "Varbourg is not Paris, of course, but even here there must be researchers and certain institutes of higher learning that have a hard time procuring sufficient . . . materials."

"Marot has read too many lurid scandal sheets," said my father. "As far as I know, there are no doctors in Varbourg who pay people to dig up corpses."

"But there must still be those who would pay for a cadaver for dissection purposes?"

My father's lips tightened, but he admitted the point. "Yes. About ten francs. Not a princely sum, but . . ."

"But seven or eight times more than a factory worker makes in a week. So if someone found an ownerless corpse, then . . ." The Commissioner said no more.

My father sighed. "I'll ask around."

And when the Commissioner had gone, he asked me to go see Doctor Lanier.

Saint Bernardine's gray façade had been undergoing repairs in the fall, and the luxurious ivy that had covered it had been cut down. I was still not used to this new stark exterior. It looked peculiarly bald, like a novitiate who had had his hair shorn but had not yet received his habit. A soft vernal rain moistened the gray walls and condensed itself into fat, tear-shaped drops on the windowpanes.

The concierge recognized me at once.

"Well, if it isn't Mademoiselle Karno," she said and lit up. She was a cheerful, stocky woman who was always referred to as Madame Bonjour, a nickname she had received as a result of the unusual almost twittering way she pronounced this word. "Is your father feeling better?"

"Yes, thank goodness. Is Doctor Lanier in the hospital?"

"Yes, he is scheduled to operate at one o'clock. The operation is drawing quite a crowd, in fact—he will be employing a brand-new surgical technique."

My heart skipped a beat. "Where?" I exclaimed. If only I could observe . . .

Madame Bonjour smiled. My eagerness was apparently obvious.

"Theater A. If you stand in the upper gallery, most likely no one will notice you." She gave me a conspiratorial wink. It was not the first time she had helped me sneak into this masculine domain, albeit usually to observe one of my father's operations.

Theater A was in the old main building's center wing, and it really was reminiscent of a theater—double balconies along three of the room's walls, the so-called galleries, allowed up to a hundred onlookers to observe what was happening in the operating theater. As Madame Bonjour had suggested, I made my way discreetly to the uppermost gallery, which was often empty because it was more difficult to observe the details of the operations from up here. But today I was not alone. A small group of medical students had been exiled because of the crowds below. They chatted while they waited for the operation to begin, nonchalantly leaning against the railing. When they saw me, however, all conversation ceased. Then two of them began to giggle, as if someone had said something funny.

"Madame . . . eh, mademoiselle . . . you must be in the wrong place," said one of the others, a tall, bespectacled young man who seemed a bit more mature than the rest. "What were you looking for?"

"Theater A," I said shortly, leaning against the railing at the opposite end of the gallery.

"But . . ."

"Thank you for your kindness, but I am precisely where I wish to be."

There was a small, astonished pause.

"I was only trying to be of assistance," he finally said, and the whispering voices of his colleagues sounded like the low hissing of a cave of snakes in the darkened room. I focused my gaze on the operating theater—*this* was why I was here, and the sibilant clique of students was merely an irritating interruption.

The patient was a boy of twelve or thirteen, and the focus of the operation was his left knee. Even from my elevated perch I could see that it was swollen and discolored, but naturally I was not in a position to determine why. Luckily Doctor Lanier was aware of his audience and began to explain, with a certain dramatic pathos.

"Tumore albus, gentlemen," he announced. "A source of intolerable pain for the sufferer. I have heard it described as having glowing hot nails pounded through the joint. The patient cannot walk, and even sitting down, the torment is difficult to endure."

The boy was not yet anesthetized. He was following Lanier's presentation with intense, almost hypnotic attention, and even from a distance the fear in his eyes was unmistakable. I hoped they would soon produce the ether mask.

"The condition is caused by osteoarticular tuberculosis, and it is irreversible. We can't return the joint's original health and painless mobility. But we can, gentlemen, ease the pain and restore the patient's ability to walk with this new technique, pioneered by my honorable colleague Eduard Albert in Vienna. By fixing the joint with these surgical screws and transplanting tissue from the healthy part of the tibia, we can provoke a fusion of the femur and tibia that will leave the patient with a painless and usable extremity, though the leg will naturally be stiff." He placed his hand on the boy's shoulder, but in spite of the gesture he was in fact still speaking to the hall. "In a month, my boy, you will be able to walk again!"

The boy looked like a paralyzed animal. Only his eyes moved. He was clearly trying to control himself, but although he did not make a sound, tears were trickling down the sides of his face, staining the thin white pillow under his head.

"The procedure is called arthrodesis, and this is only the third time it has been attempted in France," announced Lanier. "As my honored colleagues can probably imagine, an antiseptic regimen is critical for a successful result. Everything must be sterile. All linens and all instruments have been boiled, but since we can't boil the patient"—he paused dramatically so that the audience could politely offer a muted laugh—"we must use Lister's protocol and spray with carbolic acid, just as I am now washing my hands in a carbolic acid solution. Bacteria are the enemy, gentlemen, and they are everywhere in the air around us. Caution is critical! A good surgeon must be able to see them with the inner vision of his intelligence, just as we see flies and other polluting insects with our actual eyes. Do not for a moment let down your guard, it can cost your patient his life!"

This was more than the boy could take. He looked around wildly as if he expected "polluting insects" to attack him, and a thin high-pitched sobbing escaped him. It seemed as if Lanier only now sensed the child's fear. He placed his gloved, carbolic-moistened hand on his shoulder and said something so quietly that I couldn't hear the words. The boy stopped whimpering. It was hard to tell if he was really calmer, but now they finally brought the ether pump, and a few minutes later the anesthetic took its effect.

I let go of the breath I unknowingly had been holding. Ether was undoubtedly one of science's greatest gifts to the surgical patient. But it was a blessing for the surgeon and his assistants, too, who no longer needed to immobilize a screaming, half-crazed human being while they operated.

The operation began. I leaned out as far as I dared over the balcony railing, but what I could see was limited. Mostly I had to be content with Lanier's running commentary, which I carefully noted in my little notebook.

Just as Lanier was transplanting the healthy tissue, I heard a noisy throat clearing behind me. It was one of the students who for reasons best known to himself had elected to leave the pack and join me instead.

"Excuse me," he said, "but are you Mademoiselle Karno?"

"Yes," I said, without taking my eyes off the procedure.

"I thought so," he said.

He remained at my side even though I ignored him. It was extremely irritating, but there was nothing I could do about it short of leaving myself. Not until the patient was carried away and the quiet hissing of the carbolic pump had ceased did I leave him and the rest of the students to hurry down the narrow staircase and across the room to Doctor Lanier. He was in the middle of an indignant discussion with a white-haired gentleman who had kept his gray overcoat on in spite of the humid heat in the room.

"Bacteria exist," insisted Lanier. "They can be observed and described by anyone who has a microscope!"

"My good man, please do not speak to me as though I were dim-witted! Of course they exist; I don't doubt that. I am just asking how you deduce that it is the bacteria, rather than the air's miasma, that cause infections? Where is the proof that will over-turn the classic science of medicine and throw Hippocrates from his throne? It is lacking, sir. Lacking!"

Lanier saw me and lit up in a way that was unlikely to have anything to do with me specifically.

"Excuse me," he said firmly. "I have an appointment with this young lady. We must resume the discussion another time. Per-haps if you could in the meantime study Pasteur's simple experi-ments with the swan-neck flask . . ."

He didn't introduce me to the man in the gray coat but grabbed my elbow and led me quickly from the operating theater.

"Save me, dear Madeleine, from fossils and their ossified worldview. Miasma! Ffffh. This is a bright new era, doesn't he see that?" The question was apparently rhetorical, and he continued without leaving room for an answer. "How can I help you? How is your father?"

"Much better," I said. "The Mathijsen bandages have made a huge difference."

"Good, I expected they would. And get him off the laudanum as quickly as possible. I wish I could offer him an anodyne that was less addictive."

"He is aware of the dangers. That is not why he sent me."

"I see. So how can I help you?"

I told him about the corpse that had disappeared and Inspec-tor Marot's theory. "Mademoiselle!" he said. "Saint Bernardine is not in the business of stealing corpses!"

"Of course not," I said soothingly. "But who knows if the hospital's . . . purveyors . . . have fewer scruples? Would you please ask around? My father and the Commissioner are not interested in *how* the corpse has come into the hospital's possession . . ."

"It is not—"

"But *if* it were to be found here, they would naturally wish to see the good Father Abigore's remains returned. Here, I have copies of my father's detailed description. Would you be so kind as to circulate it among the hospital's personnel? Especially among the students, perhaps? Say that we are offering a reward that will fully cover the cost of obtaining another corpse."

Lanier looked at me with something that seemed close to loathing.

"I have the greatest respect for your father, Madeleine, and I understand that it can be difficult to raise a daughter without the help of a wife. But this . . . the way he *uses* you. It is *unseemly.*"

The force of his words was so violent that I blinked. I simply did not understand the depth of his outrage. Had he not just stood there talking of a new era? But certain ossified worldviews were apparently still unshakable.

"Everything I do for my father I do freely," I said, with the hollow sensation of speaking to deaf ears. "I am just happy I can be of assistance."

Lanier sighed. "That is precisely what is wrong," he said. "He abuses your praiseworthy loyalty, but you can't tell me that it does not offend your female nature when he forces you to be a witness to all . . . this." He took the description of the corpse and shook it in the air between us as if it were a papal ban.

"In no way," I said, but it was pointless. I wondered what he would have said if I had shown him the detailed notes I had taken during the operation that I had been "forced" to observe. "Will you make inquiries about the missing corpse?"

He was about to angrily refuse. I could see it. But at that moment inspiration struck and I knew how to convince him. I blinked rapidly a few times to stimulate the tear ducts. Then I placed a pleading hand on his arm.

"Doctor Lanier, I do hope that you can help us. The poor man was a priest, a pious man of faith. If we don't get him back, his poor soulless body will never rest in consecrated ground. The thought torments me, can't you see that?"

He stared at me. "Oh . . . ," he said. "Yes. That . . . I am sorry, that was insensitive of me. I shall do what I can, of course."

"Thank you, Doctor," I said, and gave his arm a hopeful squeeze. "That would make me feel so much better."

When I got home, the house was in an uproar. Madame Vogler was racing around with a broom and a dustpan all the while shouting contradictory orders to Elise.

"And make sure to buy plenty of petits fours. And get out the nice sherry glasses; they must be washed and polished. And flowers. We must have flowers. See if you can get some white lilies. No, wait. Cherry branches! Cherry branches in the Japanese style, that will be perfect for this time of year . . ."

She stopped when she saw me. Her cheeks were flushed, and her pale blond hair was frizzy with humidity and in the process of escaping the tidy chignon she normally arranged it in.

"My goodness," I said. "What has happened?"

"A professor is coming!" said Madame Vogler. "All the way from Heidelberg!" And then she hurried on, in a cloud of soap vapors and perspiration. Elise headed out the door without as much as saying hello or goodbye and raced down the street while I stood alone in our narrow hall and felt my own pulse rise. Heidelberg. It could only be Professor Dreyfuss, who apparently had decided to seek me out—or at least my father, just as he had said he would. There must be news about the mite!

Professor Dreyfuss arrived half an hour later. We could hear him a mile off, partly because of the engine noise from the automobile in which he traveled, but also because of the uproar and shouting from the children on the street. Such a thing had never been seen in our neighborhood—as far as I knew there were only two in all of Varbourg.

The professor parked in front of our door and stepped out. I had time, just, to draw back from the window when he looked up, so I don't think I was seen staring in the same openmouthed wonder as the rest of Carmelite Street. Elise ran down to let him in, in a freshly ironed apron and with her hair braided so tightly that her eyes were practically turned to slits.

He looked only a little less eccentric today, in a long khaki-colored duster and knickerbockers, along with a leather helmet with goggles, which he handed to a somewhat bewildered Elise, who was not quite sure how one handled such things.

"Mademoiselle Karno," he said, and kissed my hand just like last time.

"Professor," I said. "You have driven all the way from Heidelberg in that?"

"Not all the way," he said. "From the family's country house near Heeringen. A little more than eighty kilometers." He looked proud.

"Perhaps you should drive the car into the neighbor's courtyard? A machine like that is a great temptation for the street's children."

"I paid off two of the most scary-looking," he said. "I gave them permission to sit in the car and promised them a drive later if they made sure that no one else touched it."

That sounded to me like a direct invitation to bloodshed, but the chosen were no doubt ready to fight to the last breath for the privilege he had set before them, so presumably his divide-and-conquer tactic meant that the automobile would make it through the battle unscathed. In any case, there was nothing more I could say without being impolite.

My father was still forced to spend most of his time in the salon, but in honor of the professor's visit he had insisted on being helped onto the chaise longue so he did not look like a "damned invalid."

Professor Dreyfuss greeted him with an eagerness and a respect that warmed my filial heart.

"I have read your article about the connection between cotton dust and weaver's cough," he said, and shook my father's hand enthusiastically with both of his. "Pathbreaking!"

My father smiled. "I am glad you think so. It was not popular reading among Varbourg's elite."

"No, I can well imagine. But science can't be the servant of popularity."

"You and I have no disagreement there," said my father. And then he could not wait any longer. "I understand you arrived in an automobile?"

"Yes, Daimler's latest invention."

"Which motor?"

"Phoenix 4-cylinder. The same type that won Paris–Rouen."

And then they lost themselves in carburetor-injections, fan belts, and drive shafts with a mutual enthusiasm that ended with my father allowing himself to be carried down two flights of stairs, with the help of the professor and one of his tame street urchins, to take a test drive in the wonder. The sherry and Madame Vogler's dearly bought petits fours remained untouched. And we had not yet even broached the mite question.

"They will be back soon," I said, not quite sure whether it was Madame Vogler or myself I wanted to reassure.

They were gone for about a quarter of an hour. And when I saw the color and the excitement on my father's face, I forgave the delay.

"Fabulous machine," he breathed. "Absolutely fabulous! Believe me, Madeleine, in just a few years the suffering of the carriage horse will be over!"

I thought of the accident he himself had experienced. That would never have happened if the hearse had been an automobile.

"Then perhaps it will be safer to walk the streets," I said.

"No doubt. We will be released from the whims of brute beasts. Traffic will be regulated by technology's dependability and man's ability to reason!"

Elise served the sherry without knocking anything over, and the glasses shook only a tiny bit on the tray. And then we finally got to the mites.

The professor placed the slide on the tea table with great care.

"The past few days have been interesting," he said. "And I had better begin by saying that unfortunately I do not have a definite identification. This specimen is not identical in every respect to any that we have in our collection at the institute, even though there is one mite type to which it must be closely related."

"And which is that?" asked my father.

"*Pneumonyssus caninum*. This one is larger and has a more yellowish color. It may be an aberration."

"What is *Pneumonyssus caninum*?" I asked, hoping it was not too unintelligent a question.

"A mite that normally thrives in the nasal cavity of dogs."

"*Dogs?*"

"Yes, it is relatively common. It is easily transferred from dog to dog, possibly because its presence causes an irritation that results in violent bouts of sneezing and at times a bit of bleeding. It affects the sense of smell, so gundogs and bloodhounds can be rendered completely useless from it, but it is seldom deadly on its own."

"Do you ever see it in people?" my father asked, and leaned forward with an expression that was not entirely unlike a bloodhound's when it has caught a scent.

"I do not know of any examples, but with your permission I would like to describe the specimen in *The Journal of Parasitology*. I should be able to get it into the April issue."

"As long as you don't give Cecile Montaine's name, I see no problem," said my father.

"Of course. Will you do me the great honor of coauthoring it? The discovery is, after all, yours."

The pride this request elicited might not have been evident to the professor, but when one knew my father as well as I did, it was obvious.

"Thank you," said my father. "How are you planning to introduce the article?"

It was midnight before the professor left us to drive to the guest house where he staying. The petits fours were followed by onion soup brought from Chez Louis; Madame Vogler was up in arms at having to serve a simple soup to a professor—"from Heidelberg!"—but I think the two men barely noticed what they ate.

I sat in the armchair that was usually occupied by the Commissioner and listened while they spoke. But it was not long before the professor suddenly shot me a question.

"Mademoiselle Karno, do you recall the measurements of the mite's claws?"

"The shortest are around one-hundredth of a millimeter, the longest approximately two-hundredths."

"Splendid. That is yet another trait that distinguishes it from both *Pneumonyssus caninum* and *Ornithonyssus sylvarum*," the professor said, and continued the discussion as if nothing had happened.

But something *had* happened. Because in all the time that I had assisted my father, in all the time that I had registered, noted, sketched, and calculated for him, no one had ever before asked *me* instead of *him*. Not even if the details were ones I had immediately at my fingertips, so that he sometimes had to pass a question on to me with: "What was that again, Madeleine?"

Before the night was over, the "honored doctor" and "honored professor" had become Albert and August, and the professor had even accidentally called me Madeleine in the midst of a lively discussion, even though he quickly corrected himself.

"If this really is a different species, a human nose parasite, and not just an aberration," said the professor excitedly, "then we can call it *Pneumonyssus karnodreyfussia!*"

They toasted the idea with eyes shining with port and brotherhood. "*Pneumonyssus karnodreyfussia!*"

"You too, Madeleine," said the professor. "Where is your glass . . . mademoiselle."

It was in every way a successful and celebratory evening. At that moment we didn't know, of course, that the mites we were so happily toasting would be the cause of much more human suffering, fear, and death.

"There is a Madame Mercier here who would like to speak with the Commissioner," said Elise.

It was Sunday, and there was a heavy but comfortable mood in the salon on Carmelite Street. Outside it was raining, and we had lit the fire more to keep the damp at bay than because of the temperature. On the tea table was a tray of chocolate éclairs that the Commissioner had brought because they had been my favorite treat as a child. I did not have the heart to tell him that I now found them too sweet.

"Show her in," I said to Elise. "I hope that you asked her into the hallway so she isn't standing in the rain?"

A few moments later our guest stepped into the room. The Commissioner shot out of his chair with unwonted haste, and if my father was a bit slower, it was solely the fault of his cane.

"Madame," said the Commissioner. "How may I help you?"

I myself had trouble wrenching my gaze from her and felt a jab of unfamiliar feminine envy. The first impression was of overwhelming beauty. Shiny chestnut brown curls framed fine regular features, melting nut brown eyes, and a mouth that made even a prosaic and female soul like mine think of dewy rose petals and the dulcet tones of angels. Add to that a figure that actually looked like the illustrations in the fashion magazines.

Only at second glance did I notice how much of that impression of beauty was created with the aid of careful makeup, attention to her clothing, and an unusually effective corset.

"Are you the Commissioner?" she asked.

"At your service, madame," said the Commissioner, only a tad out of breath.

"They say that you see all the dead in Varbourg," she said with a voice that vibrated with restrained emotion. "Is it true?"

"At least all the dead that the authorities know about," he said.

She nodded. "My name is Marie Mercier. If I describe my son Louis to you, would you tell me if you have seen him?"

"Do you fear that he is dead, then?" asked the Commissioner.

"He has been gone for a week," she said, and although she still held precisely the posture that flattered her figure best, one could suddenly sense how fragile she was and how easily she could collapse. Nor was she as young as I had first thought. At least thirty, and showing the little telltale signs of it if one looked more closely.

"A week?" said the Commissioner. "So since last Sunday?"

"Yes. I did not realize it until today. He lives with my mother, you see, and I am seldom able to visit him more than once a week. Today he didn't come to meet me at the streetcar as he usually does, and when I got home, his grandmother told me that he was gone and had not been home for seven days. She thinks he has run away, but he is only nine years old, m'sieur, at that age one does not run away... And he always comes to pick me up, always."

"Did you go to the police?"

"Yes, but it was as if they were not listening. They probably think he has run away, too. He is about this tall"—she held a hand out in front of her at the level of the tight corset waist—"and dark haired like me, but with blue eyes. He was wearing his brown serge jacket, short pants, and a leather cap that our milkman gave him. It is a little too big but he loves it. He... he has a scar on his right knee, but otherwise... otherwise he is just a little boy of nine. M'sieur, have you seen him?"

The Commissioner held out a hand, whether it was to calm her or to halt her outpouring was hard to determine.

"Madame, I don't know of any dead boys of that age in Varbourg this week."

"Oh..." She swayed once, from one side to the other, then her legs seemed to collapse beneath her, and she sank into a helpless and inelegant pile on the floor. It happened so abruptly that neither the Commissioner nor I had the chance to catch her.

"I am sorry," she whispered. "I am sorry."

We helped her to her feet, and my father relinquished the chaise longue so that she might lie there and recover.

"With your permission," I said. "It would help if I loosened your corset a bit."

"The dress would not fit," she gasped. "It has an eighteen-inch waist. No, this is fine. I am feeling better now. At least Louis is not dead. At least not that."

She was not vain, I suddenly understood. All the trouble she had taken with her appearance, including the inhuman discipline it required to have an eighteen-inch waist at her age, and after having given birth to child, too . . . all of that was not due to any excessive devotion to fashion but was rather an attempt to guard the only capital she had. Her beauty was her profession.

He is just a little boy of nine. Desperation aged her face, and I couldn't feel envy or outrage at her choice of survival strategy, only compassion for the loss she had endured.

I caught the Commissioner's gaze and knew that he had seen the holes in her logic, as I had. Marie Mercier's little Louis might not be among the dead that had been found and reported to the Commissioner's office this week. But unfortunately that did not necessarily mean that he should still be counted among the living.

"I must get back to the police station," she said, and moved to rise. "As he is not dead. They must find him for me."

But the Commissioner stopped her. "Why not rest a little longer, madame, and let me arrange for the police to come to you this time?"

Police Inspector Clarence Baptiste Marot was not pleased to have his Sunday spoiled because of a runaway street urchin. He listened with ill-concealed impatience while Marie Mercier yet again described her nine-year-old son. Once that was accomplished, the Commissioner managed to convince Madame Mercier to go home to her mother's to await news. He accompanied her downstairs and hailed a hansom cab, so she would not need to wait in the rain.

When he came back upstairs, Marot's irritation had erupted. He directed a wave of indignant reproach at the Commissioner. Phrases such as "inexcusable interference" and "gross waste of police resources" flew through the air, accompanied by badly veiled insinuations as to the reason for the Commissioner's personal involvement.

"That woman is no better than a simple street whore," he hissed with such force that small pearls of spit lodged in the fringes of his bushy mustache, "and we will no doubt catch her delinquent offspring with his hand in some good citizen's pocket one day, and that will be that. Case solved. I certainly hope she has rewarded you well for your efforts, because you will not be reaping any benefits for it elsewhere!"

I have never seen an aggressive walrus butt its head against a boulder, but I believe I have a fair idea of what it would look like. The two men were of a similar age, height, and weight, but in temperament they could not have been more different. The Commissioner simply stood there waiting with a gravitas all his own, and this more than anything else finally robbed the inspector of the last of his composure.

"Have you nothing to say, man?" he exclaimed.

"Only if you are done," said the Commissioner.

"What?"

"I just want to draw your attention to the date of the young man's disappearance."

"He is not a young man, he's a nine-year-old street urchin."

"Who disappeared last Sunday and has not been seen since."

"And?"

"I permitted myself an interview with Madame Brunot."

"Madame who?"

"Father Abigore's housekeeper. The poor woman is still shocked by her employer's death and is desperately anxious about her future. Once the new priest is installed, she risks losing both her position and her place of residence. By no means easy for a woman past sixty."

"What has that got to do with the case?"

"Nothing. I am merely presenting it as an excuse for the fact that her first testimony regarding the night the priest died was not as complete as one might have wished."

It took Inspector Marot a few seconds to grasp that what the Commissioner was handing him was not really an excuse for Madame Brunot but rather for the inadequacy of that first interview. But he had not yet grasped the rest of the implications.

"I still fail to see . . ."

"Madame Brunot now describes the boy who came with the message as eight or nine years old, but she could barely see his face because his cap covered his eyes. Louis Mercier, who disappeared the same night as the priest was murdered, was most likely wearing a milkman's cap that was much too big for him."

Marot fell silent for a while. "We had better find him," he finally said.

"Yes," said the Commissioner. "I think so, too."

Four days later, two events occurred in Varbourg that appeared to have no connection but nonetheless turned out to be of significance for the investigation of our two deaths. A sudden warm front swept over the town and made flowers and trees explode with growth, and Cecile Montaine's father attempted suicide.

My father had just begun to move around a bit with the help of a crutch. Because of his broken arm he could use only one, which we constantly had to pad with fresh rags so that it would not rub his armpit raw. He grew sweaty and disgruntled from having to fight like this for minimal mobility, but at least he was now capable of descending to our modest bathroom and, of much greater importance to him, to his laboratory.

He was in the middle of taking as much of a bath as the plaster cast would allow when there was a knock on our door. Adrian Montaine Junior suddenly appeared in the hallway, unannounced and clearly shaken. He would not reveal the nature of his errand until "the Doctor himself" was present. At first he would have nothing to eat or drink, but in the end he accepted a glass of cognac, which he swallowed in one gulp without even tasting it. He began to cough and then had to drink a glass of water.

"I am sorry," he said. "It has been an utterly horrible day." He was in his early twenties, a slender and extravagantly clad young man with a smooth-shaven chin and a narrow little mustache that looked as if a child penciled it on his upper lip. The closest Varbourg came to a dandy, I presumed. I think that he typically had an open and happy nature, but the burden that weighed on him now made him restless and distracted, one foot tapping ceaselessly on our faded Boukhara carpet, and several of his sentences hung incomplete in the air between us.

The door to the rooftop garden was open, and the scent of pansies and daffodils wafted in from outside.

"Would you like me to show you the garden?" I asked to lighten the mood. "It is quite pleasant right now."

"Yes, please," he said, and got up at once, more likely because he found it hard to sit still than because of a true interest in horticulture. But he was nonetheless surprised when we stepped out into our little oasis.

"What an enchanting place," he said. "Is this your work?"

"No," I said. "My mother created this garden. I just take care of it."

"Your mother was an artist in her medium," he said.

We walked in silence among the flowerbeds, and he especially admired the corner display of ferns and climbing ivy, currently providing a dark, sylvan background for the last spring snow-flakes. My mother had not attempted to cultivate exotic orchids or palm trees from more southern climes. Instead, she had grasped the essence of our own rich nature here in the province of Varonne and had re-created it *en miniature* in the few square meters she possessed. The surrounding walls now suggested a mountain backdrop, and the very modest goldfish pond was somehow transformed into a shaded woodland lake.

"I am so sorry about your sister," I said at last.

He nodded, but I could see that he had received such condolences so many times that the words had lost their meaning.

"Thank you," he said politely.

"Please tell me if you do not wish to discuss it," I said carefully. "But have you learned more about what happened? Has the young man reappeared?"

"No," he said.

"I am sorry if I am prying."

He shook his head. "Do you know what? People are so careful not to impose, not to speak of her, not to ask. It is almost as if she is more than just dead, she has been . . . erased. Removed from the family portrait. No longer a part of us. And I find that hard to bear. Yes, it hurts to remember and to speak of her. But if we don't . . . then we are killing her all over again. Do you understand?"

I spontaneously placed a hand on his arm. "Yes, I do."

"Cecile was bursting with life—happy and warm and outgoing, and no paragon of virtue. No . . . no demimondaine, you understand? Just in love with life."

I nodded.

"In the summer she freckled because she refused to wear a hat. Mama could scold her as much as she pleased. It only worked until we could not be seen from the house, then the bonnet came off, and Cici would run and climb trees and catch frogs in the pond with me and François. She ran away from the first convent school she was sent to because she could not stand the discipline, especially being cooped up inside all day. We tried the Bernardine sisters because they are less strict and permit more outdoor activities, and that worked much better." He looked at me imploringly, repeating his plea for understanding.

"Do you understand what I am saying? She was *alive*. She hated to be closed in, could not stand not being able to move. But now . . . her body lies in a box in the ground. And her spirit . . . her memory . . . Papa would prefer to make her into a pure and pale saint who must not be soiled by coarse suggestions that she might have been something other than the most innocent and untouched lily of the convent garden. She was always Papa's little girl, but it is as if he has completely forgotten that what he loved most about her was her passion for life and her inability to be tamed. The gossip—and, yes, we hear that, too, in roundabout ways and in what people are *not* saying—the gossip paints her as a slut whose sins were justly punished. And they are all merely boxes, do you see what I mean? Whether the label on the box says slut or saint doesn't really matter. Cici would hate either just as much as she would hate the awful black coffin they buried her in."

"You loved her very much. That makes it hard now, but . . ."

"I *miss* her," he said, and stood for a moment breathing through his open mouth, as if it was difficult for him. "*Damn*

Emile Oblonski and everything he did to her. If I knew where he was, I would kill him."

"So you are convinced that he is responsible for her death?"

"If he had not brought her along . . . If he had not convinced her . . ." He shook his head several times. "You are right, she might have fallen ill anyway. But at least the illness would have come upon her at the school, where the good sisters would have cared for her, and where a doctor might have been called in time. So, yes, Oblonski has good reason to hide. And I am not going to stop looking."

Supported by his crutch, my father came limping out into the garden, in shirtsleeves and waistcoat with his hair still damp.

"I am sorry to have kept you waiting," he said to Adrian Montaine. "What can I do for you?"

Cecile's brother darted a quick sideways glance in my direction, but our conversation had apparently already been sufficiently confidential for him to feel he could speak freely.

"Monsieur le Docteur, we hope you can help us. My father . . . My father has been in an accident."

"An accident? How so?"

"His . . . a gun went off. An injury to the jaw. Our own doctor has done what he could to stop the bleeding, but he believes an operation is necessary if my father is to survive."

"Did you bring him to the hospital?"

"No. We were afraid of that journey . . . and besides . . . My mother has asked me to say that she is hoping you will be discreet."

My father looked at the young man without expression for a few seconds. He knew as well as I did what this meant. This was no accidental shot, and any doctor who was not blind in both eyes would be able to see as much. Madame Montaine was trying to protect the family and her poor husband against yet another scandal.

"I see," he said simply. "But at the moment I am not in a position to carry out an operation without assistance."

"Our own doctor . . ."

"Does he have experience with surgery? Ether? Lister's anti-bacterial regime?"

Adrian Montaine looked confused. "I don't know."

Papa sighed. "Fine. Either you must permit me to call in a colleague and inform him of the case. Or my daughter will have to assist me."

An entirely unsuitable little prayer almost escaped my lips. *Choose me. Choose me. Choose me.*

"Is your daughter . . . ?"

"Extremely well qualified, yes."

Thank you, Papa.

The Montaine family lived in one of the more stately homes along Boulevard Saint-Cyr. The family fortunes had been founded on a meat extract, Bovillion, which was sold in colorful cans with a picture of a fat soup-tasting cook who ecstatically murmured, *"Mmmmh. C'est bon—c'est Bovillion!"* But it was produced at a factory down by the railroad, and Madame Montaine's elegant salons bore no sign of that colorful vulgarity. Here all was pale rose and pearl gray, with silver and crystal accents. Adrian Montaine's bedroom had a similar aesthetic. The heavy rose velour curtains were closed and the pile in the pastel-colored Chinese carpet was so long and thick that one sank into it as if walking on a lawn.

The man in the bed lay unmoving. His breathing was a wet, animal-like snuffle, the effect of both blood and fluid in the throat, and of the massive dose of laudanum the family doctor had given him to make the pain tolerable.

He had shot himself through the mouth, but had done it at such an angle that the bullet had torn its way out through the cheek and upper jaw instead of going up through the brain, as had presumably been the intention. There was thus no visible entry wound, only the jagged, bloody exit, with a diameter of ten to fifteen centimeters. One could see bone fragments and shattered molars through the hole.

"How much laudanum has he received?" asked my father.

"Twelve milliliters," answered the family physician, a Doctor Berger.

"Then we will have to wait," said my father through clenched teeth.

"Wait? But he—"

"If we give him ether now, we risk paralyzing his ability to breathe," my father interrupted him. "We have to control the bleeding and stabilize him as well as we can, but I cannot operate until his breathing is less labored."

In the meantime, he chose the adjoining bathroom as a reasonably suitable operating theater. A frightened chambermaid was set to scrubbing the ceiling, floor, and walls with a solution of carbolic acid, and a table from the kitchen was carried upstairs and cleaned. I went down to the kitchen with the maid and asked the cook to boil some water so I could scald the instruments.

"Is it true that the master has shot himself?" she asked. There was a peculiar half-repressed excitement in her gaze, as if she were already imagining what it would be like to regale her friends with the tale: there he was, I tell you, gurgling as if he were choking on his own blood . . . She was a bony, skinny woman with iron gray hair, and I immediately disliked her. I had no desire to add grist to her gossip mill.

"There has been an accident," I said. "May I borrow a slotted spoon and a tray, preferably metal?"

She showed me two trays, one in silver and a less fancy one in pewter.

"Is he going to die?"

I looked at her. If she had been a decent person, she would have asked me, "Is he going to live?"

"I cannot say," I said. "Thank you, that one is fine." I took the pewter tray because she would presumably protest if I dumped the silver one into the boiling water.

At least the place was clean. No dirty dishes, no smell of old leftovers, and only a single winter-surviving fly buzzing against the windowpane in an attempt to get out. The cook stared at me with unfriendly eyes. I think she was having a hard time figuring out how to address me. I was dressed as if I belonged upstairs in the parlors, but then what was I doing down here, performing a task that in her eyes was probably servants' work?

"All this carrying on," she mumbled, executing a fly with a quick and efficient swat of a kitchen towel. "And all because of that little missy."

"What do you mean?"

"Well, I am not one to gossip. But you see things. And a *real* lady . . . Mademoiselle was hardly that!"

I fished the instruments out of the boiling water with the slotted spoon and arranged them on the tray. Then I went upstairs without saying another word.

It took more than an hour to remove the bone splinters and tooth fragments, tie up the largest of the damaged arteries, reconstruct the split upper jaw as well as possible, and pull the skin across the wound so it could be closed. I had to carry out a considerable part of the operation, much more than I had ever been permitted to do before, because my father still had only limited use of his left arm. His calm and precise instructions helped me through it, and I could not help thinking that this was the way it could be, the way it should be. He had taught scores of students at Saint Bernardine, not all of them God's gift to surgery, but it required two broken limbs before he treated me as something more than his occasional assistant.

It was only when the last sutures were in place that my hands began to shake and I felt a deep exhaustion that made my knees a bit unsteady. My father removed the ether mask, and I sprayed the wound one last time with carbolic acid before placing a bandage on it. Montaine was still breathing heavily, but with less difficulty now.

He had not used a powerful handgun but rather a small, ornate pocket pistol, by Flobert. Otherwise he would probably not have survived.

"Do not touch the bandage," said my father. "My daughter will come and change it once a day."

He didn't dare to leave this part of Montaine's care to the family or to the amicable but not very modern Doctor Berger. Antibacterial treatment required diligence and experience, and an infection now would most likely be deadly.

Montaine was coming around. There was a wet glint under his swollen eyelids, and his breathing contracted in an abrupt gasp. A sound came from him, an unformed word he could not finish because of the immobilized jaw.

"O! O! O!" he gasped, and it was more than an inarticulate keening. It was a denial and a desperate attempt to refuse life. He was trying to say "No."

Darkness hugged the street, and the night was still unusually warm when the hansom cab stopped in front of our house on Carmelite Street.

"Ffffff . . ." My father inhaled sharply the moment he placed his crutch on the cobblestones and transferred his weight from the cab's seat to his own legs. Or rather, his own leg. The broken one could not yet support him.

"Let me help . . ."

"No, Maddie, I am perfectly capable. If you would just take the bag."

The front door opened, and the Commissioner emerged.

"Elise said you would be back soon, so I waited for you," he said.

"You have news?" asked my father.

"Yes. You can get back into that hansom cab. We have found Father Abigore."

"Pull yourself together, Sophie," hissed Madame Ponti to her sobbing maid. "It is hardly the end of the world . . ."

"He . . . he . . . he," the girl stammered, and pointed in the direction of the ice cellar with her wobbling index finger. "I touched . . . I touched . . ."

She proceeded no further in her explanation. Her wet face looked dark and reddened against the white bonnet she was wearing. It covered her hair completely, so that one could not see the color of it, but her eyes and eyebrows were black, and there were dark hairs on her exposed underarms and a downy shadow on her upper lip. She still clutched the ice pick in her left fist, in spite of the fact that it must have been at least an hour since she had gone down into the ice cellar to get supplies so that Madame Ponti's guests could enjoy a cool glass of white wine on this unusually warm evening. No one had been able to persuade her to let go of it.

Madame Ponti turned to the Commissioner. "How long will it take to move it?" she asked.

"Not long," he said. "Doctor Karno and I just need to perform certain examinations in situ, as it were. An hour at the most, I would think."

She did not look as if this suited her. Madame Ponti was a lady of about fifty, fairly well known in Varbourg society in spite of the fact that she hardly ever stepped out. At the age of forty-five she had married an Italian manufacturer, which in itself wouldn't have been particularly noteworthy. What caused the gossip was her past as a vaudeville artist in Paris.

It didn't show. She was dressed in a dove-blue taffeta dress, which revealed a still almost perfect hourglass figure but was otherwise quite conservative. Her golden-blond hair was in an elegant evening coiffure, not boldly loose as in one of the postcards that had once circulated in the kiosks of Varbourg.

"I suppose I might as well send the guests home," she said. "Nothing suggests that Sophie will be capable of serving anytime soon."

"Madame, unfortunately I must ask that you detain your guests a little longer," said the Commissioner. "Since we are dealing with a crime, it's necessary for everyone in the house to be questioned."

Madame Ponti stared fixedly at him for several seconds.

"One of the guests is a chief justice at the préfecture," she said. "Claude Renard. I presume you know him."

The Commissioner smiled politely. "Unfortunately, that makes no difference, madame."

The Commissioner occasionally resembled his ultimate employer in his impartial obduracy; like Death, he was completely unaffected by position and class. He could not be fired, and there were no promotions to strive for. He was invited to dinner parties like that of Madame Ponti's no more regularly than my father was. But sooner or later he visited everyone.

Madame Ponti looked him over with the gaze that had once been described by the society pages as "smoldering sapphire." She determined, quite correctly, that there was nothing to be done.

"Fine," she said. "I can get the cook to set up a buffet, I suppose. You may find us in the conservatory when you wish to speak to us."

She gave one last irritable look at the still incoherent Sophie and turned to leave in a swish of taffeta and petticoats. Then she stopped in midexit.

"I assume all the ice will have to be thrown out now?" she said.

"I think that would be wisest, madame. For reasons of hygiene."

The ice cellar was not under Manufacturer Ponti's elegant Empire home but behind it, beyond the carriage shed and the stables, and was completely subterranean, so that only the top of the steep stairs was visible. I hastened to take my father's arm, not just because I knew he needed help to manage the steps, but also because it gave me the opportunity to join him in the cramped cellar.

The blocks of ice had been placed in large zinc-lined wooden stalls, and at this time of year they were all filled up, so it was like turning back the seasonal clock from spring to sudden winter. My short bombazine jacket was completely inadequate and I soon began to shiver.

Father Abigore's earthly remains lay in one of these stalls, directly on top of the ice block and squeezed in between two of the sturdy beams that supported the ceiling. One arm had slipped and stuck out into the air; otherwise you would not have noticed the dead figure right away.

The Commissioner took one of the two lamps that hung on the wall and attempted to illuminate the scene better, but it was not easy.

"I can't see a thing," he said. "We might as well take him down at once."

At this point almost twelve days had passed since death had occurred, and decomposition had naturally set in. Still, the smell was not as strong as you might expect. When we got the corpse onto the floor, my father's mercury thermometer showed that the body had cooled to between zero and three degrees Celsius, depending on the extent of its contact with the block of ice.

I was not prepared.

That is the only excuse I have.

One side of his face was his own—brow and eye socket, stubble-covered chin and jaw, and an eye that was carefully closed in the hollow of the eye socket. Death had removed much of his personality, but his humanity was still there.

But the other eye no one could have closed. The blow had been so powerful that both brow and cheekbone had been hammered flat, and there was no longer a socket in which the eye could rest. It had popped out and instead ran and melted down the remains of the nose cartilage.

I had just assisted at an operation of a person who had been equally disfigured without feeling any need to swoon or tremble. Why I reacted so strongly now puzzled me. I thought I had long since left behind my fear of the dead.

But the dead were not usually familiar. I had never before seen a murdered human being whom I had met and known in life.

Suddenly, I could not breathe. At least not enough. The cellar darkness swirled around me, and I grasped frantically at the nearest object on which I could steady myself. This happened to be the Commissioner's left arm.

"Madeleine . . . what is wrong?"

His words echoed at once far away and much too close. And it was too late to pretend that I was not affected, even though I tried.

"I just stumbled," I said, lips clenched. "Nothing happened."

But I had become visible again. I had revealed myself. Woman. Young. Fragile. Everything I did not want to be.

"You had better go up, Maddie," said my father.

It was no use arguing. I had to leave the cellar and sit and wait in the hansom cab while they brought a stretcher down and carried the body up and across to the ambulance that served as a hearse while the Commissioner's own vehicle was being repaired.

By the wrought-iron fence that separated the property from the street a number of curious bystanders had gathered. Two nursemaids, each pushing a pram, stood staring uninhibitedly. An older couple had interrupted their evening walk and were observing the scene with slightly more discretion. On the other side of the street, a broad-shouldered man in tweeds had stopped, even though the dog he was walking was whining impatiently. A newspaper boy halfheartedly announced that the evening edition of the *Varbourg Gazette* could be had for ten centimes, but it was clear that his real interest concerned what was happening on the other side of the fence. That was probably why he noticed me.

"Mademoiselle," he shouted. "Please."

"What is it?" I asked.

"Is it old Ponti? Has he shot himself?"

Shot himself?

"Why on earth would he do that?" I could not help asking.

"Is it him?"

"No," I said. "It is not someone from the house."

The gossip mill was clearly already grinding. How thrilling for Madame Ponti, I thought. But then, she was probably used to it.

Even though it was late, and he was presumably about to keel over with exhaustion, my father insisted on performing yet another examination of Father Abigore's body that very evening. This time, a constable from the préfecture stood guard outside the morgue, and I was not allowed to assist. To my great regret I was sent home in a hansom cab and thus was not present for the autopsy that the Commissioner gave my father permission to perform.

When he came home, I could see at once on his face that something had happened. The Commissioner had to help him up the stairs, and while I presumed he was again in severe pain, this was not what disturbed him. "Turn up the light, Maddie!"

There was an edge to his voice that made me obey without question.

"Sit there. Put your head back."

"Here?"

"Yes, so the light falls properly."

On what? Perhaps I understood that he wanted to examine me before the Commissioner handed him the magnifying glass but not why. He bent over me, and I could smell the distinctive perspiration caused by pain even through an otherwise penetrating smell of carbolic acid.

"Raise the lamp," he ordered the Commissioner. "No, a little higher."

With a speculum held clumsily with the fingers protruding from his cast, he dilated my left nostril first and then my right, examining them thoroughly with the magnifying glass. Then he extracted some of the nasal fluid with a pipette. He held the pipette up to the light and studied its contents at length.

"Open your mouth," he commanded, and carried out a more normal examination of my throat.

"I am fine," I said when he was done depressing my tongue and observing my tonsils.

He did not answer but at least allowed himself to drop down onto the chaise. I could now see that his healthy hand was also trembling with exhaustion or agitation.

"Papa . . . what is wrong?"

He exchanged a glance with the Commissioner.

"I will have to do it again in the daylight," he said. "But it does not look as if there are any."

Suspicion began to dawn. I felt slightly queasy.

"Thank God," exclaimed the Commissioner, and only now did I notice that his normally unshakable calm was also showing some cracks.

"What has happened?" I asked.

The Commissioner silently handed me my father's notes from his examination of Father Abigore. They were even more hurried and illegible than usual, but I had, after all, had years of practice in deciphering my father's handwriting.

His conclusions regarding the cause of death remained the same, of course. Father Abigore had been killed by a powerful blow to the head, presumably with a shovel or a spade. But there was more. Abigore had not been in good health when he died.

Punctiform hemorrhage around the eyes indicates advanced respiratory struggles; this is borne out by the examination of the lungs, which revealed six abscesses the size of a coin, as well as another half dozen in initial stages. In addition, in the throat and nasal cavity were found three dead parasites of a type similar to but not identical with the mite Pneumonyssus caninum.

I looked up. "Mites?"

"Yes," said Papa. "The same as on Cecile Montaine."

"He must have been infected while he sat beside her bier."

"We must assume as much. And I am fairly confident that I

76

would have found the same abscess formations in Cecile Montaine's lungs if a proper autopsy had been permitted." He ran his hand across his face, and his exhaustion was visible in the gesture. "That means that we are faced with what is probably a parasitically transmitted and potentially deadly lung disease, the type and vector of which we are now only beginning to investigate, after a delay of several weeks."

I looked across at the Commissioner, who had let himself subside into his favorite armchair.

"Do we know if there have been other deaths?" I asked.

"It is hard to say," he answered. "Every year, and especially during a winter like this one, many people die due to lung infections, and few are autopsied. There have not been more than usual."

"Yet," added my father grimly.

"Tomorrow I will ask the préfecture for a decree that will make autopsies mandatory for every death from lung infections in Varbourg and its environs," the Commissioner continued. "But it is far from certain that I will get it. The City Council prefers not to frighten the public."

Epidemic. That was the word that neither man was saying out loud. It hung in the air like a shadow. It was a cholera epidemic that had taken my mother's life, and my father took such events extremely personally.

Prevent the spread, I thought. Identify, isolate, treat; somewhere out there was the source. I suddenly remembered the three fresh droplets of blood in the snow at Cecile's burial and understood that Father Abigore had been sick even then. The mites had wandered from her to him while he sat by her dead body and prayed for her soul.

But how had she acquired them?

II

March 20–25, 1894

I found it hard to keep my eyes off the wolf.

It was so bizarre. The creature was sprawled on a hearthrug in front of the fireplace in the abbess's office with its head resting on its front paws, its eyes half closed. Yet there was no way it could be mistaken for a large dog.

"Does he bother you?" asked Mother Filippa. "We can sit in the front office instead."

"No, no," I said quickly. "I was just . . . surprised."

She smiled. She was younger than I had expected, perhaps about forty-five, with smooth sun-freckled skin and olive-green eyes. The habit of the Bernardine sisters hung loose on a figure that I still somehow perceived as athletic. Perhaps it was the way she moved.

"He is old now, and I do not have the heart to put him with the others," she said, glancing at the wolf with a look that I could only interpret as loving. "The new pack leader will not tolerate his presence."

The Bernardine sisters kept wolves. I knew that, of course. The story of the Gray Miracle of 1524 was known to every child in Varbourg. It was said that as long as the wolves remained with the Bernardine sisters, no foreign tyrant could reign in Varonne. As a border province, we needed all the help we could get. We were like a shuttlecock constantly batted from one side of the net to the other, in a game played by nations much greater than our little state. Only a couple of decades ago, in 1870, Varonne could have been swept up into the German empire the way Alsace-Lorraine was, and that would have been the end of spoken and written French in schools and public life. As it was, we were still an independent province under the more or less protective wings of the Third Republic, and there were people who believed that this was due to the wolves, rather than to diplomats and politicians. All the same, I had not expected to find one of them lying comfortably in front of the fireplace.

I cleared my throat and tried to concentrate on my errand.

"As you can see from the Commissioner's letter, it is of the greatest importance that we find the source of the infection and determine its extent. I know that there are some very competent nurses among the sisters here. Perhaps one or more of them could help examine all the students and teachers who were in contact with Cecile Montaine."

"It was considerate of the Commissioner to send a woman," said Mother Filippa. "Some of the sisters prefer to remain in the cloistered part of our community. But—excuse me for saying so—you seem a bit young."

"Yes. But I am used to assisting my father, and besides, I am one of the four people in the world who can identify the mite with any certainty—if we find it."

She still looked at me with a challenging skepticism in her olive green gaze. Just then the wolf got up from its place by the fire. It stretched and yawned, allowing me to see a set of teeth that although yellowed and marked by its advanced age, still featured canine fangs that were about four centimeters long. The yawn became a small disarming sneeze, and it rubbed its nose with one paw. Then it came over to the desk where we were sitting, I on one side, the abbess on the other. It nudged her with its snout, a single powerful push, and she let her fingers slip through the thick gray-white fur of its neck for a moment. Then the wolf continued around the desk and approached me.

Its eyes were almost white. The pupils were like shiny black buttons in the middle of irises pale as miniature moons, and it stared at me without blinking, without lowering its gaze. I was distantly aware that I had stopped breathing, just as most of my thought processes had ceased.

It studied me in this way for an endless moment, and it was entirely impossible for me to look away. When the wolf finally blinked and lowered its head, its nose briefly touched my hand. It was not a peremptory poke like the one it had given Mother Filippa, just a fleeting and damp touch. A greeting, a marking of invisible lines. Yawning once more, it lumbered back to its hearthrug and lay down.

"I think he likes you," said Mother Filippa. "Very well. The Commissioner would presumably not have sent you unless he felt you were up to the task."

I was left with a clear impression that the wolf's judgment was more important than that of the Commissioner.

In 1524 the convent had been remote and secluded, surrounded by deep forests. This probably played a part when Black Pierre and his mercenaries had found themselves so harassed by the local wolf packs that they gave up their attempts to seize the convent and the citizens of Varonne who had sought refuge there. These days, the outskirts of Varbourg could be glimpsed between the hills; farming and human habitation had replaced much of the original wilderness, and apple orchards and wide sprouting fields smelling of spring and rain surrounded the convent walls. The forest was still there, a low dark shadow on the edge of the open landscape, but only as a distant reminder of another, less protected time. The convent was no longer a fortress, crouched behind moats and buttresses, but was now reminiscent of a cross between a country estate and a village. The convent chapel and the cloister itself were still sequestered from the world by walls and iron gates, but the school and the old hospital, the cider barn, the stables, the orphanage, and the almshouse lay along tidy lanes bordered by budding chestnut trees, with some fifty cottages spread a little more haphazardly in the shadow of the solid institutional buildings. All in all, just over a thousand people lived here, and I sincerely hoped that it would not be necessary to examine everyone. It depended entirely on what we found among those who had been in close contact with Cecile.

Two hospital sisters, who really should have been having a well-deserved rest after their night shift, had been woken up and agreed to help with the initial examinations. One, Sister Marie-Claire, was young and energetic and apparently found it easy to brush off her sleepiness; the other, Sister Agnes, showed the strain of her night's work more clearly, and every other move was accompanied by a soft, unconscious, "Oh dear. Oh dear."

The examination was simple. With the aid of a bright light and a loupe, the nostrils and oral cavity were studied for signs of mites, and samples from the mucous membrane were collected with the aid of a pipette, to be examined later under the microscope. Fortunately, one wing of the school had a coal-powered generator that provided electricity to the entire first floor, and it was possible to find three lamps suitable to our purpose. I started by examining both Sister Marie-Claire and Sister Agnes, partly to demonstrate how it was done and partly to make sure that neither was carrying the infection.

"As you can see, it is a simple procedure," I said to Mother Filippa, who had accompanied us to observe events.

She smiled. "Nothing is simple when you are dealing with three hundred girls," she said. "What are you planning to tell the students?"

"The truth, of course," I said. "That we are here to investigate whether the mites we found on Cecile have infected anyone else."

"I would not recommend using the word 'mites,'" said Mother Filippa.

"Why not?"

"Because I would like to keep the hysteria to a minimum. How do you think the average sixteen-year-old reacts if she is informed that she might have potentially deadly mites in her nose?"

"Umm . . ."

"We try to discourage tight corseting for health reasons, but not everyone follows our suggestions. In addition to shrieks and screams and hyperventilating, you should probably expect some fainting."

"But . . . This is hopefully only to determine that the mites are *not* there."

"Nonetheless . . ."

"That is not rational!"

Mother Filippa looked at me for a few seconds. "We do in fact try to encourage our young pupils to become thinking human beings," she said. "But not all of them are as rationally inclined as you seem to be, Mademoiselle Karno."

"So you want me to lie?"

"Not at all. But perhaps you could leave the explanations to me?"

Fifteen minutes later I thus heard Mother Filippa explain to the first group of Cecile's previous schoolmates that the hospital sisters and I were going to perform a preventative and painless *Pneumonyssus* examination that would be "over in a few minutes." Eight girls in gray uniforms nodded seriously and sat down in turn on the three chairs we had arranged, allowed themselves to have their nose and throat illuminated, and accepted the pipette sampling with minimal objections. Cecile Montaine was not mentioned, and no one used the word "mite."

The rest of the morning passed with student examinations. Luckily, we did not find any signs of mites, a result that microscopic testing later confirmed. A few had irritations in the mucous membrane, but as far as I could determine, they were simply the result of a common cold. Then it was the turn of the adults who had been in contact with Cecile, which was more or less the school's entire faculty and the sisters and novices and lay sisters who took care of the laundry, cleaning, cooking, and so on. There was no sign of a mite infection among them, either, though two of the kitchen maids were found to have lice.

As the afternoon wore on, I was becoming thoroughly tired of staring into nostrils of varying sizes and degrees of hygiene and hairiness. When I closed my eyes briefly, a procession of noses flickered past my inner eye, and every time I was introduced to someone new, I initially saw nothing but this one organ.

"Are we done?" I asked Mother Filippa, who had patiently remained with us.

"Not quite," she said. "But all that remains now is to see to the sisters who do not go out into the world."

"How many are there?"

"About a dozen. We are not a cloistered order, but even so, for some the convent is a refuge and a retreat. Some of the older sisters in particular have withdrawn from the world to live out the rest of their lives behind the walls of the enclosure in prayer and contemplation of God. But there are a few younger ones among them, too. Until a month ago, one of them was Cecile's teacher in physics, biology, and chemistry. Would you follow me?"

I cleaned the magnifying glass, mirror, and pipette with carbolic solution—I had insisted that this be done after every examination; we were there to stop infections, not to spread them—and wrapped them in a clean cloth before I put them back into my bag.

"So she has only recently . . . withdrawn from the world?"

"Yes, she is still a postulant."

"Why?"

"In the case of Imogene Leblanc, it was probably not only God who called to her but also the world that frightened her. It is too bad; she was a good teacher and worked tirelessly to develop her pupils' abilities. She offered them individual tutorials, Cecile, too, I believe. And sadly it is not so easy to find female lecturers in the sciences. We can hope that she returns, but unfortunately I doubt it."

I expressed my surprise that the natural sciences were a part of the school's curriculum at all. They certainly had not been at Madame Aubrey's Academy for Young Ladies, where I had passed entirely too many years of my life.

"It is the belief of the Bernardine sisters that the world cannot afford to waste the intelligence of young women," said Mother Filippa with a small sniff. She had an unusually well-formed nose, I noticed. "The founder of our order, Saint Bernarda, wrote one of the most treasured works of her time, on fever illnesses and their treatment. We do not teach our girls only French poetry, hymns, and embroidery; history, geography, biology, chemistry, physics, and of course mathematics are all equally important to their education. We have a very good teaching laboratory. Would you like to see it? We can pass it on our way."

"Very much," I said.

When we left the school to walk back toward the convent, a feeling of unfairness burned in my veins. Why had I not been allowed to go to school here? My father had chosen Madame Aubrey because he preferred an education with less emphasis on religion and especially Catholicism, for which he harbored a deep mistrust. We did not go to church very often, and when we did, it was to the small Huguenot chapel in Rue Colombe. But I would have been prepared to swallow a substantial portion of holy water and saint worship if it had given me admission to the institution we had just left. Well-lit workbenches, Bunsen burners, microscopes, copper spools, magnets . . . and, first and foremost, *knowledge*. Knowledge instead of posture and good manners. I could not refrain from sighing.

Mother Filippa glanced at me.

"Are you tired? Would you like to rest a moment before we continue?"

"No. No, I am just a bit envious of your pupils."

"In what regard?"

"I am afraid Madame Aubrey's Academy for Young Ladies

found female intelligence much less indispensable than you do," I said, and silently wished that we had used more time to discuss the subject matter of books and less time wandering around with them on our heads.

"Imogene?" Mother Filippa pushed open the door to the sisters' refectory. "Imogene, we have a visitor . . ."

"No!" The woman in the postulant habit looked up abruptly, and there was a terror in her gaze that stopped me short. "I do not want to see him! I . . ." Then she saw me, and she realized that she had misunderstood the situation. "Oh, pardon me. Good afternoon." She had been in the process of scrubbing the long table with soapy water and was still clutching the brush in one hand. Her throat and face flushed unevenly with nerves or effort, and there was a worried furrow between her eyebrows that looked as if it was more or less permanent. Of whom was she so afraid?

"Mademoiselle Karno is conducting a health examination of the school's pupils and teachers. We think it best that you also participate, since you are still officially on the teaching staff." Mother Filippa spoke with a calming authority that would have made any animal or child relax and lie down. It had no visible effect on Imogene Leblanc.

"Health examination?" she said suspiciously. "How so?"

"I would like your permission to examine your nostrils and throat," I said. "It will only take a moment."

Her expression did not change. Her eyes were very pale, gray or perhaps a watery blue, it was hard to determine. What you could see of her hair was frizzy and auburn and as lusterless as the fur on a dead animal. She looked at me for so long that I began to wonder if she would refuse, and what I would do if she did.

"If you really feel it is necessary," she said at last. "But I have my work to do."

"Thank you, Imogene," said Mother Filippa. "The value in these tests lies entirely in being thorough and complete."

There was no electricity in this part of the convent, and the refectory was so dim that it was impossible to perform the examination there. Mother Filippa led us out through a side door to a small enclosed courtyard where sunlight fell bright and sharp onto the old sandstone tiles. I asked Imogene to sit on one of the four benches and tilt her head back. She moved a bit stiffly, and her fingers were crooked with arthritis in spite of the fact that she was presumably still in her early twenties. The flush had not been just the result of nervousness, I could now see. She had patches of old eczema on her cheeks and neck. But her throat and nostrils were normal, and there was no sign of mite infection. I thanked her, and she returned to the refectory to resume her work.

I could not help asking Mother Filippa who it was that she had been so anxious to avoid meeting.

"Her father does not approve of her decision to devote herself to convent life," said Mother Filippa. "He has attempted to prevent her from returning several times, the last time he physically locked her up, as far as I understand. She was in a very bad way for a long time afterward, both physically and mentally. As you can see, her health is delicate. I think it was her fear of her father that made her give up her teaching and seek permission to join the order. I think she was afraid just now that he had come to force her to leave us."

"Can he do that?"

"Not without a fight. But . . . he is her father, after all. Until she takes her full vows, she is still under his authority. Come, we can go through here. I think we will find the last two sisters in the west wing."

Sister Bernadette and Sister Beatrice were in a courtyard almost identical to the one we had just left, except that here an old mulberry tree grew between the sandstone tiles. The sisters were both quite old. One was clearly almost completely blind but sat crocheting with hands that saw more than her eyes did, and the other had clearly entered a second childhood and hugged a rag doll tightly, singing a lullaby in a high, clear, and astonishingly beautiful voice.

"This is Sister Bernadette," said Mother Filippa, indicating the crocheting nun. "And this is Beatrice."

"She is in a good mood today," said Sister Bernadette. "When she is sad, she sings nothing but funeral psalms from morning to night. Poor dear."

"Sister Bernadette was Cecile's closest spiritual adviser," said Mother Filippa. "I thought the two of you should meet. Perhaps a short stroll in the garden? I will sit with Beatrice in the meantime."

Bernadette got up quickly and set her crocheting aside. "Thank you. She is the sweetest creature . . . aren't you, Beatrice? But a little stroll will do me good."

"Sweet Beatrice. You have to keep an eye on her," said Sister Bernadette, with no apparent acknowledgment of her own sightlessness. Her hand was resting lightly on my arm, but I was not sure that she needed my support at all. It seemed as if she moved without difficulty, in spite of her blindness, at least on the neat garden paths where she presumably knew every stone and tree. "Otherwise she begins to walk around looking for her siblings, in spite of the fact that one has been dead for many years and the other is seventy-two and is unlikely to need her supervision any longer. But I understand that you are here because of Cecile?"

"Yes," I said. "We are trying to determine with whom she has been in contact so we can trace the source of the illness she died from. Mother Filippa said that you knew her well?"

"I must be the sister that knew her best. But she was a girl with many secrets."

"What do you mean by that?" Her brother had described her as open and alive, not secretive.

"Cecile was not suited to a life such as ours. But for her family, anything other than a convent school was unthinkable, and, as you know, we are more liberal than most others. We do not believe in too rigid a discipline. Still, Cecile kept butting her head against the rules again and again, especially in the beginning."

"In what way?"

"She could not sit still. She had to get out, had to move, she was more like a boy than a girl in this respect, and then . . ." Sister Bernadette hesitated, and I think she changed her mind several times before she at last continued. "She was not of a contemplative nature. I might even call her . . . sensuous. Even though she was very independent, she was constantly hanging on some classmate's arm, had to touch and be touched, could not tolerate isolation and enclosure. The one time we attempted to confine her to her room, she cried like a small child and hammered on the door with such force that we feared she would harm herself. In time, she got better at following the rules, but . . ."

"But what?"

A small and somehow sad smile pulled one side of the sister's mouth out, not up.

"I do not think we taught her to obey the rules, just to pretend and cheat so that it was noticed less frequently when she broke them. That is not the kind of effort I think we should be proud of."

"And now she is dead . . ."

"Yes. And Emile has disappeared."

"Did you know him?" I asked.

"Yes. He came here when he was ten or eleven, orphaned and very alone in the world. He, too, was . . . different from most. When he got older, he helped out in the stables and especially in the wolf pen; he had an amazing way with animals. Probably got along better with them than with people."

"So they met each other here?"

"Yes. That must have been the way it was. Cecile loved animals, too."

"But no one suspected that they developed an affection for each other as well?"

Even though she presumably could not decipher anything at all about my expression with her weak sight, she still looked directly into me.

"You know . . . everyone talks as if it was Emile who lured Cecile to run away. But I think it was the other way around."

When we returned to the bench where Mother Filippa sat with Beatrice, Beatrice had moved on to a singing game that I had played as child.

The maid goes into the dark forest
picking berries
picking berries
Father Wolf, he is in the dark forest
Prowling here
Prowling there
First she drops one shoe
Then the other, then the other
First she drops one ribbon

Then the other, then the other
Father Wolf in the dark forest
is hungry for little girl pie
When the little maid does not come home
Oh, how her mother must cry, must cry
Willy-nilly
You're in the wolf's belly
Rip, nip, nip, you're dead!

Suddenly I clearly remembered the prickling sensation of going through the "forest"—usually two older girls who stood with their arms in the air and pretended to be trees—waiting to see if the one caught in the "wolf's belly" was me. If you were caught on the "Rip, nip, nip," they pinched your arms and legs and especially your midriff and belly, and some of the most merciless pinched so hard the bruises lasted for weeks. Still, it was one of our favorite games.

I examined the two older sisters on the bench in the sunlight, and, as I had gradually come to expect, got a negative result.

"Then you are the only one left," I said to Mother Filippa.

"Let us go back to the office," said the abbess. "It is closer to the gate."

This time I was prepared for the wolf, so it was not quite as disturbing to see it get up and come over to greet Mother Filippa, with lowered head and tail. It did not demean itself by anything so submissive and puppy-like as wagging its tail, and it was still not possible to mistake it for a dog. It ignored me completely this time.

I asked Mother Filippa to bend her head back and directed

the lamp at her nostrils, not without a certain gratitude that this was the last nose I needed to examine for now. As I had gradually come to expect, her mucous membranes were healthy and normal, without a trace of irritation or mite infection.

"That was it, I believe," I said and straightened, with a soreness in my lower back from having bent over so many times in so many hours. "I will return when we have examined the samples in the microscope, but I am happy to say that it looks as if both the school and the convent are free from infection."

"Should I ask our coachman to drive you back to town?" asked Mother Filippa.

"No, thank you. The Commissioner is picking me up himself when his investigations are concluded." He and my father had earlier that day taken samples from the entire Montaine household and were presumably now examining Father Abigore's circle of acquaintances. The task of tracing the infection was daunting, but necessary, and the fear that we were not going to do it thoroughly enough was a nagging uneasiness in my stomach.

The abbess looked at me with clear, calm eyes. "I understand that you are not a Catholic?"

"No," I said, somewhat surprised by the sudden change of subject. "We belong to the Reformed Church."

"I do not wish to offend you," she said, "but I would like to ask permission to bless you."

I discarded the first responses that occurred to me—"Why?" and "Well, it can't hurt"—and just said, "Thank you." After which I just stood awkwardly, waiting.

"Would you kneel?" she asked. "It is not necessary, but . . . that is usually what one does."

I hitched up the skirt of my traveling suit and got down onto my knees. Suddenly it felt natural, as if I had been doing it my whole life. She touched my forehead lightly while in a low voice she chanted the ancient Latin invocations and ended with an even quieter "Amen."

At that moment the wolf sneezed several times and rubbed its snout energetically between its front paws. And I realized that Mother Filippa's nostrils were not in fact the last that I would need to examine that day.

The wolf looked at me with its moon-pale eyes. Mother Filippa's hands lay on either side of its broad skull, and its jaws were open so I could see the dark ribbed throat, the meat-colored tongue, and the yellowed, worn teeth.

"I promise you, he will not harm you," she said.

Her words brought back memories from my childhood that I would have preferred to have forgotten. Big wild dogs that came running toward me, tongues hanging out, even more enormous and fear inducing because I myself was so little, while the owner cheerfully yelled, "Don't worry, they'll not hurt you," from his comfortable position on a distant park bench.

And this was no dog.

I directed the lamp so that its light fell as directly as possible on the wolf's face. It blinked once but otherwise stood completely still. I raised the mirror and the loupe, but my hands were shaking so badly that I could not see a thing.

Empty your heart of fear.

"What?"

I broke off my eye contact with the wolf for a brief moment and instead looked at Mother Filippa.

"I said, 'Empty your heart of fear,'" she said.

But she had not spoken out loud. I was almost certain of that. Or had I just been so focused on the wolf's gaze that I could no longer distinguish what I saw and heard from what I was merely thinking?

All at once I felt an extraordinary clarity and calm inside. The world was as it was. The wolf lived in it, and so did I. Its breath enveloped me, its body was as warm as mine. It breathed, and I breathed. Right now, in this moment, we breathed in the same rhythm and shared the same life.

My hands stopped shaking.

I directed the loupe first at its throat and, later, with great care, at one damp, dark nostril. Even with the mirrors it was almost impossible to see anything. But when I drew the delicate instrument out again, it was covered by yellow mucus. And something in the mucus was moving.

I reached for a pipette and managed to suck the struggling organism into the narrow glass tube and raised the tube to the light. In spite of the filaments of phlegm that had been sucked up with it, I could see it now: a mite, about two millimeters long, with a pale white abdomen. Until I placed it under a microscope I would not be able to identify it with objective certainty, but in my mind there was no doubt. *Pneumonyssus*, and the same species as the ones we had found on Father Abigore and Cecile.

The sadness that seized me had no place. Even though I immediately understood that the wolf's life had to end, it ought not to have touched me in this way—more strongly than Cecile's death, more strongly than Abigore's. Where did that pain come from?

"You have found something, have you not?" whispered Mother Filippa. "You are now going to tell me that he has been infected by the parasite you are seeking."

"I am afraid so."

"What will happen now?"

"I must examine it under a microscope to be certain, but . . ."

Mother Filippa bent her head and hid her face in the wolf's bushy neck for a moment. "He has had a long life," she said without looking up. "But what about the others?"

"How long has he been separated from them?"

"For a few months. We lost a wolf in the fall, and that unsettled the pack. It was only then that the new pack leader began to bully him."

"Lost? How?"

"It was not sickness, so it probably has nothing to do with this. But at feeding time, one of the females was missing. Emile found her all the way up the hill, at the far end of the pen, with one hind leg in a fox trap. We had to put her down, she had gnawed her leg almost all the way through in an attempt to break free. Poor Emile. He had nightmares for several days. It has been a long time since we were bothered by poachers, but a wolf pelt brings in a tempting sum for people of limited means."

"Emile—that must be Emile Oblonski?"

"Yes. He was the one who took care of the wolves most of the time."

"Before he ran off with Cecile."

"They disappeared at the same time, at least." She looked up and her eyes shone damply in the light from the lamp. "What are you suggesting?"

"I hardly know." I shook my head. "I have no idea how it is all connected. We will have to examine the other wolves as well, of course, and take whatever measures are necessary." I could not bring myself to use the words "put down." "But it is just as important that we find your Emile. He might be seriously ill." Or dead—but I did not say that out loud. "Do you have any idea at all where we should look for him?"

"If I had, don't you think I would have told Cecile's family when they disappeared?"

"Yes. I am sorry."

The abbess was not lying, I thought. Still, there was something about her answer that bothered me, though it was not until sometime later that I realized what it was: her answer *was* no answer, just a counter question. And as my old school friend Hélène, who had been raised as a good Catholic, once taught me, this is how you avoid lying when you do not want to speak the truth.

"A professor of parasitology is on his way from Heidelberg," said my father, and invited first the Commissioner and then Inspector Marot to look in the microscope. "You can await his judgment if you wish. But there is really no doubt. The mites from the wolf are identical to the ones we found on Cecile Montaine and Father Abigore."

My father would not admit it, but I could see that he was in pain again. It was to be expected when you considered what he had done to his healing bones in the past few days, and I had therefore carried the microscope up into the salon so as to at least spare him the stairs. Similarly, the Commissioner had presumably discreetly twisted Marot's arm until he agreed to meet in Carmelite Street, though the official excuse was that he had come to see the mites for himself.

"What bearing does this have on the case?" asked Marot, straightening from his inspection of the slide. With an unconsciously feminine gesture, he smoothed his forelocks. They did not need it; significant amounts of macassar oil ensured that the two dark spit curls stayed exactly as they had been arranged, on either side of a neat middle parting.

"We have most likely found the source of the infection," said my father. "The wolf in question must of course be put down and that holds for the rest of the pack, too. Even if we do not immediately find mites in all the others, it would be too risky to let them live. Also, it would be difficult to accomplish an examination safely as long as the creatures are alive."

Marot looked at him with an unusually expressionless face, possibly because he found my father's priorities extremely peculiar.

"I meant the murder case," he said. "What does all this have to do with my homicide?"

"The mites form a connection from the convent wolves to Cecile Montaine, and from her to Father Abigore," said the Commissioner. "It could be pure chance: the wolves infected Cecile, Father Abigore then contracted the disease after sitting with her in the chapel all night—after which he was murdered for a completely different reason by person or persons unknown. But that does not explain why Cecile and the young man, Emile Oblonski, disappeared in the weeks leading up to her death. It is necessary for both the murder investigation and in order to stop the spread of disease that we find Oblonski, healthy, sick, dead, or alive, and determine where the young couple went, with whom they have been in contact, and why they acted as they did. It is also of increasing interest to determine who removed Father Abigore's body from the scene of the accident and why it reappeared in the Pontis' ice cellar."

Inspector Marot was not stupid. Choleric and impatient, to be sure, and with an unfortunate tendency to jump to conclusions and go for the fast result rather than the correct one—indubitably a great failing in an investigator. Nevertheless, he did possess both a sense of logic and the ability to scrutinize things closely when he gave himself the time to do so.

"The cold," he said. "First the chilled boxcar that was supposed to go to Paris, then an ice cellar. That suggests first of all that it *was* the murderer who stole the body and next that the cold itself was in some way a significant part of his intention."

"To keep the body fresh?" the Commissioner suggested. "But why? It seems bizarre, and it is not otherwise a bizarre murder—a single powerful blow, like putting down a steer."

"Perhaps it is because the cold kills the mites?" I said. "After a certain amount of time, anyway."

For a moment, the room was still, and I cursed myself and my eagerness. Normally I did not say anything during this kind of discussion unless I was asked. I did not want to draw attention to myself for fear that they would then avoid any subjects that were not considered appropriate when ladies were present. But I was the one who had looked the wolf in the eyes and found the source. They could not claim that I had nothing to contribute!

"That is a possibility," said my father hesitatingly. "But it would be simpler and more effective to use fire."

"It is no small matter to burn a corpse," objected the Commissioner. "And a fire can create unwanted attention."

"It all assumes a kind of consideration that I think strongly contradicts the nature of the crime," said Marot. "We are speaking of a priest, a man of the cloth. And because of the false message, we know that the murderer had full knowledge of the victim's name and calling, and in fact used it to lure him into a trap. He is unlikely to have been killed by a conscientious God-fearing good citizen."

"This Oblonski," said my father, "what do we know about him?"

"He is an orphan and apparently also a bit disturbed. Barely speaks to anyone and mostly keeps to himself. He grew up in the convent and for some years has had the main responsibility of the tending of the wolves. Cecile Montaine was apparently interested in the animals, and that was how they met. It is hard to imagine what a beautiful young woman from a family like the Montaines

99

would see in a wretch like Oblonski, so I sincerely doubt that she went along voluntarily," said Marot.

That entirely contradicted what both Sister Bernadette and Mother Filippa had said, and I felt obliged to say as much.

"In fact they believe that Cecile could have been the one who initiated the elopement," I added.

"I find that very hard to believe," said Marot. "She was engaged to a young man from one of the city's best families, I've heard. Why on earth would she ruin her reputation and her future in this way? I know that young women occasionally allow themselves to be dazzled and throw all good sense to the wind, but by all accounts Oblonski was practically a half-wit and not very attractive. Not exactly love's young dream."

"How did the family react to her disappearance?" I asked. "Did they call the police?"

"No," admitted Marot.

"Don't you find that odd?"

"They must have feared a scandal."

Avoiding scandal was certainly a significant goal in Madame Montaine's life, as her actions in connection with her husband's suicide attempt demonstrated. But if a family had reason to fear that their daughter had been abducted by a disturbed half-wit, would they not do everything to find her?

"To whom was she engaged?" I asked.

"Rodolphe Descartier."

"Descartier? Of Varonne Commerce?"

"Yes."

You could only describe that as a sensationally good match. Not only did the Descartier family stem from a branch of Varonne's nobility, they also owned and directed Varonne's largest bank. For the daughter of a meat extract manufacturer, this was something of a coup.

But one thing struck me.

"He did not attend the funeral, did he?"

"No," said my father.

None of this particularly interested Inspector Marot, it seemed. He was, perhaps understandably, more concerned with Father Abigore's murder and impatiently returned to that trail.

"These mites," he said, and gestured in the direction of the microscope. "Are we certain that Father Abigore got them from Cecile Montaine?"

"It is the most obvious explanation," said my father. "He was not the convent's priest and has never been in contact with the wolves."

"But could he have been in contact with Oblonski?"

"We cannot say for certain, but there is nothing to suggest it."

"Are you sure?"

"Why do you ask?"

"Because I am trying to connect the pieces. Let us say that Oblonski has kidnapped Cecile. She becomes ill. Perhaps she escapes, or perhaps Oblonski has a crisis of conscience and brings her to her parents' house. He cannot knock, of course, so he just leaves her in the snow. The family discovers her, but she is dying. They call a priest, he hears her confession and administers the last rites, and she dies. Oblonski now realizes that the priest knows of his crime and fears that he will be exposed. That is why he kills Abigore. Oblonski is strong and used to physical labor, and he would be able to use the weapon with sufficient power."

My father opened his mouth, but Marot beat him to it.

"No, no, I know it. The brother said that she was dead when he found her. I guess we have to believe him."

"The clinical facts support his explanation."

"Perhaps Oblonski sent for the priest when he saw that she was dying? Can one assume he had that much decency?"

"Then Father Abigore would presumably have told the family," said the Commissioner.

"The Seal of Confession?" Marot shook his head in frustration. "No, I know. It does not fit together. Perhaps there is no connection whatsoever between the murder and Cecile's disappearance. Perhaps mites and illness and wolves are entirely without significance for Abigore's death."

"Except for one thing," said my father.

"And that is?"

"If the body was in fact put on ice to prevent the mites from finding another host, then the murderer must have known that Abigore was infected with them."

The look that Marot sent my father was almost tormented. He got up abruptly and walked over to the window, where he stood rocking back and forth on the balls of his feet for several minutes.

"It makes no sense," he mumbled, "no sense at all."

"Is there any news of Marie Mercier's little boy?" I asked.

"Unfortunately, no," answered Marot. "I have three policemen out taking statements from people in the area near Espérance, so that we may try to trace his movements. I am expecting a report soon." He consulted his pocket watch. "I am afraid I have to get back to the préfecture. But this has been most interesting."

I got up as well to see them out. When the inspector noticed that I was putting on my hat and jacket, he paused in the doorway.

"Where are you headed?" he asked. "The Commissioner and I have a coach waiting downstairs. May we escort you?"

"If it is not too much trouble," I said. "I am going to Monsieur Montaine's to change his dressing."

"Ah, yes. They say it was an accident with a gun?"

"Yes. That is what they say."

Inspector Marot nodded. He could easily read the subtext.

"Poor man. To lose a daughter in that way must certainly make life appear burdensome and meaningless. Will he survive?"

"If we avoid infection."

"Poor man," he repeated. He performed a sort of salute to my father, who had followed us onto the landing at the top of the stairs. "Thank you for your effort, Doctor. Although you have mostly just contributed to my confusion."

"We should not fear confusion," said my father with a small smile, "but rather embrace it. It leads to questions, and with a bit of luck, to answers."

I thought about the Montaine family. About a beloved daughter who was not reported missing although she had disappeared. About a fiancé who did not appear at her funeral. About a mother who would do anything to avoid scandal. About a father who was a practicing Catholic and still in sufficient despair to commit a mortal sin by attempting to take his own life. Very well, I thought. I will embrace my confusion and ask a few questions of my own.

You could hear it as soon as you entered the Montaine family's mansion. A low but penetrating moan, drawn out and rhythmic like breathing.

"Aaaaaah . . . ahhh . . . Ahhhhh . . . ahhh . . ."

It affected everyone. The maid who showed me in had bright red spots on her cheeks and glistening eyes. And when Madame Montaine met me on the first landing, I could see that she had developed a nervous tic in one nostril, like a slightly too purebred racehorse.

"Has he not been given laudanum?" I asked.

"As much as we are permitted," said Madame Montaine, her jaw so tense it vibrated. "It makes no difference. I have asked him to try to pull himself together for the sake of the children, but . . ."

I remembered Cecile's little sister from the funeral, her rigid paralyzed shock. I hoped that someone was taking care of her now.

"Can you help him?" she asked. "This is . . . unbearable."

"I will try," I said. "But . . ."

"No, what can you do that our own doctor cannot? And his visits have no effect."

The moans stopped for a breath or two when I entered the bedroom. My patient was conscious and had registered my presence. But after that it continued unchanged, a long whine of anguish followed by a short moan, yet another long moan, then another short one, on and on.

I observed him for a while. His eyes were closed, but there was a wet glimmer behind sticky eyelashes, and I knew that *he* knew who I was and why I had come. His hand, which had been lying limply on the blankets, moved slightly.

His fists were not clenched. There was no tension in the body, no rocking or throwing back of the head. The suffering that made him moan was not a simple message of pain from nerves in the torn tissue; even if the laudanum drops could not eradicate this physical pain, it was not this, but rather something different and more deep-rooted that tormented him.

"Monsieur Montaine," I said, "is there anything I can do for you? Should I send for a priest?"

He opened his eyes abruptly and gave a single shake of the head. "Ooohhhh."

I waited a moment, but there were no more words from the abused mouth.

"Madame," I said without turning around, "may I be permitted to be alone with your husband?"

I could almost feel her stiffen.

"Why?" she asked.

"Tending the wound can be painful," I said. "I do not think your husband would wish you to observe it."

"Oh. No. If you are sure . . ."

She quickly left the room. She was already witnessing more of her husband's pain than she could take.

I sat down next to the bed but did not yet open the bag.

"Monsieur," I said, "would you tell me what it is that is troubling you?"

There was no answer. Just another moan.

"I cannot help you if you will not tell me. You do not need to speak. I can bring you pen and paper."

The moaning ceased.

". . . ehhh," he said, but it was not a moan, it was an attempt to pronounce the word "yes."

I opened the door. Madame Montaine stood right outside, so I could present my errand with no delay.

"Why?" she said again, and her nostrils vibrated more strongly than ever. "What is it you want him to write?"

Her resistance puzzled me. I did not understand how she could refuse so simple a wish.

"Madame, you have seen yourself how difficult it is for him to speak. I simply wish him to describe his symptoms for me, so I can ask my father's advice on how best to alleviate them."

She still hesitated a moment but perhaps sensed how odd her reluctance must seem to a stranger.

"Naturally," she said. "I'll ask Odette to bring his writing instruments up from the office."

"Thank you, madame."

When the writing implements arrived and I helped Monsieur Montaine to sit up a bit so he more easily could use them, there were only three words, printed in careful script and with much space in between:

Let me die

"I cannot, monsieur."

He looked up at me with eyes that shone alarmingly and were full of hate. Then he lashed out at the pen, tray, and inkstand, so they scattered in all directions, and a shower of blue-black ink soaked the wool blanket and the sheet that covered his lower body. The stains imprinted the white surface like some alien form of calligraphy, but if there was a meaning hidden in their arbitrariness, it was not one that I was capable of deciphering.

"I would like to speak with the young master," I said to the unappealing cook whose pots I had borrowed on the day of the operation.

"Monsieur is in the garden," she said, and pointed at the green back door. Then she added with a grim smile, "Mademoiselle can just look for the smoke."

The smoke?

But she was right. I could smell it as soon as I entered the back garden, and it was not long before I saw a thin column of bonfire smoke rising from among the fruit trees a little farther away.

He stood with folded arms, observing the fire. It was a small, untidy bonfire, quickly thrown together from dried grass, old asparagus stalks, twigs, and damp leaves, and it smoldered more than it burned, except when the flames reached a new asparagus stalk and blazed up in a crackling, short-lived explosion.

"Monsieur," I said.

He started, turning around only slowly. Something had happened to him since I'd seen him last. His face had closed up, had become expressionless and plaster-like. The happy, extroverted young man I had glimpsed last time was now gone.

"Mademoiselle," he said measuredly. "Have you come to help my father?"

"I have done what I could," I said, fully knowing that it had been insufficient. "He is sleeping now."

"Thank God."

"Yes." But he would soon wake up again, and it would start over, unless I could find a way to ease his mind as well as his body. "Monsieur, there was one thing I wanted to speak to you about."

"And what's that?"

"When your sister disappeared . . . You did not go to the police. Why is that?"

"We had no reason to believe it was a matter for the police."

"Why not? Inspector Marot is not convinced that her disappearance was voluntary. And the last time we spoke, you yourself believed that Emile Oblonski was responsible for what happened."

He did not answer, just stared at me with his new, dead face.

"Have they found him?" he asked.

"No."

"You must excuse me," he said. "They are expecting me at the factory. There is a lot to do in Papa's absence."

"Of course."

But still he took the time to burn old asparagus stalks in the backyard?

"Monsieur . . ."

"Goodbye, mademoiselle," he said quickly. "I must go now."

He walked rapidly up the garden path to the house. I had to hurry if I wanted more of my questions answered.

"I understand that Cecile was engaged," I said, rushing after him.

"Yes."

"To Rodolphe Descartier. But he did not attend the funeral. Do you know why? Was it because of the Emile Oblonski affair?"

He stopped suddenly and turned toward me.

"There was no Oblonski *affair*. Descartier broke off the engagement several days before my sister disappeared from the Bernardine school."

"Why?"

"You will have to ask him that. And now I really must go. Louise or Odette can show you out."

He disappeared into the house and left me on the garden path with the scent of bonfire smoke in my nostrils and a dissatisfied itch under my skin. My attempt to embrace my confusion had not led to answers, only to more questions.

Bonfire smoke. Asparagus stalks.

There was no doubt that the Montaine family had a gardener who normally took care of such menial duties. And I remembered the grim glint in the cook's eyes when she said, "Just look for the smoke."

I hurried back to the bonfire, found a branch, and scattered the smoldering stalks, grass, and twigs.

At the center of the fire lay a book, blackened and charred on the outside but not yet burned through. I could still see that it had been bound in leather, with a clasp and a lock of the kind found on some diaries. I did not doubt for a moment that it was Cecile's.

I managed to maneuver it out of the fire with the stick and attempted to pick it up. I burned myself and had to let go of it, then tried to douse the embers by pushing the book through the wet grass, but I did not succeed. The pages curled and crumbled, and only individual words were visible briefly when a page burned through and I could see the next page beneath it.

Skin, I read. *Dream. Tongue.*

Yet another page disappeared.

. . . kisses . . .

. . . breath . . . my thighs
. . . penetrated deeply . . . inside . . . melted
. . . when I long to . . .
. . . told no one . . .

And then a last amputated sentence before the embers took the rest: *is not enough!*

I felt my own breathing change. There was something about the disappearing, smoldering words that made me tremble inside, a shiver I could not control. I pressed the palm of my hand so hard against my mouth that one of my canines cut into my lower lip, and a brief taste of blood mixed with my saliva.

Is not enough. No. It was not. I wanted more, wanted to know more. It was intolerable that Cecile was dead and could no longer tell me who she was.

"I came as soon as I read the telegram," said Professor Dreyfuss. "The circumstances are, of course, unfortunate, but I have to admit that I find them interesting professionally."

Sufficiently interesting that he had not hesitated for a moment to climb into the Commissioner's resurrected hearse to go with us to the convent. He was somewhat more conventionally dressed today, in a gray suit and a derby hat, with a burgundy silk waist-coat as the only flamboyant note. He had not had the automobile with him in Heidelberg and so had been obliged to travel by train like ordinary mortals.

The hearse was necessary because we wished to bring home at least one wolf for autopsy and further examination. Large quantities of ice we had procured from the town's fish market made sure that we did not spread living mites all the way to Varbourg.

The Commissioner sat silent and inscrutable and reacted only sparingly to the professor's attempt at conversation. I myself had the irritating thought that the professor had now seen me three times in the same slightly worn traveling suit, this time at least with a short beige linen jacket in a bolero cut that was more comfortable in the hot weather than the woollen one that matched the skirt. He must think that I had nothing else to wear, which was sadly close to the truth. At least I had occupied a couple of winter evenings with adding a border of dark-brown ribbon to the edge of the collar, the sleeves, and the hem to hide the most threadbare places.

The heavy wagon swung into a lane bordered by chestnuts, and the Belgians' replacements, two coal-black boulonnais horses, leaned forward to get up the last incline.

"Are they expecting us?" asked the professor.

"I promised Mother Filippa to return today with news of the fate of the wolves," I said. "She does not know that I am not coming alone."

"How do they keep the wolves? In cages?"

"No." I pointed north to where, just beyond the almshouse, one could glimpse the tops of the elderberry bushes growing along the fence around the wolf pen. "They have a fairly large area to roam around in, five or six hectares, I believe, with boulders and trees and a variety of shrubbery."

"How are we going to get hold of them, then?"

"They are used to being fed, and I even think it is possible to call them. They are not truly wild. But there have to be sufficient numbers of hunters because as soon as the first shot is fired, the rest will naturally run away."

"If I can be of help, I would be happy to," he offered. "I am an excellent shot."

"I will tell Mother Filippa."

I was not looking forward to informing her that all her wolves were sentenced to death. But there was no way around it.

Sister Marie-Claire let us in.

"Mother Filippa is not here right now," she said. "Can I help?"

"We had better speak to the abbess herself," I answered. "When will she be back? Unfortunately, it is of some importance."

Sister Marie-Claire looked from the Commissioner to the professor and then at me again.

"The gentlemen will have to wait here," she said. "If Mademoiselle will come with me ..."

The "gentlemen" had to sit nicely in the visitors' room, while Sister Marie-Claire led me through the cloistered part of the convent and to the hospital wing.

"She is attending a birth," Marie-Claire confided in me. "It is one of our former pupils, and it is her first, so she is a bit anxious."

The woman giving birth was hardly older than I, and *a bit anxious* was clearly an understatement. She feared for her life. The terror could be read clearly in her sweaty face and in the jerking, panicked gaze. She waddled up and down the wide corridor, dressed only in a birthing smock, with Mother Filippa on one side and an unfamiliar nun on the other. They held her arms out, away from her body, so that it looked as if they were teaching her to fly.

"Why are they doing that?" I whispered.

"If we do not stop her, she will hit herself in the stomach," said Sister Marie-Claire. "Some get like that, as if they are trying to punish the child for the pain it is causing them. Mother, Mademoiselle Karno has returned."

Mother Filippa looked up. There was a movement in her

face, and it was clear that she understood at once what message I brought.

"We are far from done here," she said, "but I assume that this cannot be postponed?"

"It must happen as quickly as possible," I said. "To minimize the risk of further infection."

"All of them?"

"I am afraid so."

The laboring woman looked mutely from one to the other and of course had no idea what we were talking about. But when Mother Filippa wanted to let her go and allow Sister Marie-Claire to take her place, she grabbed on to the abbess's sleeve with a grip that made her knuckles shine white.

"No," she said. "No."

"My dear child. I will return soon. I promise."

Her promise did not make much of an impression. Mother Filippa had to loosen the white fingers from her sleeve one by one before it was possible for her to go. At that moment there was a contraction that made the woman bend over and moan, not unlike Monsieur Montaine's cries:

"Aaaaaaah . . . Aaaaaahhhh . . ."

It could have been me. The same thought that had felt so urgent when I had stood by Cecile's dead body reappeared with similar force. It could just as easily have been me, married, impregnated, conquered by biology. I looked at the distorted features, at the rigid back trembling under the birthing smock, at the claw-like fingers. I shuddered. And the girl, the woman, lifted her head for a brief moment. Her gaze was blank and empty, her personality erased, there was no room for anything except the pressure and the pain.

"Nggahh. Nggahhh. Nggahhh." Her breathing came in short gasps.

"If it is just about time . . . ," I said hesitantly.

"Oh, no, my dear," said Mother Filippa. "We have many hours to go. Time enough, unfortunately, to see to death before we take care of this new life."

The wolves were uneasy. Though they could smell the fresh goat meat, they nonetheless continued to crouch, half hidden by the shrubbery, while they observed the row of men waiting among the elderberry bushes by the fence.

But they were tame animals, not wild. They were used to being fed here, and finally one of them ventured out onto the worn grass toward the dead goat that had been tied to a pole so that they would not drag it off into the shrubbery.

"Wait," said the professor quietly to the other hunters. "Wait until they are all eating."

The wolf in front reached the goat and closed its jaws around its throat with a growl. That was too much for the others. In a gray and white furry wave they tumbled from their hiding place and closed in on the dead animal.

"On my count," said the professor, and raised his borrowed rifle. "One. Two. Three. Fire."

The shots rang out. Most of the wolves fell at once. One managed to leap back for four or five meters before it, too, was hit and fell to the ground, and another was left wounded and howling for a few long seconds before the professor ended its suffering with a precise shot through the head. Then all was silent, and what had been a wolf pack a moment ago was now just a collection of bloody carcasses.

Two of them were carried out to the hearse by men with cloths tied across their lower faces and gloves on their hands, to join the old wolf that already lay half buried in ice and sawdust, just as dead as his previous pack mates. A big bonfire of straw and wood was built and set on fire in the wolf pen, and the remaining corpses were slung onto the pyre with pitchforks, like tossing coal into the furnace of a locomotive. The singed smell of burned fur tore at my nose, and I turned away.

Mother Filippa stood a few steps from me. She had hidden her hands in the sleeves of her habit, her eyes were closed, and her face was calm as usual. But in her eyelashes, a teardrop glittered, and it took a little while before she raised her head and opened her eyes again.

"Are you sad?" asked the professor when he helped me up into the wagon. A sharp whiff of gunpowder still emanated from his hands, hair, and clothes. "You are so silent."

"I hate to see life wasted in that way," I said. "Even if it is only animals."

"It was necessary."

"Yes. I know."

But I did not say much more on the trip home.

We performed autopsies on the three wolves the next morning after they had lain on ice all night. Presumably, all the mites were dead by this point, but the three of us, the professor, my father, and I, nonetheless covered our mouths and wore gloves. If there were still living mites, the risk of infection would be greater now than when the wolves were alive, since they, as in Cecile's case, would have left their host in search of a new one.

Despite the refrigeration, the three bodies smelled rancid and decayed already. One of the hunters had offered to gut them for us and had seemed perplexed at our insistence that we most certainly did not want the innards removed. It had also been hard to make them understand that the remaining animals were not to be skinned but must be burned, pelts and all.

However, the three unburned wolves now lay before us, complete with stomach contents and internal organs, and since my father still had only limited use of one arm, it was the professor and I who had to open the chest and crack the ribs apart so we could lift out the lungs and the heart. It took real strength; one could not fiddle delicately with one bone at a time. I took a small secret pride in the fact that I was almost as fast as the professor.

The lung tissue was darker now than it would have been if we had performed the autopsies immediately. But even though I studied both the bronchial tubes and the lung membrane carefully, I saw no sign of the abscesses we had found in Father Abigore. The cavities of the throat and the nostrils were irritated, and under the microscope one could see the tiny lesions and scars that the mites had left, as well, of course, as a number of dead mites. We now had plenty both for our own use and for the Forchhammer Institute's parasite collection, I thought. But the lungs were healthy.

"It doesn't look as if the animals have any abscess formation," said the professor. "It appears that they can host the parasites without suffering the same type of lung disease that the human hosts were afflicted with."

"Perhaps it is not the mites themselves that cause the abscess formation," I said. "Might they merely act as vectors for the bacteria?"

Once again there was a moment where the professor just *looked* at me. Perhaps I was getting used to it; at least it did not seem quite as paralyzing as before.

"I have read everything I could get hold of on Pasteur's work with pébrine in silkworms," I said a bit defensively. "Bacteria *can* be transferred by a parasite!"

"That is a very valid point," said the professor. "But have we actually determined that the abscesses are caused by a bacterial infection?"

My father rubbed his forehead with his healthy hand. He still looked a bit pained, although it was better than the day before.

"If only the family had let me perform an autopsy on the girl," he said. "And if only we had found Father Abigore while it was still possible to do a proper bacteriological examination."

"Do we have any tissue at all from the priest?"

"Yes, a bit. But at this stage, we are unlikely to find much."

"So. Let us study the wolves first."

We took samples from all the wolves where the mucous cavities and throat were most attacked by the mites and placed the bloody tissue lumps in gelatin-filled petri dishes. I marked the dishes so that we would know from which cadaver they came and set them aside for cultivation. Unfortunately, we did not have a proper temperature-controlled cabinet for that purpose but had to make do with placing the petri dishes in a glass box on the windowsill and hoping for the best. I resisted an urge to apologize to the professor for the primitive conditions. He must be aware that this was not the Forchhammer Institute but simply a rebuilt kitchen with modest facilities.

The professor removed his bloody gloves and dried a bit of sweat from his forehead.

"It is quite hot in here," he said. "We had better put the wolves on ice again as fast as possible."

The ice from the hearse had been poured into three big wooden crates that reminded me of the circumstances under which Father Abigore had been found. The professor and I hauled the cadavers off the laboratory bench and back into the boxes. Some of the ice had melted in the course of the night, but there was a significant cooling effect left.

As we were closing up the boxes, I noticed that Professor Dreyfuss had touched the wolves with his bare hands.

"Professor," I said, "you did not put your gloves back on."

He held up his hands, wet from the melted ice and blood.

"That was careless of me," he said.

"Don't touch anything," I said quickly. "I'll get the carbolic solution."

I poured plenty of carbolic solution into a tin water basin. The professor was still standing with his hands held stiffly out in front of him. I held the basin while he washed and rinsed them carefully in the pungent liquid. There was an odd form of intimacy in that moment, which for some reason made me remember what it was like to be bathed together with my cousin Claude in my aunt's kitchen, when my mother was still alive and we occasionally visited Aunt Desirée and Uncle Georges. I must have been about four, Claude a year younger.

The water in the white basin was colored pink with wolf blood, and why that would remind me so much of two naked children in the same bathtub, lobster red from the hot water and with white soapsuds in their hair, I did not understand.

The professor dried his hands and arms carefully in a clean towel I handed him. "Should we look at the priest's abscesses now?" he asked.

I brought out the glass jars with Father Abigore's specimens. The pale growths floating in the alcohol looked more like some kind of marine polyps than something that had once been a part of a human being.

"Alcohol or formaldehyde?" he asked.

"Alcohol," I said, again a bit apologetically. Formaldehyde preserved better because it killed the bacteria instead of just slowing their growth. But it was also more expensive.

"All the better!" he said enthusiastically.

He was right, of course, I suddenly realized. Precisely because it was *not* formaldehyde, the chance of finding some kind of bacterial remnant was significantly greater.

The professor fished the infected tissue from the jar and with practiced, precise cuts sliced through one of the abscesses. I prepared a new set of petri dishes with gelatin and transferred what I hoped was sufficient bacterial material to begin a cultivation.

After a fairly humble lunch—just a cold platter of pâté and Brie that Elise had fetched from Dreischer & Son—we returned to the laboratory to observe the results. Professor Dreyfuss seized the first petri dish, from one of the wolves, and without comment I handed him the solution of methylene-blue alcohol and caustic potash that we used for bacterial identification.

The microscope was back in its usual place on one of the workbenches.

"It is not from Zeiss, unfortunately," I apologized.

"Dear mademoiselle, it is a fine instrument and entirely sufficient," said the professor somewhat distractedly, while he adjusted the lens. "Hmmm. Yes. Hmmm." The last was apparently a running, unconscious commentary to what he was observing.

"Have a look," he said, and waved at my father with one hand while still crouched over the apparatus himself.

"Yes," said my father. "Clear chains . . . and quite a lot of them."

"Is it streptococcus?" I asked, and had to hold myself back from pushing both men aside so I could get a look. "May I . . . ?"

The professor gallantly took a step away from the microscope. "Of course."

The methyl had taken effect and had colored the bacteria, and I could clearly see the drop-shaped microorganisms and the short S-chains they formed. When Pasteur described streptococcus for the first time, he had compared the bacteria chain to a rosary. However, these chains were shorter, in some cases only a single pair.

"Some kind of micrococcus," said my father. "I am not sure which. It is a bit like Fehleisen's erysipelas-causing bacteria but . . ."

"Micrococci can be frighteningly difficult to distinguish one from another," said the professor. "We still know too little about their various forms. And even less about their effect."

"Rosenbach describes erysipelas bacteria as fern shaped, while pyogene cocci are supposed to look like acacia leaves," I said.

"Pyogene micrococci might cause pyaemic lung abscesses," said the professor thoughtfully.

"Apparently not in wolves," said my father dryly.

"No. You are right about that."

All the wolf samples showed traces of micrococci. It was time to turn to Father Abigore's samples. I did not have the greatest expectations for the tissue samples that the professor now— somewhat disrespectfully—simply referred to as the "priestly abscesses." Not after the freezing, and after that, the alcohol solution. However, the professor studied the culture even longer and even more intensely than he had done the wolf samples, all the while accompanying his efforts with his unconscious "Hmmm. Hmmm."

"Well," he said at last, "the material is of course not the best, but ... well, have a look." His gaze fell on me when he said it. My father and I almost bumped into each other because I followed his encouragement.

"Maddie!" said my father, surprised and perhaps a touch annoyed. He was not used to my pushing ahead.

"Pardon me," I said. "I was too eager ..."

His smile was warm but also overbearing.

"Do calm down," he said. "I will let you have your turn in a minute ..."

While he bent over the sought-after microscope, I felt a certain unfamiliar irritation. It was not just my usual impatience; it was that I did not want his permission, I wanted the *right*. Laboratory work was more than just an odd and rather unsuitable hobby for me. It was a part of the profession I was planning to devote my life to, regardless of what my father thought.

I realized that the professor was observing me again, and I wondered whether my rebellious thought was visible. I quickly pushed it back where it came from, as if it were a strap from a chemise that was not supposed to be visible to the general public.

"There *is* something," said my father. "But whether it is the same organism ... is difficult to determine."

Finally it was my turn. And I could see why neither of them would speak categorically. The growth was poor, the pigmentation weak, and the morphology consequently difficult to determine. All the same, a conviction was born in me that was no doubt entirely unscientific.

It *was* the same bacteria. It had inhabited the wolves without making them sick, but it had been deadly for Cecile Montaine—and would presumably have killed Father Abigore had not someone got to him first with a coal shovel.

Rodolphe Descartier looked at me with a certain lack of enthusiasm.

"I understand that you wish to discuss a deposit?" he said.

"Not really."

"No?" He frowned. "Did Monsieur Lavalle misunderstand something?"

"No." I cleared my throat. I was not used to this kind of deception and forward behavior. "I am afraid I misled Monsieur Lavalle. You see, I am here because you were engaged to Cecile Montaine."

His reaction to this simple statement was extraordinary. A scarlet tide surged across his otherwise pale skin, and he got up clumsily from his stool behind the counter.

"How dare you!" He gasped. "Leave. Now. At once!"

His outburst provoked curious glances in the bank, which neither he nor I cared for.

"Unfortunately, I cannot help you," he said in a more normal tone of voice.

"I think you misunderstand me," I said quietly. "The Commissioner was of the opinion that it was better if you and I were to discuss a banking matter quietly. But if you would prefer a more official inquiry, then I am sure . . ."

"No," he said. "You are right. If you would come this way?" He lifted a part of the counter and indicated that I should follow him.

It was hardly likely that all apprentice clerks in Varonne Commerce could just walk into the assistant director's office and say, "Excuse me, Maurice . . . I need to discuss something with this young lady . . ."

But though Rodolphe Descartier might officially still be a lowly clerk, the assistant bank director knew very well that it was only a matter of time before this gangly and still somewhat pimply-faced twenty-year-old would be sitting in the director's office next door. He got up and bowed politely in my direction.

"Of course. Mademoiselle, will you have a seat? Would you like tea or coffee? Or perhaps a glass of sherry?"

"Thank you very much. A cup of tea if it is not too much trouble."

"Not at all. I will see to it."

After which he managed to turn over his office to the bank apprentice and his "young lady" without it in any way seeming awkward. Clearly a man with a well-developed sense of diplomacy.

Rodolphe Descartier was not nearly as well versed in this area. He stared at me with poorly disguised affront.

"What is it you want, then?" he asked.

"We are attempting to track Cecile's movements in the weeks before her death."

"Why?" Again the lurid flush as if the sound of her name alone initiated processes he could not control.

"It is of critical importance for the public health," I said with all the authority I could muster. "We need to trace the infection Cecile died from. I will also need to take a specimen from your nostrils." It was probably best not to mention the mites.

"Nostrils?"

"Yes."

Did I imagine it, or did he look relieved?

"I am not sick," he said.

"Nevertheless . . ."

"Oh, very well. If it is only my nose you are concerned about . . ."

"The Commissioner appreciates your cooperation." The Commissioner had no idea I was there. But *if* he had known, he would definitely have appreciated it, I assured myself.

We had found no traces of mites anywhere in Cecile's circle of acquaintances either in Varbourg or at the Bernardine School, and Cecile had not displayed any sign of illness before her disappearance. I needed to study both Koch's and Fehleisen's work with micrococci more closely, but I seemed to remember that they reproduced quite quickly when they became pathogens. Therefore, it was most likely that the mite invasion had occurred after Cecile's disappearance, perhaps as a result of long and close contact with Emile Oblonski. But he had not yet been found in spite of Marot's search, neither "healthy, sick, dead, or alive" as the Commissioner had expressed it, and we could therefore not be sure.

In other words, I did not expect to find much in Rodolphe Descartier's nose apart from thoroughly normal nasal discharge. But if I did find mites . . . then it would suggest that he had been in contact with Cecile after she had disappeared. And that would be an extremely interesting piece of news for both the Commissioner and Police Inspector Marot.

I got out my loupe, my mirror, and a fresh pipette. Descartier looked, if possible, even less enthusiastic. His Adam's apple, already fairly prominent, moved uneasily under the skin of his throat.

"What do I need to do?" he asked.

"Lean your head back and relax."

I directed the lamp at his face and bent over him. He smelled strongly of cologne and shaving cream, and once again I noticed how the blood rushed into the tiny capillaries of his facial epidermis. His breathing became quicker and more shallow, and that was probably what suddenly made me perceive this simple examination, which I had performed literally hundreds of times before, as something far more invasive and private.

"I am sorry," I said. "But it really *is* necessary."

He went along with having his nostrils and throat illuminated, but when I directed the pipette at his second nostril, he suddenly jerked his head aside and batted at my arm.

"No," he said. "That will have to do."

His flailing blow had been uncommonly hard, enough so that I had dropped the pipette. I picked it up. The glass tube was full of clear, only slightly white fluid, and I could not immediately see any sign of mites.

At that moment there was a knock on the door.

"Come in," said Descartier, thankful for the interruption, I think, and slightly out of breath.

It was the tea, arranged on a small trolley, which was being pushed across the threshold by a middle-aged woman the size of a sparrow.

"Milk or lemon?" she asked as she poured a strong orange-colored liquid into the cups.

"Lemon," I said. "One sugar."

Apparently she did not need to ask Descartier. His cup received a generous helping of milk before she retreated with a small curtsy.

A short pause ensued while we sipped the tea.

"I apologize for my behavior," said Descartier at last. "Cecile is a painful memory."

"I understand that, of course," I said. "Was that why you did not attend the funeral?"

He looked up sharply. "Yes. I . . . did not feel up to it."

He was lying. I couldn't say exactly how I knew he was lying, but he was. It was not just the blush that raced across his face again. After all, it seemed to appear almost constantly. Perhaps it was something about his voice.

"Have they determined precisely what kind of infection it was . . . ?" he asked, his eyes rigidly focused on his teacup. And then it dawned on me. I suddenly understood why he had been so relieved when he realized that it was "only his nose" that I wanted to examine.

"Not yet," I lied. "But we know that it is primarily transmitted by certain forms of intimate contact."

He choked on his tea. Orange droplets sprayed the assistant director's desk.

"Mademoiselle . . ."

"Did you know that Cecile Montaine kept a diary?" I asked innocently.

He set the teacup aside with such force that a thin crack appeared in the porcelain glaze.

"What has she said?" he asked. "What has she written? It is not true. She was the one who—the one who—"

"Perhaps it is best if you tell your side of the story," I said. "In the interest of thoroughness."

What emerged under many protests and angry comments was the following:

Cecile had attended Sunday lunch at her future in-laws' home by the Place de Triomphe. After lunch the two young people had been permitted to stroll together in the nearby park. Cecile had been happy and lively and had started a snowball fight.

"She was always happier outside," said Descartier. "Like a child out of school. And when she was happy, she was . . . incredibly attractive."

It was a cold day, hazy with frost, and the park was nearly deserted. Descartier had suggested that they sit for a bit in the empty closed-up tea pavilion. And there, in the cold room, behind closed shutters, he had kissed her. It was not the first time, but it was the first time they were alone for an indefinite time without interruptions and invasive looks. And he had been completely taken aback by the reception he received.

If one was to believe Rodolphe Descartier, his fiancée had transformed herself into a fury. She had unbuttoned his pants and taken his member into her mouth. And as soon as he was ready, she had offered her sex to him, from behind, like an animal, and insisted until he performed.

He told the story with his back to me, standing not by the window but facing into a corner of the office.

"It was revolting. Shocking. I have never experienced anything like it. No man . . . I say, no man could have . . ."

He stopped. But while he had related the story, I could tell that he was reliving it, too, and it was not exactly distaste that made his voice hoarse and his shoulders tremble.

And suddenly he turned around. The buttoned-up scion of the bank, the polite apprentice, hurled his words at me in an almost unrecognizable voice.

"I gave her what she had coming. You had better believe it. Until she was steaming. Until she bled. Until she screamed in pleasure. Is that what you want to hear? Are you enjoying this? Are you jealous? Her ass was baboon red by the end. She was so wet that she was dripping. Is that what you want to hear? I hammered her, and she just wanted more. She lay across the bench with her cunt straight up in the air, and *then* she suddenly started to bawl. But you had better believe she was asking for it. What about you? Are you like that, too?"

I sat with my mouth open and did not know what to say or do. I had never actually heard the word "cunt" before. He grabbed both my upper arms, so that the teacup fell out of my hands and tinkled quietly against the carpet. In one powerful motion he pulled me to my feet and pushed me up against the mahogany panels.

"Are you like that, too?" he repeated. "You come here and insist . . . You make me tell you . . . things . . . use words . . . that no lady would . . ."

"Would you be kind enough to let me go," I said, and tried to sound calm and controlled. "Monsieur, you forget yourself!"

He did let me go. His young face was completely naked, his gaze dark with barely restrained horror.

"Leave," he said. "You got what you came for." The last was said with a contempt so searing that I could not help blushing myself.

"Was that the day you broke off the engagement?" I asked.

"Of course," he said, suddenly much more collected. "I wanted a wife, not a whore."

I went directly from Varonne Commerce to Boulevard Saint-Cyr and the Montaine family home. Odette, the parlor maid, let me in without first announcing me to Madame, a definite sign that in her eyes I had crossed an invisible line and was no longer a guest of the master's. Not quite one of the help, either, perhaps, but a sort of service provider on a par with tutors and craftsmen.

Monsieur Montaine had stopped moaning. But I sensed that it was not because he was feeling better but because his family had given him such a dangerously large dose of laudanum that he could barely breathe. There was hardly any reaction when I removed the thin layer of gauze that protected the wound from impurities, and even though his eyes were open, his gaze was veiled and unclear. Only once during the treatment did he look directly at me and say, almost clearly, "Like ahn ahimal. Ahn ahimal."

Then he closed his eyes, shutting out both me and the rest of the world. Who or what was he speaking of? *Like an animal.* It was the same expression that Rodolphe Descartier had used about Cecile, and it occurred to me that the last conversation the tormented man in the bed had had with his daughter presumably concerned the broken engagement and its cause.

There was no sign of infection, thank God, but if his loving family did not reduce his laudanum doses, they risked killing him. I therefore asked to speak to Madame.

She received me in the orangery, where she was tending to a collection of orchids worthy of a botanical museum.

"How do you judge his condition?" she asked.

There was no doubt that her concern and care were deep-felt and genuine. I could see the signs of weeping and sleepless nights in the pale violet shadows around her swollen eyes, and I think she had lost weight as well. But her dark hair was carefully arranged, and though the dress was black, the elegant cut and the neat lace were a far cry from sackcloth and ashes.

"The wound is healing well. But, madame, you must adhere to my father's instructions regarding the laudanum."

"Are you suggesting that we are not?"

"Perhaps there is an uncertainty about who administers it and when?" I suggested diplomatically. "I can see that he is affected to a degree that is a threat to his health, madame. Laudanum inhibits respiration. If your husband receives too much, he may simply stop breathing."

"I see. Thank you for your warning."

Had she understood it? I could not tell. Her gaze was cool, her politeness so distancing that it almost felt like rudeness instead.

"Madame, he seems very troubled," I ventured. "Not just from the physical injuries, but in his mind."

"Of course he does. He has lost a daughter."

"Yes, I understand that. But forgive me if I say that it seems to me to be something more than just sorrow."

If she had been a bird, she would have hackled her feathers at me. Her gaze grew narrow and sharp.

"What are you suggesting?" she said.

"Perhaps a kind of guilt?" I said. "It often happens that bereaved parents will blame themselves unreasonably. I am in no way suggesting that your husband has *reason* to feel guilty, just that he may do so anyway. Could there have been some occurrence that would normally have been trivial, an argument or a reprimand, that now has taken on terrible proportions for him, because it was the last communication he had with Cecile?"

But I made no impression on her armor.

"Mademoiselle Karno, I think this conversation is over." She turned her back on me and picked up a delicate brush that she proceeded to guide into the flower of an opulent, pale red orchid until she made contact with the stamen. A judicious prod released a copious amount of sticky pale yellow pollen.

I had the choice between leaving or being terribly rude. I chose the latter—not without misgivings from the sense of propriety my upbringing had instilled in me.

"I have spoken with Rodolphe Descartier," I said.

She stood as if turned to stone for several seconds. A blush not unlike his washed across the slightly sunken cheeks and the thin neck, and the pollination brush shook slightly.

"I see," she said at last. "And what does he have to say in his own defense?"

A quick unwelcome image flashed through my mind. His face, so close to mine that tiny bubbles of spit exploded against my chin and upper lip, the pressure from his body against my corseted abdomen. *You had better believe she was asking for it. What about you? Are you like that, too?*

"You already know that, madame."

Now it was not just the brush that shook. Her entire slender, black-clad figure was rattled by a force she could barely contain.

"Leave," she hissed. "Doctor Berger will be in charge of my husband's care from now on."

"What I'm wondering . . . ," I began. "What I am wondering

is this. Did your husband and Cecile part in anger? Did he scold her? Is that why he is so tormented right now?"

Then the dam burst. She turned toward me and screamed like a fishwife.

"Go away! Get lost. What the *hell* does one have to do to get rid of you?" She hurled the brush at me, so that the yellow pollen left a smear down the front of my gray blouse. Then she began to cry, with the same unrestrained, jagged sobs as at the funeral. She had to support her hands on the plant table's zinc top and lean forward to get enough air. If I had wanted to pierce her armor, I had certainly succeeded. But all that emerged was pain. No words. She was beyond words now, and the only sound that came from her was more like a howl than a sob.

"Why were you gone so long?" asked my father when I returned home. "Has his condition worsened?"

I had not told him that I was also planning to visit Rodolphe Descartier. And I couldn't tell him what had happened in the assistant director's office.

"No, the wound is healing well, in fact," I said. "But they are giving him too much laudanum."

"You must get them to stop that!"

"I tried. But . . ."

"But what?"

"Madame Montaine was offended."

"Why? What did you say?"

My cheeks burned and I knew that they—again—were bright red. My pale complexion was one of the few features I possessed that Madame Aubrey had considered a feminine advantage, but occasionally I wished that I had a less revealing skin type.

"Nothing special," I lied.

"I will go over there myself!" He got up from the chaise longue, with somewhat less difficulty than before, I noticed.

"No," I said quickly. "She . . . She got so upset that she no longer wants our help. Doctor Berger is to see to her husband's care from now on."

He observed me carefully. His narrow face was damp from the heat, and his gaze clear as water. I had the sense that he himself had completely given up on the laudanum drops even though the bottle still stood on the tobacco table next to the chaise longue.

"Madeleine, what is going on? It is unlike you to be rude to our clients."

"Should I have let her kill her husband with an overdose out of sheer politeness?" I protested, more sharply than I had intended.

A surprised and somewhat affronted expression crossed his face.

"Maddie!"

"Sorry, Papa. But . . . you were not there."

He looked down at his broken leg with a grim expression.

"No," he said. "I know I am asking a lot of you right now, perhaps more than you are ready to cope with. I am sorry."

"No," I protested. "That is not it at all." My gaze fell on the collection of medical journals on the tobacco table next to the laudanum bottle. "What are you reading?" I was not asking merely in order to change the subject. My interest was genuine.

"I was trying to find something that resembles our micrococci," he said.

"Did you succeed?"

"I'm not sure. Fehleisen's work with erysipelas is interesting. Did you know that he managed not just to cultivate the bacteria but also to inoculate several terminally ill patients with the erysipelas culture with amazing results?"

"Yes. I read the article. I believe he actually managed to get a cancerous tumor to shrink?"

"Yes. And cured a patient with lupus. But what is interesting in this connection is that although erysipelas is not restricted to humans, there are apparently distinct erysipelas bacteria for different species—one for humans, one for swine, one for horses, and so on."

"If we are dealing with a species-specific bacterium of the micrococci type . . . ," I began.

". . . Then that might explain why the wolves did not get sick while humans do."

"But erysipelas does not normally cause lung abscesses," I said. "And if it is a human-specific bacterium, then what is it doing in wolves in the first place?"

He shook his head. "I have no idea. And my stomach is growling so loudly that I cannot think. Where on earth is Elise? Isn't it almost seven?"

"I will go find her," I said. "Or else I will run over to Chez Louis myself to pick up something."

"I know this is a tough time for you," he said. "But it will get better soon. Lanier will put a new plaster cast on my leg next week, one I can walk on."

"That is good news," I said, smiling. But as I went down the stairs and headed for Chez Louis, conflicting feelings stirred inside me. Of course I wanted my father to get better and regain his mobility. But at the same time I had to admit that his temporary handicap was not just a burden to me. It had also given me a certain freedom, a freedom that I did not wish to lose again.

"I thought that you might want to bury him," I said to Mother Filippa as the driver of the hansom cab hauled the meter-long wooden box from the rack at the top of the carriage. "Fire is not necessary; the ice has had the same effect now."

"That was thoughtful of you," she said. "Not many people would understand. Thank you."

The two other wolf cadavers had been cremated in the hospital's furnace, but in spite of my father's puzzlement, I had insisted on bringing the old wolf back to the convent.

"I understand that you have already acquired some new wolves?" I said.

"Yes. Someone higher up in the hierarchy than I felt that it was necessary because of the myth."

"The myth? Don't you believe it?"

She smiled. "Yes and no. I firmly believe that God's mercy gave us the wolves three hundred years ago, and that He had a purpose in doing so. Perhaps we were supposed to learn to understand ourselves better through living with them? But that the mere presence of a few wolves at the convent is enough to save the nation from defeat and human stupidity . . . that I doubt. Do you want to see them? Sadly, they are a bit of a sorry sight right now; we have to keep them caged in quarantine for a couple of weeks."

She was right. It was a depressing sight. There were only three, a male and two females, the male from Varbourg's Zoological Garden, the two half-grown females caught in the mountains and brought here in the cage they still crouched in.

One pup lay listlessly and had apparently withdrawn into herself completely; the other snapped at us and bit the bars as soon as she caught our scent. The grown wolf also lay flat at the bottom of its cage, not as panicked as the two wild ones, but his eyes were rheumy and his nose looked dry and crusty.

"He does not look well," I said.

"No. I don't know if it is just the trip and the change of environment, or if he is really ill," said Mother Filippa. "I wish Emile was here. He had an instinct for getting them to thrive."

I noticed that she said *had* not *has*.

"You do not believe he is coming back?" I asked.

She sighed. "I don't know what to think. Police Inspector Marot has been here several times now, and he seems convinced that poor Emile was responsible for all kinds of crimes, from abduction to the murder of a priest."

"But you are not?"

"No. Emile is a very gentle soul, but most people misunderstand."

"Did Cecile understand?"

The abbess shook her head doubtfully. "She was the only one of the girls who was not afraid of him."

I thought of what she had done with Rodolphe Descartier and of the diary's smoldering soot-stained words: *Kisses . . . breath . . . my thighs . . . penetrated deeply . . . inside . . . melted.*

And that last despairing cry: *is not enough!*

Generally speaking, Cecile did not seem overly afraid of men, I thought.

"May I see Cecile's room?" I asked.

The abbess raised an eyebrow. "Why?"

I could perhaps have said something or other about the importance of finding Emile Oblonski, especially if he was sick. And something about "signs a man would not notice." But I had the feeling that it was better just to be honest.

"Because I would like to understand her better," I said. "And understand her death. My father always says that the dead can no longer speak, and that we must therefore help them tell their stories."

"There is certainly a great deal about this story that I do not understand," said Mother Filippa. "And the police have already gone through everything. I can't see what harm it would do for you to satisfy your curiosity."

The younger girls slept in a dormitory, while the older ones, like Cecile, slept four to a room on the floor above the dormitory. The school's facilities did not permit much in the way of privacy, I thought, at the sight of the narrow room that was made even narrower by the bunk beds along the walls. Any illusion of finding a secret diary hidden under her pillow evaporated at once. Two of the beds were tidily made up with white sheets and gray blankets, the third, the one I assumed had been Cecile's, was covered only by a bare mattress. On the fourth, a chubby schoolgirl lay on her side, crying quietly.

"What is it now, Christine?" asked Mother Filippa.

"My stomach hurts," said the girl.

"Shouldn't you be in the infirmary, then?"

"Sister Marie-Claire said I was in the way. They are having a big cleanup."

Her pudgy face was red and tear streaked, and Sister Marie-Claire's slightly insensitive comment had probably been prompted by a suspicion that Christine was not physically ill. That she was sad and miserable was, on the other hand, quite obvious.

Suddenly I realized that my feeling that I had seen her before was caused not just by the likelihood that I had studied her nose intensely. She had attended Cecile's funeral—she was the school friend who had cried most openly and loudly.

I held out my hand. "Hello, Christine. My name is Madeleine Karno. We met at the funeral." *Met* was of course a bit of an exaggeration since we had been about twenty meters apart at the time. But Christine took my hand and snuffled even more loudly.

"She was my best friend," she said, runny nosed and tearful. "I miss her so much."

"I can understand that," I said, and sat down on the bed across from her. "It must be hard." I looked up briefly at Mother Filippa. She nodded her permission for me to speak with Christine and perhaps give her a little attention, which she clearly needed.

"I will be in the wolf stables," she said. "Come say goodbye before you go."

"Thank you, Mother," I said.

"It is all so terrible," said Christine. "I keep thinking that I will wake up and it will all be just a bad dream."

"How long have you known Cecile?" I asked.

"We roomed together for a year and a half. I knew her before as well, of course, but it was not until then that we became friends."

"What was she like?"

"She was wonderful."

That did not help me much.

"Did you talk a lot?"

"Every evening. She would climb down and get into my bed, and we would hold each other and talk. Anette once got so mad that she threw her pillow at us, but we did not care. It is so strange that she is no longer here. I can't sleep without her; it feels all wrong."

"Did you ever talk about Emile Oblonski?"

Christine stopped sniveling. "Him," she said. Her brown eyes grew a shade darker.

"Did she talk about him?"

"Not really. She just said that the others did not understand him."

"What did she mean by that?"

"All the girls—they did not think that he should be allowed to be here. Some of them even got their parents to complain. That made Cecile angry. She said they were a bunch of narrow-minded, cruel ninnies."

"Why did they think he did not belong here? Because he was a man?"

"No. There are other men employed here, not in the school and in the actual convent, but on the farm and the apple orchards and so on. Of course there are men."

"What was it about Emile, then?" Inspector Marot had called him unattractive and slow-witted. I wondered to myself if that was the reason for the complaints.

It sounded almost as if Christine was giggling.

"Well, he couldn't help it. It was a kind of illness. But . . ."

"But what?"

"Well, if he was scared, or angry, or . . . well, it did not take much. Then it got hard."

I stopped myself the second before asking her what she meant by "it."

"Oh," I said.

"Yes. That must have been why he was so shy, too. But there were those who thought that a convent couldn't have someone like him around. Even though he lived in the wolf stables and kept to himself, and never came to the school."

"If he never . . . Then how did you . . . ?"

"Oh, everyone knew. And once there were some girls who sneaked down with sheets over their heads like ghosts, just to scare him. Just to see . . . well, it."

"Did you?"

"No! But . . . some girls did. Aprile Beauforte, for one. I think it was her idea. At least, she was the one Cecile took revenge on."

"How?"

"She pulled her out of bed in the middle of the night and dragged her into a cold shower. Aprile was screaming her head off, but Cecile had the strength of a man almost. Aprile did not stand a chance."

"But you did not know that Cecile was going to run away with Emile?"

The giggling ceased. Christine's face grew blank and expressionless.

"No."

"Or where they were planning to go?"

"No. I . . . I knew something was wrong. She was not herself for the last two days. And someone had hit her. She was terribly sore and could barely sit. And she . . . she . . ."

"What is it, Christine?"

"I just wanted to hold her as usual. That was all." Now it was no longer just sniveling; tears spilled heavily from her eyes.

"And then what?"

"She bit me. Really hard. First in the shoulder and then . . ." Christine's hand flew unconsciously, protectively, toward her left breast. And I thought of the many marks we had found on Cecile's own dead body. Her chest, her stomach, and the inside of her thighs, human tooth marks. Old marks and new. Who had taught her to bite this way?

When I approached the wolf stables again to say goodbye to Mother Filippa, there was a large chestnut horse tied to the fence, and from inside I heard a man's voice shout very loudly and with uncontrollable anger, "You are not God's servant. You are Satan's!"

I stopped, taken aback. At that moment an unusually

broad-shouldered man in a riding habit came tearing out, wrenched the reins loose from the fence, and threw himself onto the chestnut. He spurred it so hard that it jumped more sideways than forward, and then disappeared along the road between the farm buildings at a clattering gallop.

Mother Filippa came out. She looked as calm as always. "Is your curiosity satisfied now, mademoiselle?" she said, a bit pointedly, I thought. Maybe she thought that I had not just probed into Cecile's background but had also eavesdropped on her conversation with the angry man. And so I refrained from asking her, "Who was that?" which was on the tip of my tongue.

"I understand from Christine that Cecile was not quite herself the last few days before she disappeared," I said instead.

"Her young man had broken off their engagement," said Mother Filippa. "And I have the sense that the news was not received well at home. Are you suggesting that that is why she ran away with Emile?"

"Maybe," I said. "But you believe it was her initiative?"

"I assume so. Emile was not like that."

"Not even if you take his handicap into consideration?"

"What do you mean?"

"I understand he had certain . . . troubles."

"What has Christine told you? There was nothing wrong with Emile."

"Inspector Marot seems to have got the impression that he was not quite right in the head."

"Mademoiselle Karno, I am about to get angry. Emile may need a bit more kindness and understanding than most people are willing to offer. But there is nothing wrong with his mind. And as far as Christine's gossip goes, let me describe it precisely, so that there is no misunderstanding. When he is strongly moved, Emile gets an involuntary erection. It is an unhappy condition for him and it makes it difficult for him to be among people, which is one of the reasons he has found a haven here. And if you in your human charity cannot understand and accept that, I can assure you that God does."

I felt as if she had just pulled down my pants and given me a well-deserved spanking.

"I . . . I just came to say goodbye," I managed to stammer.

"Of course you did, Mademoiselle Karno. Thank you for your visit. And thank you for bringing my old friend home."

I just nodded mutely and fled with my tail between my legs.

That night Sister Marie-Claire was awakened a few hours after compline when someone knocked quietly on her door. In the hallway stood Mother Filippa, still in her nightdress, with a knitted shawl thrown hastily over her shoulders and just a scarf covering her short hair.

"The new wolves are restless," she said. "I heard them howl several times. And I thought I saw a light. I'm just going to check on them."

"Do you want me to come?" asked Marie-Claire.

"No. Best if I go alone—in case it's him . . ." It was not necessary to use names. "But I want you to go down to the kitchen and get some food. Bread, cheese, perhaps some smoked meat if we have it. Apples, there must still be some apples. Things that will keep, things that are easy to carry. And plenty of it, please. Just set it outside the wolf stables. Do not go in. It is enough that one of us may have something to hide from the authorities and Father Augustine." Father Augustine was the sisters' confessor.

Marie-Claire smiled. "I think we have some smoked duck," she said, "and ham."

"Thank you." The two women exchanged a warm, conspiratorial look. But then a shadow crossed the abbess's face. "I shall have to explain to him what happened to the old wolves," she said. "It will be hard for him."

She disappeared down the corridor, with bare ankles in the frayed brown shoes she usually wore in the stables and the garden. An odd pairing with the nightdress.

Marie-Claire listened but could not hear any wolf howls, only an owl from somewhere over by the apple orchards.

In the cool cellar under the kitchen, she found the duck, kept in a jar covered by fat, and she also cut some generous slices from one of the smoked hams that hung from the ceiling on large iron hooks. Two whole loaves of bread, one white and one dark. Nine apples. But it had to be portable, Mother Filippa had said, so she emptied the last potatoes out of a sack and used that to pack the food in.

When she came back up, the night was completely still. The owl was silent, and the moon shone pale and calm on the convent courtyard, so bright that the tall yews cast long blue shadows. She walked through the colonnade that connected the convent with the oldest stable buildings where the wolves were. And then she suddenly did hear a noise. She spun around but saw nothing out of the ordinary. Only moonlight and columns, yews and long shadows.

She put down the sack by the stable door as she had been ordered to do and returned to the convent. It was not until Mother Filippa failed to appear at the matins prayer that her unease led her to look for her in the wolf stables.

Later she often asked herself just what she would have seen if she had opened that stable door the night before.

III

Mother Filippa lay on her back on the bare earth of the wolf pen with an odd neatness to her dead limbs—her arms along her sides, her legs straight and together, the nightdress smoothed so it almost covered her ankles. Her feet were bare. The morning light touched the white folds of the dress with a soft golden glow and lent the scene an air of false serenity, making me think of gilded icons and portraits of martyred saints.

But there was nothing serene about this death. A bloody gash ran down the abbess's face and continued along her neck and chest, under the nightdress. It looked almost as if someone had attempted to cleave her in two, like a log.

"I suppose we may put 'homicide' on the certificate without further ado," said the Commissioner.

"Yes," said my father. He could not kneel by the body, and stood awkwardly leaning on his crutch. "But I will have to get her on a table before I can say with certainty what kind of instrument was used."

A few paces from the abbess lay another dead body—the new male wolf's. His fur was matted with blood, and a coil of his intestines hung out through an incision in the abdomen. A grimy trail of blood and feces led from the beast to the abbess, or perhaps the other way around. The Commissioner made a note in his book.

"Inspector Marot will not be able to get here for a few hours, and I would like to have her examined before rigor mortis sets in," he said. "Dear Madeleine. Could you draw a sketch for the inspector?"

It was the first time I had been at the scene of a murder. And once again it was a person I had met when she was alive. I could feel my saliva dry up, and the muscles in my abdomen contract in involuntary spasms. But I just nodded with my mouth closed, in order not to release the vomit I was fighting off.

Oddly enough, it helped to draw it. To notice angles and lines, shadow and light, instead of looking at the terrible totality. I was even able to make a closer study of the abbess's cloven face.

Then a stretcher arrived from the hospital, and with the help of the Commissioner, two sisters carefully lifted the abbess's body onto it.

"Where may I perform my examination?" asked Papa.

That simple question caused some uncertainty. The sisters clearly believed that their dead abbess belonged in the chapel of the convent church, but that was one of the places to which they could not allow my father access. They settled on a compromise. The examination could take place in the hospital wing, and only when it was over would Mother Filippa come to rest where she belonged.

"What about the wolf?" I said. "Does he need to be examined as well?"

"Later," said my father with a glance at the sisters. "Humans first, then the animals."

Predictably enough there were more protests when my father and I wanted to undress the body. In consideration of the nuns' sense of propriety, both my father and the Commissioner had to leave the room while I and Sister Agnes took off the abbess's nightdress and underwear and covered the dead body with a sheet.

At that point I was already conscious that something was not right.

There were several things to note about the naked body. In addition to the bloody incision that continued down between the abbess's small, pointed breasts, most noticeable were the bite marks that covered breast, stomach, and thighs, eleven in all. On one breast, the bite was so deep that there was actual tissue missing.

But that was not all. On the stomach, lower body, and the inside of the thighs were smeared splotches of blood and some uneven brownish tracks that, judging by smell and appearance, were feces. It looked as if someone had attempted to wipe it off, but in the daylight the smears were clear. I had to look a little more closely to discover the long dark animal hairs that stuck to the blood.

Sister Agnes cried quietly during our work, and her usual, "Oh dear. Oh dear," had been replaced by a despairing little, "Oh no. Oh no. Oh no."

Together we spread the clean white sheet and let it fall around the abused body. At this point I hardly knew if it was for the sake of the dead woman or for ours. It was a mercy in any case.

This morning I was glad that my father would come in and take over. His even voice noted the facts with a calming objectivity, and all I had to do was write them down:

"Height: one hundred sixty-two centimeters. Build: normal. Hair color: dark chestnut brown. Eyes—"

"They were olive green," I said.

The sheet was lifted from one body part at a time, which not only removed the general impression of exposure and nakedness but also isolated the relevant area and made it an object of inquiry rather than an arm, a leg, a breast. My father had me place a piece of silk paper over each of the eleven bite marks and carefully draw them on a 1:1 scale. As I had, he noted and described the animal hair, the bloody tracks, "which do not seem to originate from the victim's own wounds," and the smears of intestinal contents.

"The bite wounds are generally shallow and possibly made after death. The lesions in the head, throat, and chest . . ."

"Knife?" asked the Commissioner.

"I do not think so. The edges of the wound are too jagged, too torn. A knife would have made a cleaner incision. I think we should be looking for a saw."

"But she would not have just stood there while the killer started sawing through her head," objected the Commissioner.

"No. That is why I also looked carefully for other lesions, a blow that might have knocked her unconscious, for example. But I could find nothing like that. Perhaps some kind of anesthesia?"

"And the bite marks. Did the wolf bite her?"

"Probably not. They are almost certainly from a human being."

"As with Cecile Montaine."

"Yes. But Cecile was not murdered."

"So you think these are the murderer's teeth?"

"That was one of the reasons why I got Maddie to trace the marks. As I said, the victim was most likely bitten postmortem, so it is at the very least strong circumstantial evidence."

"Anything else?"

"The abbess was naked when the damage was done. She was dressed later."

"Do you mean that the murderer dressed her?"

"It is possible. But . . . it could also have been someone else."

Sister Marie-Claire sat with her hands folded, but there was no serenity in the gesture, one hand was gripping the other so tightly that the knuckles whitened, and occasionally they performed a spasmodic leap in her lap, like a wounded rabbit. Her voice was oddly monotonous; it was as if her attempts to control her emotions squeezed all other expression out of it as well.

"Mother Filippa woke me up shortly after midnight to say that she was going to check on the new wolves. She thought they were restless."

"But you did not go with her?"

"No. I . . . went back to bed. It was not until she did not show up for matins . . ." The hands jumped, and Sister Marie-Claire did not finish her sentence.

"How much time passed from your last words with her until you found her dead?" asked Inspector Marot.

"Perhaps two hours," she said. "I had, as I said, gone back to bed, but I didn't completely fall asleep."

"Did you notice anything during that time?"

"No, I cannot say that I did."

"It is important, Sister."

"I am well aware of that. But I drifted off, I wasn't really awake." Then she suddenly raised her head, but not to look at us. Her eyes were unfocused and became distant. "It cannot be true," she said.

"What?"

"I thought I heard a dog bark."

"That is hardly unusual, is it?"

"Yes. At least so close by. Because of the wolves, we have no dogs at the convent."

"Why is that?"

"Wolves can be quite aggressive toward those they consider invaders of their territory. As recently as last fall, we found a puppy that had somehow got into the pen. The wolves had practically torn it in half."

"But you think you heard a dog bark," said Marot and made a note. "Would you be kind enough to describe how you found the dead woman?"

The hands jumped again. "I went down to the stables. I could see that the sack was gone . . ."

Inspector Marot immediately took note. "What sack?"

Sister Marie-Claire stared at him with her mouth half open, stopped midsentence.

"Oh . . ." She sighed.

Inspector Marot waited. My father, the Commissioner, and I did as well. She bent her head under our probing eyes.

"She thought . . . that is, Mother Filippa thought it might have been Emile who had come back. She asked me to get some food for him."

"Why did you not say so right away?" asked Marot.

She looked up.

"People *misunderstand* Emile," she said. "It has perhaps become a habit to protect him. It was for Mother Filippa as well."

"So this sack of food, where was it?"

"I had placed it right outside the stable, as she asked me to. Now it was gone."

"So one may assume that the murderer took it with him." Marot stroked his walrus mustache and made a note.

Sister Marie-Claire protested. "I cannot say that. I did not see it."

She was still protecting Emile, I thought. Perhaps she thinks he was the one who took the sack. But would she still try to shield him if she thought he was the murderer?

"So I assume you went into the stable?"

"Yes. The male wolf's cage was open, and there was blood on the floor. That was when I knew something was wrong."

"But you did not go for help?"

"No."

"And then?"

"Then . . . I followed the trail of blood into the wolf pen and . . . found her."

"Would you please describe what you saw?"

"The other gentlemen saw it themselves," she said, and bent her head lightly in the direction of my father and the Commissioner. "I do not have much to add. It . . . It was a shocking sight."

Papa leaned forward. "Sister," he said, "were you the one who dressed her?"

She tilted her head back as if trying to make the tears subside into her eyes. She did not succeed.

"How did you know?" she asked.

"It was clear that someone had done so," said my father, without going into detail. "It was either you or the murderer."

She took a deep, shaky breath.

"She was an incredible person," she said, her voice roughened by the tears. "So much humanity, and so firm a faith. I do not know if she ever doubted her calling, but it did not seem that way. To see her . . . *violated* in that way . . . I could not . . . I didn't want anyone else to . . ."

She could not continue. Weeping overcame her, and it was only slowly and with great patience that we succeeded in getting her to tell the rest.

That Mother Filippa had lain naked on her back, her arms and legs spread wide. And the dead male wolf had been placed on top of her, between her thighs, in a grotesque parody of the human act of love.

"I couldn't . . . You must understand, I could not let . . ."

"Yes," my father said quietly. "I understand."

"I am sorry, M'sieur L'Inspecteur, but God's laws are greater than man's."

That was the message Police Inspector Marot received when he wished to gain entrance to Mother Filippa's cell. So while Marot searched the priory office in the open part of the convent, and my father and the Commissioner looked more closely at the dead wolf, I was given the job of cataloging possessions of the abbess in situ before I packed them in boxes so they might be brought to the inspector, rather than the other way around. I was closely monitored by Sister Agnes, as if the nuns feared that I might somehow harm their abbess further through my prying.

There was not a lot to catalog.

The cell was about three meters long by two and a half meters wide. A window faced a sunny walled courtyard and a colonnade that allowed the nuns to reach the stables without getting their shoes wet even in the rain. In the yard grew a large linden tree with light green buds on the brink of bursting into leaf.

The cell's walls were whitewashed and without decoration. The narrow bed was made up with white sheets and a gray blanket, just like the beds in the hospital wing. It was still as she had left it, with the blanket thrown to one side and the pillow crumpled between the bed and the wall. I felt a small stab of pain. There was so much living personality in the impatient gesture that had tugged the sheet and the blanket free of the mattress, the hands that had crammed the pillow together, the body whose weight had rested on that mattress, leaving a faint but permanent indentation in the center. The crucifix that hung above the bed was a simple black cross with a white figure of Christ, the suffering suggested more by the lines of the body than by the expression on the face. It did not look as if a professional artist had carved it.

I drew a sketch of the bed for the inspector. Then Sister Agnes and I folded the blankets and sheets together and placed them in the first box. Sister Agnes would have routinely shaken and smoothed out the sheets first, but I stopped her, though without telling her that the inspector would want to examine the sheets for any stains or hair that did not come from the abbess herself.

"When was the last time these were changed?" I asked.

"A few days ago," said Sister Agnes uncomprehendingly. "Are they dirty?"

"No," I said, "of course not. Do you know precisely when?"

"I think it was Thursday morning. That is when it is normally done."

She was beginning to look uneasy. She had a slightly shapeless nose, thick eyelids, and almost no eyelashes, which together with the veil and the habit made her look like something Bruegel might have painted.

"Why do you ask?" she wanted to know.

"For technical reasons," I said. I lifted the mattress, but, as with Cecile's bed, there was a disappointing lack of a hidden diary or private letters.

In addition to the bed, the cell was furnished with a washstand, a white-painted chest of drawers, a small writing desk in darkened, unvarnished oak, and a simple wooden stool with the seat woven from rushes, such as might be found in any farm cottage. Above the chest of drawers hung a bookcase with two shelves, and on the inside of the door was a row of hooks. The only luxury in the room was the worn but colorful rag rug beside the bed, which meant that the abbess's first daily contact with the world did not have to be the cold granite flagstones. When we rolled it up, I noticed several five- to six-centimeter-long grayish-white hairs stuck to the rug's fibers.

"Did she keep the wolf here at night?" I asked.

"Usually," said Sister Agnes, and she was overwhelmed by a fresh batch of tears. "Oh no. Oh no."

I drew the bookcase and noted how the books were arranged before I began to take them down, page through them rapidly, and put them in the box. Some of them were of course religious— *The Confessions of Saint Augustine*, several lives of the saints, an unusually worn prayer book with the inscription "To Louise-Clemente on the occasion of her confirmation on April 7, 1871." But there were works on botany as well, a book about cultivating roses, one about insects and butterflies, a bulky work about Kaspar Hauser, and a more curious one, *Peter Stumpp, the Werewolf of Bedburg*. It stopped me for a moment because the title page featured a bizarre medieval woodcut. In the foreground a man crept around on all fours with an infant in his mouth, which he apparently was planning to devour, while the landscape behind him was marked by torn-off body parts and disemboweled bodies. An overall scene of human horror and panic.

I paged through the book a little before I put it into the box, but all I got out of it were sentence fragments such as "... in an unnatural relationship with his own daughter" and "... so possessed by the devil that he, when he wanted, could take the shape of a wild animal ... ," which did not make me much wiser as to why someone like Mother Filippa had possessed such a work.

It was less unexpected to encounter works by Voltaire and Rousseau; *Émile, ou de l'éducation* looked as if it had been especially diligently read. But it was another book, a ragged, stained edition of *Shockheaded Peter*, which made my heart jump. Not because of the contents or the drawings, even though I had been terrified by them as a child, but because of the carefully printed name on the inside of the jacket. The letters leaned haphazardly in opposite directions and were obviously written by a childish hand. The name was Louise-Clemente Oblonski.

"What was Mother Filippa's name before she became a nun?" I asked Sister Agnes.

"I don't know," she said. "That is precisely why we change names—to leave the secular world behind."

"Is there anyone here who knows?"

"There probably is." It was clear that she found my probing unpleasant and inappropriate. "If you must know, it is probably best to speak with Sister Bernadette. She has been here the longest, and she was the convent's archivist until her sight started to fail."

I wanted to rush out to find Sister Bernadette right away, but I controlled myself. Inspector Marot had given me an assignment that required orderliness and care, and he expected me to conclude it as quickly as possible.

Unsurprisingly, the dresser contained mostly clothing, but also, hidden in the bottom drawer under an apron, was a box of dried dates. I could not help smiling. It was so innocent a vice, and I was glad she had had it.

The washstand also had a drawer and a little cabinet. It was here Mother Filippa kept the few toiletries she had found necessary to own. A comb, a small bar of soap, a bottle of mouthwash, a nail file, a pair of clean, freshly folded towels and washcloths, as well as some crocheted hygiene pads that somehow took me by surprise. But of course nuns would also menstruate; the body did not stop ovulating just because the woman in question had decided to refrain from reproducing.

If in fact Mother Filippa had not reproduced . . . because I could not help but wonder whether she was Louise-Clemente Oblonski, and whether poor, parentless Emile Oblonski perhaps was not so parentless after all. That would at least explain her desire to protect and defend him.

I was just about to close the washstand drawer when the bottom of it caught my eye. It was covered by a sheet of faded and worn shelf paper in flowered pastels, carefully fastened with two upholstery tacks in each corner. But the pattern was not worn consistently. When you looked closely, there was something like the outline of a rectangle, almost corresponding to the drawer's dimensions, but slightly smaller.

I used the nail file to work the tacks loose. Hidden under the paper was a yellowed newspaper—the front page of *Varonne Soir* dated seven years earlier, April 24, 1887. The main story, which filled the entire front page, was the Schnaebelé Affair, and the newspaper's editor banged the war drums in a peculiarly half-hearted way. On the one hand he demanded that Bismarck be "held accountable for his treasonous and brutal behavior toward a French citizen," if necessary by the French army "saber in hand"—an army that was naturally ready to give the Prussians a good trashing. On the other hand, the editor pointed out, it was necessary to behave with dignity and consideration and leave no diplomatic effort untried. One sensed through the veil of rhetoric that he knew that the costs of a war would fall heavily on border districts like Varonne.

I could not understand why Mother Filippa had so carefully saved and hidden an article about something so generally known and so thoroughly discussed. I read it twice and still could not see that there was anything in it that was especially notable. Other than the article and some advertisements at the bottom there was nothing else. In those days, the Schnaebelé Affair had been *the* news, the only thing that was really worth writing about.

I carefully refolded the front page and put it in the box with the books. Then I turned around and looked the room over.

It had taken less than an hour and a half, and I had succeeded in removing every trace of the person who had lived here for more than ten years. In the physical world she had left only a light and fleeting mark, and it seemed brutal to remove it so quickly, and so soon after her death.

When I had delivered my boxes to Marot, I mentioned the name scribbled in *Shockheaded Peter* and told him where I had found the newspaper page. The newspaper did not really interest him.

"My wife uses newspapers as shelf paper," he said. "She must just have failed to remove the old paper and placed the new on top. But the name is interesting. What was Mother Filippa called before she joined the order?"

"Sister Agnes suggested I ask the convent's previous archivist. She is blind and no longer goes out into the world, but I have met her, and her mind is not weakened."

"Yet another inaccessible witness?" His mustache stuck out aggressively. "How am I to conduct a murder investigation in this way?"

"It is just a simple question," I said. "She is not a key witness, after all."

"No, I don't suppose she is, especially since she is blind. Fine. Go ask her and come back as quickly as possible with the answer."

"There is something I should mention," I said. "I overheard some kind of disagreement between Mother Filippa and a man yesterday. He was not someone I know, or have seen around the convent, but he was shouting at her, and I got the impression that she would rather not tell me why."

"What did he shout?"

I tried to recall the words as precisely as possible.

"He called her the devil's servant," I said. "Not God's."

"What did he look like?"

I described him as well as I could—about fifty, dark haired, tall, and stocky, with broad shoulders, somewhat carelessly dressed but still clearly a man of a certain wealth and position—and I told what I could remember about the horse, which unfortunately was only its color.

"Someone must know who he was," said the inspector. "I will make inquiries. Now, go talk to the blind nun."

Sister Bernadette was still in bed. The news of the abbess's death had hit her hard, and she simply did not have the strength or will to get up and face the trials of so cruel a day. Imogene Leblanc sat at her bedside, reading to her from the Book of Psalms.

"'The Lord is my shepherd; I shall not want. He maketh me to lie down in green pastures: he leadeth me beside the still waters. He restoreth my soul . . .'"

She turned the page with her arthritis-knotted hand and continued.

"'He leadeth me in paths of righteousness for his name's sake. Yea, though I walk through the valley of the shadow of death, I will fear no evil . . .'"

Her eyes no longer followed the text; she knew it by heart. Sister Bernadette no doubt did as well, but there must have been consolation in the ritual, in the sound of the rustling of the pages, in the companionship of the familiar words.

"Excuse me," I said.

Imogene looked up. "What do you want, mademoiselle?"

"Inspector Marot has requested that I ask Sister Bernadette a few questions."

"She is not well."

"It will not take long . . ."

Sister Bernadette pushed herself up so she sat leaning back against the pillows. Her face was even more lined than it had been when I saw her the first time, and the folds of skin around her blind eyes were swollen and red.

"It is all right, Imogene. Thank you for your concern, but if I can contribute in any way, it will do me good. Have a seat, Mademoiselle Karno."

She had recognized me without hesitation, and when Imogene remained standing by the door, Sister Bernadette turned her face to her and said quite firmly, "Thank you, Imogene."

And then the postulant was obligated to leave us alone.

"No one will tell me how she died," said Sister Bernadette. "Only that she was killed."

For a moment I imagined what it was like to sit there, helpless and unable to see anything but the pictures in her own mind.

"What do you want to know?" I said. "I am happy to answer if I can."

She wanted to know everything. Not just the cause of death but all the circumstances, how it had looked, how and when the male wolf had died. She managed to extract from me even the body's nakedness and the grotesque placement of the wolf, though I would have liked to shield her from that.

At last she sighed. "Oh, I don't know. I can hardly believe it, and yet I fear . . ."

"What, Sister?"

"They still have not found Emile?"

"No."

"Is he suspected of the crimes?"

"I don't know." But I could imagine that Marot's thoughts were leaning in that direction.

"Ohhhh . . ." This last utterance was a long, frustrated hiss, perhaps an expression of uncertainty.

"Sister Bernadette, there is something I need to ask you. What was Mother Filippa called before she joined the order?" When she hesitated, I decided to be more direct. "Was her name Louise-Clemente Oblonski?"

She shook her head slowly. "It is not as you might think."

"What do you mean?"

"When Emile came here seven years ago, he did not have a name. She gave him hers. She always said that even though several hundred people called her mother, he was the only child she would ever have."

Seven years. 1887.

"I thought he had been here longer."

"No."

"But he was not a baby. Why did he not have a name? He must have been ten or so by then."

"He could not speak."

"When I asked Mother Filippa, she said there was nothing wrong with his mental faculties."

"No. He was intelligent enough. But how will someone who has grown up without human contact receive the gift of language?"

Suddenly I saw the newspaper in my mind's eye. Not the article, though it was, naturally enough, what I had first focused on . . . but the advertisements at the bottom of the page. Among the ads for hair tonic and variety shows, there had been one for a traveling menagerie, which in addition to showing "deadly lions and tigers directly from Africa" boasted a true curiosity: "The Wild Boy from Bois Boulet. Half beast, half human. He speaks with wolves, and they do not harm him!"

"The Wild Boy," I said.

"Yes. That is what they called him. But he was no more wild than you and I, just abandoned, and later caught and abused and exhibited like an animal."

"He already had his . . . handicap back then?"

"Are you referring to his priapism? Oh, yes. That was a part of the attraction. And since he was terrified most of the time, it was presumably the high point of every performance."

"And now you are wondering if he has killed Mother Filippa?"

"No. No, I cannot believe that. He worshipped her."

"But?"

"No, it is just that . . . if you damage a child that badly, that early, and for so long . . . He is not *guilty*, don't you see—no matter what he may have done."

The hunt for Emile Oblonski officially commenced a few hours later. They hunted him as one would hunt a wild animal—with horns and horses, beaters, dogs, and riflemen on foot. Throughout the day one could hear the distant shouts, the baying of the bloodhounds, and now and then the sharp report of a hunting rifle.

"Oh no, oh no. May God prevent them from shooting each other," said Sister Agnes, who had arrived together with Sister Marie-Claire and six other nuns to escort Mother Filippa on the short trip from the hospital to the convent's chapel.

"Amen," said the Commissioner with particular emphasis. "I am not sure that it is wise to allow so many amateurs to participate. But, on the other hand, the professional effort to find Oblonski has admittedly failed miserably up to this point."

Perhaps I had been infected with a hint of the protectiveness that Mother Filippa had felt, because my concern was not so much for the hunters as for the one they hunted.

"I hope they do not kill him," I said quietly. "They are so angry and so . . . self-righteous."

The Commissioner loosened his collar with an index finger. His night had been interrupted twice; before Mother Filippa, by a kitchen maid who had chosen to fill her apron pockets with rocks and throw herself into the river from the Arsenal Bridge, presumably because she was five months pregnant and could no longer hide her condition from her master. The lack of sleep was evident in the Commissioner's bloodshot eyes and the increased heaviness in his movements.

"Inspector Marot has made sure that every group has a responsible leader with either police or military experience," he said. "Men who can maintain discipline. Do not worry, dear Madeleine, we will catch him alive."

But I knew him too well. He was far from serene himself.

Mother Filippa's body was now dressed in the habit she had worn most of her adult life. The crucifix from her cell lay on her chest, and there were no outward signs of the incisions my father had performed during the autopsy. Even her face looked less disfigured—we had pulled the skin over the injury and closed the long wound with tiny, almost invisible stitches.

Four nuns carried her, while two others walked in front, and the two last, Marie-Claire and Agnes, made up the procession's rear guard.

"Salve Regina," they sang while they walked, not especially beautifully or loudly, but with great sincerity. "Mater misericordiae." And when they reached the wrought-iron gate to the closed part of the convent, they were met by a gray host of Bernardine sisters, who added their voices to the old antiphon, so that the notes gained strength and fullness and carried the abbess home.

It was at that very moment that we heard a series of shots from the woods behind the field, and several hunting horns blew the signal "Hunt Over." They had found Emile Oblonski.

He lay curled up on the bed of the wagon on which they had transported him. His face was swollen and discolored, and it later turned out that his chest, abdominal cavity, and especially the genital region were bloated with blood and damaged by numerous kicks and blows. He was mercifully unconscious.

"Maintain discipline?" said my father in an unusually sharp tone. "If this is discipline, I would hate to see the result of anarchy."

"He is alive," said Inspector Marot. "And the use of force is necessary when a suspect resists arrest."

I did not say anything, but my jaw hurt from remaining silent.

"He must not be moved any farther," said my father with his teeth similarly clenched. "God knows what kind of internal bleeding he has suffered, and whether he will survive the night. Besides, we will need to isolate him until we know whether he is infected. If he is, we will have to examine all those who have been in close contact with him during the arrest."

Eventually, the captive was placed in a private room in the convent's hospital wing, with two armed policemen at the door. They were there not so much to prevent Oblonski from running away—he was not going anywhere in his condition—but to make sure that no vengeful mob broke in "to finish the job."

While my father placed cold cloths and ice on Oblonski's bruises with the aid of one of the nursing sisters, I took several pipette samples from his nostrils. They were so full of blood, however, that it was impossible to tell if mites were present with the naked eye.

"You will have to go home to examine it," said my father. "We must know whether there is a risk of infection."

"That is not necessary," I said. "There is an excellent microscope in the school's laboratory. Better than ours, in fact."

"Very well. Hurry. The sooner we know, the better."

There were no classes that day. Those students who could had gone home to their families as soon as the terrible news of the abbess's death had spread. Those who remained, for the most part because they did not live close by, had gathered in the school's dining hall, from which you could hear the faint and somehow unsettling sound of hymns. I could not find anyone to ask permission, but the laboratory was not locked, so I just sat down with my samples and began. It was quiet there. A window was ajar, and the scent of wet earth and daffodils from the garden mixed with the smell of floor wax and book dust, and the sharper reminiscences of Bunsen burner gas and chemicals. For some reason, a part of the school's collection of stuffed animals and birds was stored here. A jay with spread wings, a marten and a squirrel, the skeleton of a bird of prey and a glass-lidded case full of carefully mounted beetles . . . There was not much of a system to it, so perhaps it was just a random overflow from the biology room.

I dripped saline solution into the bloody mucus in order to see better. But even though I studied all the samples carefully, I found not a single mite.

I got up from the stool and stretched my sore back. Could it be true? We had been so convinced that the close contact with the wolves had transferred the mites from Emile Oblonski, who thereafter had infected Cecile. There was perhaps a possibility that she had been infected directly from the wolves; Mother Filippa had said that she was interested in them, and that was how she had got to know Emile. But why did he, who lived with the wolves in the stable and had been in close contact with them every single day . . . why did he have no mites whatsoever in his nostrils?

I sat down to look through the samples one more time. But while I was looking at the next to last, I suddenly had an odd feeling of being studied myself.

Behind me, a few meters away, stood Imogene Leblanc. I had not heard her come in, and the unexpected sight sent a jolt to my stomach and made my hand jump so that I almost dropped the last slide.

She stared at me silently, and I felt a need to explain.

"I am sorry," I said. "But it is of critical importance that we get these results without delay, and since there are no classes today . . ."

She had taught physics, biology, and chemistry, I remembered. Perhaps that was why she succeeded so well in giving me the sense that I had invaded a room in which I did not belong.

"I will be done in a minute," I concluded and controlled a desire to curtsy.

She nodded briefly. Then she walked deliberately to one of the cabinets along the wall, the one that was crowned by the slightly worn jay, and opened it. She had a light-blue cardboard box in her hand that she apparently wanted to put away on the cabinet shelf. But at that moment the box slid from her hand and hit the floor with a flat tinkling. The lid came off and four or five glass pipettes rolled out. She stood for a moment staring at them with a disapproving look, as if they were naughty pupils who did not know how to behave as was expected.

Then she slowly and with difficulty squatted down, and I remembered that she suffered from arthritis.

"Let me," I said, and jumped down from the stool to help her.

"No."

It was so abrupt and harsh, with no attempt at courtesy, that

I automatically stopped in my tracks. She picked up the wayward pipettes, placed the box in the cabinet and closed it, and left the room, still without saying more than that one word.

An odd woman, I thought. What was it Mother Filippa had said? Something about it being less the love of God and more the fear of the world, and in particular of her father, that had made her seek the safety of the convent walls.

"There were no mites," I said.

My father looked up from his own examinations, astonishment written across his face. Both he and the sister helping him were wearing white mouth covers.

"Are you sure?"

"Yes. I examined all six specimens three times."

"How very odd."

His gaze fell to the still form of Emile Oblonski. There was a touch of reproach in his manner, as if the unconscious boy in his miteless state were guilty of a breach of conduct far more serious than anything he had done with Cecile Montaine. My father had taught me to receive all results with the same clearheaded acceptance, whether they supported my hypothesis or not, but it was a dogma to which he was not himself always able to adhere.

In the yard outside, the last men, dogs, and horses were dispersing. You could hear the men exchanging greetings and slapping shoulders and could sense their reluctance to dissolve the brotherhood of the hunt. It would be dark soon; the sister had already lit the kerosene lamp in the ceiling and now raised the glass on the table lamp to light that as well.

"How is he?" I said quietly.

"He is fairly stable," said my father. "There is no doubt that there are internal injuries, but how serious they are . . ." He left the sentence unfinished.

It is always difficult to determine how tall a person is when he is lying down, but my impression was that Emile Oblonski was rather short. As he lay there, still curled up and on his side, with filthy and unkempt hair and a thin and patchy beard covering his throat and chin, he shifted constantly in my perception between boy and man. Other than the bruising left by the blows and kicks he had received, he had no deformities as far as I could see. Whether he was ugly or not was difficult to determine with his face so battered. For some reason I had imagined that he was dark haired, but he was not. The greasy locks were straw colored, and the beard a shade darker and more reddish. His ribs were clearly defined beneath the skin, and under the sheet that covered his lower body I could, even now, see the contours of what Sister Bernadette had called his "priapism."

I turned my head in order not to stare and instead caught my father's gaze.

"It is an entirely involuntary and uncontrollable reaction," he said. "You have to consider it simply a symptom."

The heat washed up into my cheeks.

"Of course," I said firmly, and felt hopelessly unprofessional.

Throughout the night the sisters kept vigil at Mother Filippa's bier in the convent chapel, while I sat next to the person she had considered her adopted son. Papa, who like the Commissioner had had the previous night interrupted by the unfortunate kitchen maid, lay in the room next door, catching a bit of much-needed sleep. I had strict orders to wake him up if Oblonski's breathing, pulse, temperature, or color changed significantly.

This was an unusual duty for me. Most of my father's living patients were admitted to the Saint Bernardine Hospital and thus in the sisters' care, and the dead did not require watching. Toward morning I must have dozed off a bit because I had the dizzy sensation of waking up and being in the process of sliding down from the chair on which I had been sitting.

His breathing was different, but it was hard to determine whether it was worse or better. A bit more rapid, yet at the same time less congested. Then I caught a liquid shimmer under the half-closed eyelids and understood that the change was caused by the patient being conscious.

"My name is Madeleine," I said. "I am here to take care of you."

Why did I immediately feel this need to console and soothe? Was it a legacy Mother Filippa had managed to pass on to me? Perhaps it was because I had seen the newspaper page she had hidden in her drawer for seven years and thus knew precisely how inhumanely people could behave toward someone like him.

He lay completely still and looked at me through his eyelashes. He did not say anything, but after a few seconds he placed his free hand discreetly over the erection bump and pressed it against his thighs in an attempt to make it less visible. Why that gesture seemed so heartbreaking that it came close to making me cry, I did not completely understand.

"Are you thirsty?" I asked. "Does it hurt? I can get my father. He is a doctor."

He did not answer and did not in any way show that he had understood me. His eyes closed again, but I did not think he was sleeping. It was merely the only way he could hide.

I let him do so. In this way we remained, silently next to one another in the faint glowing circle of the lamp, and waited for it to be morning.

Emile Oblonski did not resist when my father pushed the thick wax plate into his mouth and made him bite down on it with a light pressure against his chin. He just seemed confused yet eager to do what was asked. He still had not said a single word, but his eyes followed our every move, as if he constantly had to make sure that we did not want to hit him.

I mixed plaster powder with water and poured it carefully into the tooth print. In this way we would soon have a model of Emile's teeth that could be compared to the bite marks on Mother Filippa's body.

"Has anyone told him that Mother Filippa has died?" I quietly asked my father while we waited for the plaster to set.

"Not that I know of," he said, and tried to scratch himself under his own plaster cast. "Of course one cannot rule out that some of the proud hunters may have run their mouths."

"But . . . shouldn't he be informed?"

"You assume that he does not already know because he didn't kill her himself."

Papa was right. I did. And I had no cause for that assumption.

Still I insisted. "She considered him her adopted son. And if he is innocent . . ."

"*If* he is innocent, you will ruin a great deal for him by giving him that kind of information before Marot has questioned him," said my father sternly. "The more you tell him about the crime, the harder it will be for him to appear ignorant and unimplicated."

The questioning. It was of course necessary and unavoidable, but when I looked at the poor battered human being lying curled up in the hospital bed, trying to hide behind his closed eyes . . . I could barely stand the thought.

"Go home, Maddie. You need to sleep."

"I can do that here."

He looked at me for a few seconds. He needed a haircut, I noticed distractedly, it was starting to curl at the ends, which did not suit him.

"I will have Marot find a carriage," he said.

I wanted to protest. I did not want to be packed up and sent home as if I were a fretting child; I wanted to know what was happening.

"You need me here," I said.

"No, Maddie, I do not. Go home and sleep."

The house in Carmelite Street did not feel homey or safe; it closed around me like a shell that I would have preferred to be without. The air was stale, the sound of the mantel clock in the salon ear-splittingly loud. My stomach rumbled with hunger and a sense of injustice. I knew why my father had sent me home. It was not because he did not need me, though he could probably manage the rest of the work with the assistance of the Commissioner and the nuns. It was because I had defended Emile, because I had revealed that my feelings were biased. But he was not as impartial and objective as he believed himself to be. He also was working on certain assumptions that did not all have a basis in cold, objective facts.

I ate a small handful of raisins but could do nothing to ameliorate that other feeling of discomfort. Finally I went upstairs and tried to sleep for a few hours. I was only partly successful. My semiwakeful thoughts continued to circle around Emile, and when I was woken up completely and suddenly, it was with an unreleased and shameful feeling in my entire body.

Elise Vogler was knocking on my door.

"Maddie, you have a visitor."

We had played together as children even though I was five years older than she. When we were alone, I saw no reason to insist on "Mademoiselle" and other stupid formalities.

"Who?"

"The professor from Heidelberg."

I sat up with a jolt.

"What time is it?"

"Almost twelve thirty."

"Good God, Elise, help. Offer him a glass of sherry or something. Say I will be down in a moment."

There was no time for my so-called health corset and no Elise to help me with it in any case. I pulled on an old bodice belt that I could manage myself, and perforce had to grab a loose blouse with a ruffled front and a gray skirt from my school days. I rolled up my night braid, stuck a few hairpins in it, and shook my head quickly to make sure it was fairly firmly in place. Damn the man. Had he never heard of *announced* visits?

The air in the salon was musty and somehow off. It had been neither aired nor dusted yesterday, I guessed, because my father and I had both been away.

The man waiting on the edge of the chair I thought of as the Commissioner's was not at ease, either.

"Madeleine," he said the moment he saw me. And that alone told me something was wrong; where was the gallant hand kiss, the usual courteous urbanity? He looked as if he had slept as little as I had.

"Professor. Elise will have told you that my father is not at home?"

"Yes."

No more than that. What was wrong with the man?

"More sherry?" I asked, because I could see he had already emptied his glass.

"No."

He was being decidedly impolite. I remained standing, somewhat at a loss, and did not know what to do with this person who was staring at me with a look that resembled that of a condemned prisoner. Perhaps I should not be alone with him?

"Madeleine, I need to ask you . . . Will you marry me?"

Expecting anything but that, an astonished "Why?" shot out of me.

"I . . . I have the greatest respect and admiration for you," he said. "If you would do me the honor . . . no scientist could have a better wife. And I for my part would do everything to ensure that your intelligence receives the education it deserves. A woman like you ought to study at the country's highest centers of learning. Why aren't you already at the Sorbonne? They accept women."

The Sorbonne. That name, to me, had exactly the same kind of ring as Jerusalem probably had for a priest or a nun. But how could I leave my father? He had no one else. And where would we get the money?

"That is unfortunately not possible," I said.

"What? The Sorbonne—or marrying me?"

"I thought you were already married . . ."

"Me? Why did you think that?"

"I assumed . . . in your position."

"You were wrong. And you have not answered my question."

"No," I said. "I can't."

He looked completely helpless, but I did not understand why. Something was hidden under the surface, but it was not anything as simple and straightforward as the erection Emile Oblonski had tried to repress. I had previously noted the intense attention with which the professor observed me in certain situations, but if it had been head-over-heels love or simply physical desire, then why

170

this odd way of presenting his errand? *I need to ask you.* As if he would really prefer not to. And still it was clear that he sincerely hoped I would say yes.

"Why is it suddenly so urgent for you to have a wife?" I asked.

He got up. I unconsciously took a step backward, and he held his hands up in an odd disarming gesture, as if he were calming a frightened horse. "It is not just 'a wife' I want," he protested. "It is you. Yes, I admit that it would be convenient for me to be married. As you said yourself, it is expected of a man in my position, and there *is* a position at the Sorbonne that I would like to apply for. But that is not the only reason. And you . . . you also need a husband, a marriage that will not limit you and trap you in *mediocrity* . . ." The last he said with a passion that had otherwise been markedly absent in his odd proposal. "I believe I know you well enough to realize that you are not a woman taken in by flowers and banalities, so I have made my suggestion in rational terms. But that should not lead you to believe that I do not have strong feelings for you."

Would I have taken him seriously if he had got down on one knee and waved a bouquet of pink roses at me? No, I did not think so. And there were elements of the "offer" that were definitely tempting. Especially the part about allowing me to develop my intellect. Why, then, was I feeling insulted and belittled in spite of the fact that he had offered me what Madame Aubrey in her commencement speech had called "the highest honor a man can show a woman"?

I would soon be twenty-one. Many would be of the opinion that marriage was long overdue.

Then I remembered another scene—the terrified woman in labor and her animal-like bellows, and the empty blank gaze. *Married. Impregnated. Conquered by biology.*

"I don't think I am ready to be married," I said. "And if I am to be totally honest, I do not know if I ever will be. There is so much more I want to be than just . . . a wife."

He nodded and actually looked as if he understood.

"I am willing to take that chance," he said. "If we can just announce the engagement, you may decide when the wedding will be. Or *if* it will be. I think you will be convinced in time, but if I am wrong, I promise you that we will part without bitterness."

An engagement. It sounded less categorical and monumental than a marriage. An engagement could be long, several years, if necessary. During all that time I would have a practical shield against the courting behavior of other males. And I knew how much it would mean to my father and the concerns he had on my behalf. It would be living proof that he had not ruined my chances of a respectable marriage with his unorthodox way of raising me.

"I will think about it," I said.

His face changed entirely. It was as if he lit up from the inside, and at that moment I felt that he perhaps might in fact have feelings for me and not just have a rational need for a wife.

"And does that mean you are planning to say yes?" he said with a smile that contained at least some of the gallant charmer I had met that day in Heidelberg. "Once you have finished thinking . . ." Damn him. I could feel a tugging at the corner of my mouth, but I was *not* going to smile.

"It is a theoretical possibility," I said pointedly.

He came close to me for the first time and placed a hand on either side of my neck. His palms were warm and a bit damp, and I could smell the precise mixture of cologne and formaldehyde that I was beginning to associate with him. Goodness, was he planning to kiss me? It would, of course, be not entirely unnatural, given the circumstances, yet I had not given him a "yes." At the most a "perhaps."

But yes, that was what he was planning. It was a bit abrupt and choppy, so that my upper lip made unexpected contact with his front teeth and later swelled up as if he had hit me. Nor was I entirely sure what I thought about the tongue that hastily slid across mine, probably resulting in a not insignificant transference of microorganisms. What my body felt about the rest of him, however, was disturbingly unequivocal. Yes, please, it begged, with an intensity that was not all that different from Cecile Montaine's. *Yes. Now. Come to me.*

Did he know what he was doing to me? Did he know that I stood there feeling certain muscles contract, certain physical processes start up? Oh, God. The answer to Rodolphe Descartier's question had suddenly become quite clear. Yes. I was like that. True, I did not have the courage to unbutton the man's pants as Cecile had supposedly done, but had he pushed me down on the chaise longue and performed the coitus then and there, my body would have been altogether ready to receive him.

He did not. He let his hands rest around my waist a moment, then he let go of me completely. I was left with the sensation of having been betrayed by the body I had believed myself to be the mistress of. Deep in my abdomen there was still a muscle that trembled faintly and sent a quivering warmth both down and up. Married, impregnated, conquered . . . I had made my decision not to end up like that. *Damn* the man, and damn biology. Was it really so easy for it to topple the intellect?

"I have to speak with your father," he said. "Where is he?"

"At the convent," I said, attempting to collect the shreds of my dignity and my good breeding around me. "There was a death . . ."

"Lung abscesses?" His gaze became scientifically focused.

"No. It does not look as if it has anything directly to do with the mites."

I told him about the circumstances of Mother Filippa's death.

"And now they think that this Oblonski is responsible? What is his motive supposed to be?"

"I do not think they believe he needs a motive. It is enough that he is who he is."

"Has he been violent before?"

"Not as far as I know."

"If it is him, then something must have happened that has brought on this change in behavior."

"Yes."

"But you do not believe it is him?"

"I did not say that."

"No. But I can see it on your face."

If he could see that, perhaps there were other things he could see as well. I half turned so that I was no longer facing him directly.

"The most peculiar thing may be that he did not have any sign whatsoever of mite infection," I said.

"Yes," he said. "That is very peculiar."

My father came home half an hour later. You could see his exhaustion in the way he handled the crutch and in the shadows on his face. But he lit up when he saw the professor.

"August," he said and held out his hand. "It is so good to see you."

"Albert," said the professor and shook his hand warmly. The thought occurred to me just then that it was a bit peculiar that the two of them had a less formal and more openly cordial rapport than the professor had with me, the woman he wished to marry. Perhaps one of these days we might progress to a mutual first-name basis?

"I brought a few copies of *The Journal of Parasitology* for you," said the professor to my father, who had collapsed gratefully onto the chaise longue. "Hot off the press!" He opened his briefcase and gave one copy to my father and another to me.

I peeled back the buff-colored cardboard cover and paged through it eagerly. And there, in black on white, was the article "by Albert Karno, MD, and Professor August Dreyfuss, Forchhammer Institute" about our *Pneumonyssus* variant, with an addition written by the professor about its ability to transfer an abscess-forming bacterium—all of it illustrated with a quarter-page drawing of the mite executed by M. Karno. That is what it said—"drawings by M. Karno." I could feel my smile growing, a foolishly vain reaction in the midst of much more serious events, but all the same, I was happy.

"Wonderful!" said my father, looking decidedly cheerful. "Wonderful, August!"

"And then I have a request," said the professor.

"Ask away," said my father.

"You see, today I have asked Madeleine if we might become engaged to be married."

My father was caught by surprise—at least as much as I had been, I think. He was still sitting with *The Journal of Parasitology* in his hands, peering at us across the top of a page that announced a breakthrough in the treatment of intestinal worms in cows.

"Madeleine! Is it true?"

"She has *almost* said yes," said the professor with a teasing smile.

"Dear friend! I . . . I must say . . ."

"So we have your permission—once I manage to convince Madeleine to give me a date?"

My father cleared his throat. "Dear August. Dear Madeleine. Nothing could make me happier."

So far, so good. But would it also make me happy? I looked from one smiling man to the other, and I still had my doubts.

"I am afraid it really is Oblonski," said my father as he sipped his Gewürztraminer. "They caught him near a hunting cabin where he had apparently been living for weeks. Perhaps that was also where Cecile Montaine stayed during the weeks she was gone."

"And where is the proof in that?" I said, a more strident challenge than I had intended. It was after all supposed to be a celebratory evening, and I had no wish to appear like an officious harpy on the very first day of my peculiar engagement.

"The food sack was in the cabin," said my father. "There is little doubt that he went to the convent to beg for provisions and then—for some reason known only to himself—turned on the one human being who was closest to him. He had even eaten some of the food. He still had traces of duck grease on his fingers."

I looked down at the duck confit I was in the process of consuming myself. There was little risk that I would get grease on my fingers, the silverware was Minerva, and were it to happen anyway, I could always make use of one of the starched white damask napkins. The contrast to the battered and confused creature they had dragged home like some kind of hunting catch was suddenly nauseatingly huge.

"Did the tooth prints match?" I asked.

My father shook his head slightly, not so much a definite no as an indication of doubt.

"I would not be able to convict him on that basis," he admitted. "And I have asked the inspector to make sure that a dentist takes a more precise print so we can get firmer evidence."

"What you are saying is that it does not match."

"No. I just said that the match is not sufficiently precise."

Above our heads, the crystal chandeliers twinkled like captive stars, and all around us at the other tables dinner-jacketed gentlemen conversed with ladies in elegant décolletage. I myself was wearing the only evening gown I owned, a midnight blue taffeta gown from Magasin Duvalier. Madame Duvalier was one of my father's living patients, and she had let me have it cheaply. It was perhaps not this year's fashion, but according to Madame Duvalier it "flatters your fair complexion, *chérie*, and your lovely blue eyes." She had not mentioned my unbelievably ordinary middle-brown hair.

"Has he confessed?" I asked.

"No," said my father. "In fact he still has not uttered a single word. The inspector is beginning to doubt that he *can* speak, but the nuns have assured us that he has the ability. Or had. Perhaps what has happened has robbed him of it again."

"He was like a son to her," I said. "And no one has ever accused him of being violent. *Why* would he suddenly 'turn on her'?"

The professor looked from one to the other.

"Perhaps he is what Mr. Darwin calls an atavism," the professor said. "A return to an earlier and more primitive stage of human development."

"Are you a supporter of Darwin's theories?" My father seized—with a certain gratitude, it seemed to me—this less personal topic.

"The arguments are convincing," said the professor. "Scientifically speaking, creationism must be considered dead. Regardless of what theological consequences it may have . . ."

I let them change the subject. But though I definitely considered Darwin's evolution theories fascinating and worthy of numerous discussions, my thoughts still continued to center on Emile Oblonski.

When we reached dessert, I tried again. "Where exactly is that hunting cabin? How far from the convent?"

"A few kilometers," said my father. "It actually belongs to the

Vabonne family, but old Jacques Vabonne has sold off the hunting rights for that part of the forest and hasn't used the place in years."

"I would like to see it," I said tentatively. "Is that possible?"

"Why?"

"Because we still do not know where or how Cecile Montaine fell ill."

"I will ask the Commissioner," said my father. "If you really believe it can help us solve that riddle."

The professor escorted us home to Carmelite Street in a hansom cab and then continued on to his lodgings after a warm back-patting embrace of my father and a fairly modest peck on the cheek for me.

My father stood for a moment looking after the hansom cab that clip-clopped down the night-damp cobblestones and disappeared around the corner and onto Rue Perrault.

"That was a surprise, Maddie," he said.

"Yes."

"I value the man greatly."

"I know." Why was there, then, an unspoken "but" in the air? *Nothing could make me happier*, he had said. Had he not meant it?

Silence fell, but my father did not move and made no sign that he wanted to go inside.

"When . . . ?" he asked at last. "What is your plan? This fall, perhaps?"

Something had cracked in him, something that was no longer whole.

"Papa. No. It will be a long time. And I am not sure that we ever will be married; I have only promised to consider it."

"Of course you will marry," he said in a voice that sounded

as if he had just bit into a mealy apple. "That is the point of an engagement, after all."

He turned abruptly and clumsily at the same time and unlocked the front door. He would not let me help but struggled up the stairs on his own. I did not know what to say or do.

The next morning he was carefully kind and cheerful, but to me the apparent good humor seemed forced.

I cannot leave him, I thought. I have to tell August (we had at least achieved that much in the course of the evening) that it is impossible. It is unfair to lead him on.

And yet, the second I came to that conclusion, I felt unreasonably angry. I stabbed the knife into my brioche as if it were an animal I wanted to gut, and forced Madame Vogler's strawberry jam into it with furious force.

"What is wrong?" asked Papa.

"Nothing. Why should there be anything wrong?"

He did not have anyone else. I thought of the photograph on his bedside table. The little family—father, dead mother, and child. For ten years it had been the last thing he saw before he turned off his bedside lamp, and perhaps the first thing he looked at in the morning.

"Papa?"

"Yes?"

"Would you ever consider . . . ?" I stopped. We never discussed this kind of thing. Never.

"What?"

"Getting . . . married again?"

He looked at me for a long time across the edge of the copy of *Médecine Aujourd'hui* that had arrived in the morning mail.

"I do not think so," he said calmly.

Damn the man. The thought resounded in my head, and still I barely knew which one of them I was cursing. It was a relief when the Commissioner arrived shortly thereafter in a rented carriage to escort me to Jacques Vabonne's old hunting cabin.

This part of the forest had once provided oak for ship planks and masts, but now only the most crooked and thus useless trees were left, and a new, younger forest had come up, a mixture of alder thicket and hornbeam and an occasional dark pine. The new forest was dense and impenetrable, and you could see why Emile had been able to hide here for so long without being discovered.

Vabonne's gamekeeper pointed down a narrow path that was barely more than an animal track.

"You will have to make your way on foot," he said. "It is about an hour's walk. Or . . ." He glanced at me and was probably calculating how much my womanly weakness would slow us down. "Maybe two. Just continue until you get to the lake. If Monsieur Leblanc should appear, give him my regards and tell him you have my permission."

"Monsieur Leblanc?"

"Yes. He has the hunting rights." Leblanc. Like Imogene Leblanc?

"Does he have a daughter who teaches at the convent school?"

"No idea," the gamekeeper grunted. "Don't really know the man. He occasionally takes part in the hunts, but he never says much."

The Commissioner considered the narrow path with skepticism.

"Dear Madeleine, are you sure this will do any good?"

"I am sure, at least, that we will feel negligent if we do *not* go," I said.

He sighed. "Very well. Onward, onward, ho, ho, and away we go . . ."

It took us almost an hour and a half before there was finally a glimpse of water through the branches, and the path dipped sharply. The earth under our feet became blacker and more swampy, and it was necessary to climb across a couple of fallen trees. The Commissioner offered me his arm, and I needed it. My poor abused traveling suit would not survive this trip without harm, I noted with a certain sadness. The hem of the skirt was already dark with mud and lake water, and I had both felt and heard the seams rip under my left arm.

The sun glinted off the waters of the lake, but here in the shadows the mosquitoes were dancing. We followed the path along the slippery bank for another fifteen minutes. The Commissioner, who was not used to such physical challenges, was red faced and out of breath, but he did not suggest that we turn back. At heart, he was probably as stubborn as I was, and just as curious.

Now we could finally see the cabin. It rested on a rough platform that overhung the surface of the lake. The walls were built of black, tar-smeared logs, with faded silver-gray wooden shingles on the roof. This was not the sort of cabin meant for parties and drunken brotherhood; it was little more than a glorified duck blind, a primitive sanctuary and night shelter for a lone hunter who wished to catch the sunset from the worn wicker chair on the veranda and watch snipes come in to land in the reeds at dusk.

The door was closed and the windows covered by shutters. You could see tracks in the mud around the lodge, presumably from the men who had hunted and caught Emile Oblonski, but otherwise there was a feeling of abandonment about the place.

A split log served as a step to the veranda.

"Watch out," said the Commissioner. "Some of the boards look as if they've rotted through."

I stepped around a few of the worst places and pushed the door open.

The room was dim and smelled of damp and old ashes. There was a brick oven at one end, providing a crude source of heat and the facility to cook a simple meal, and a curtained-off sleeping alcove at the other. In front of the window facing the lake stood a small table with yet another wicker chair.

I had imagined it bigger. It was hard to picture Cecile Montaine in these surroundings, even though her room at the convent school had been even more spartan.

The Commissioner opened the shutters to let the light in.

In the alcove there were several gray blankets that seemed very similar to the ones at the convent. The bed frame was covered by a rough burlap-covered mattress, presumably filled with straw. A shelf above the fireplace held a couple of tin cans and a blue enamel coffeepot. On the table stood a water basin and a pitcher covered by a checkered dishtowel. There were also two books, which I immediately examined. One was an almanac, the other a Bible. Both had numerous notes in the margins, with small closely spaced letters that did not resemble Cecile's loopy handwriting.

The Commissioner's interest had been caught by a faded green dress carefully hung on an improvised hanger cut from a thick branch.

"We can probably assume that this belonged to Cecile Montaine," he said.

"It is hard to imagine that it could have been anyone else's," I said. "Unless the good Monsieur Vabonne has a mistress with a passion for nature."

The Commissioner offered a small, dry "Ha."

"Unlikely," he said. "I believe he is over eighty. And if this was a love nest, the décor would probably be somewhat less spartan. Two glasses, for example. Another chair on the veranda. Not to mention sheets."

He took out a large white handkerchief and dabbed his neck and forehead.

"Do you think we can drink the lake water without contracting dysentery?" he said.

"Most likely," I said. "There are probably greater health risks associated with the municipal water in Varbourg."

I lifted the dishtowel. The water pitcher was almost full. I poured a glass for the Commissioner and took the porcelain cup myself. I, too, was thirsty after the hike, and the water tasted fresh and clean. Then I began my search. I lifted the mattress, looked in the tins, shook the Bible and the almanac to see if any loose pages were hidden among the printed pages.

"Dear Madeleine, what is it you expect to find?"

"Cecile Montaine kept a diary," I said. "I found her brother burning it."

"Then it can hardly be here," said the Commissioner dryly.

"No. But if you had developed that habit—would you stop? If you were sitting in a cabin like this one, during a couple of freezing weeks in February, with no company other than a peculiar young man—who from what we have heard does not talk much—might you not feel the need to put down your feelings and thoughts?"

The Commissioner looked around the small room. It was as if he imagined for the first time what it was like to be Cecile and to be *here*, in the winter cold, alone with Oblonski.

"She would not have been able to spend much time out of doors," he said. "And what happened to her shoes? She was barefoot when she was found."

"If he took her boots, with the weather we had in February, that would be about as effective as chaining her to the wall. She would not get far."

"Do you think that is what he did?"

"The thought is frightening," I said. "And when she fell ill . . ."

"Yes. She would have been utterly helpless. Completely dependent on him."

But though we searched high and low, we found neither boots nor diary, and traces of Cecile were on the whole depressingly scarce. Other than the dress, the only evidence were two blood-splotched handkerchiefs with the initials *CM* embroidered in satin stitches, and some bloodstains on the gray blankets.

I thought about the long trip home and felt a need to apologize to the Commissioner.

"I was so sure that we would find something," I said.

"We did," he said, and put the handkerchiefs in his pocket. Then he carefully folded the faded green dress and placed it on top of one of the blankets. He folded the two other blankets with the same care and then tied the corners of the first together into a travel bundle. "We can now tell her family a little more about what happened before she died. It all counts."

I hoped Cecile's father was still free from infection and wondered if I could use the handkerchiefs as an excuse to see him again. Probably not. But perhaps I could ask the Commissioner for a report.

"Can we take the Bible and the almanac with us?" I asked.

"Presumably they belong to Old Vabonne or possibly to Leblanc," said the Commissioner.

"Yes. But I would like to have the time to look through them properly and see whether Cecile has written something after all."

"Very well. I don't think the owner will object."

We both had another drink of water, and I dried the glass and

cup with the dishtowel before putting them back in their place. Then we closed the shutters and began the homeward trudge.

My feet and legs were sore and my throat covered with mosquito bites when we finally reached civilization, or at least the forest lane that led to civilization. I walked often and happily, but I was more used to the city's short distances and smooth streets and sidewalks. I was definitely not some kind of female Doctor Livingstone.

"Wait here," said the Commissioner, who must have seen my exhaustion. "I will go back to Vabonne's farm and get the carriage. It shouldn't take me more than half an hour. Here, you can sit on the blanket in the meantime."

For once it was nice to be treated as a delicate feminine creature. I sat down gratefully and wished that we had thought to bring some kind of water bottle.

Here in the sun, the mosquitoes left me alone; they were still not as numerous as they would be later in the spring. When the Commissioner had disappeared down the lane, I unlaced my boots and took them off. I was quite convinced that I had acquired at least four blisters and considered removing my stockings as well, but refrained. I would have had to shimmy up my skirt and loosen the garter belts, and this was, after all, not the East African jungle. Someone might walk by.

While I waited, I studied the notes in the almanac. They were for the most part hunting observations—this and that kind of bird or animal spotted in such a place, at such a time, carefully registered on the relevant dates. Once in a while the observations were mixed with comments of a more personal kind: "J d' A could not hit a barn door at three paces. But his cognac is good." "AB boasts of his conquests. Unpleasant human being." Apparently these were character judgments Old Vabonne had made of various hunting friends. Most were very brief, but in one place there was a slightly longer note: "Lb's dog is a devil. It attacked MP's brown gelding and bit it so severely in the left hock that the tendons were damaged. Have forbidden him to bring it on hunts from now on. At first, he was furious and cursed me to my face, but that same evening he came over to apologize. The man is choleric but has a good heart. Has offered me a nice sum for the hunting rights, too. Considering it. Maybe next year? These old legs aren't what they used to be, and he knows what he is doing. But will miss this place."

My attention was abruptly sharpened. Lb had to be Leblanc, since I knew from Vabonne's own groundskeeper that he *had* in fact taken over the hunt now.

Leblanc had a devil of a dog. A dog that attacked horses. Or at least he had had one when Vabonne had made his notes.

I quickly flipped through the rest of the almanac to see if there was any more about Lb. There was not. Only one carefully filled margin after another about snipes, pheasants, ducks, wild rabbits, and an abundance of other living creatures.

I picked up the Bible to see what kind of thoughts Old Vabonne had set down there. Here there were fewer comments, and they focused almost exclusively on the First Book of Moses, the Book of Job, and a few places in Revelation. "Myriad is God's creation" it said next to the creation in Genesis with a neat line under "myriad." And in Ecclesiastes, a section was underlined with the same ruler-straight precision: "For that which befalleth the sons of men befalleth beasts; even one thing befalleth them: as the one dieth, so dieth the other; yea, they have all one breath; so that a man hath no preeminence above a beast: for all is vanity." A brief "So true!" was added in the margin. But either Vabonne had changed his mind or someone had felt the need to express disagreement. A wild and clumsy hand had crossed out the first declaration and scrawled a denial—NO NO WILL NOT BE-LIEVE IT, in awkward capitals and with no punctuation.

Was it Cecile? It was hard to determine because the block let-ters and the obvious difficulty the writer had had in forming them blurred any personal characteristics. It had very little similarity to the handwriting I had seen in the burning diary, but if she was ill and desperate, it might be possible. Or could it be Emile Oblon-ski? He could both read and write and must have his own reasons to think about the natures of men and animals.

In Revelation, a single passage was marked, not with the pre-cise and straight line I had assigned to Vabonne but with a much less tidy undulation: ". . . and they worshiped the beast, saying, Who is like unto the beast? who is able to make war with him?"

And again there was a note in the same clumsy block letters as the first. This time a sincere prayer: HAIL MARY FULL OF GRACE HELP ME PREVAIL NOT SUCCUMB FILL MY MIND WITH WISDOM GIVE ME COURAGE.

Were those Cecile's words? Or Emile's? And what kind of beast was it that had to be conquered?

The last underlined passage I did not find until I noticed that someone had torn a page from the Good Book and concealed it between the dust jacket and the cover. A hidden message, I thought, and hoped to finally find something I could definitively say came from Cecile Montaine.

I unfolded the page with eager fingers, but it was not essen-tially different from the others. It was from Leviticus, and again it was the messy hand that had done the underlining: "And if a woman approach unto any beast, and lie down thereto, thou shalt kill the woman, and the beast: they shall surely be put to death; their blood shall be upon them." The word "death" was underlined twice and repeated in the margin: DEATH DEATH.

My brain was slower than my spine. The skin along my vertebral column contracted so that I would have raised my hackles if human beings had still been equipped with fur. And only afterward did rationality catch up with base reflexes.

Blood, feces, and wolf hair on Mother Filippa's stomach and the inside of her thighs. And Sister Marie-Claire's choppy and reluctant narration:

"It lay . . . someone had placed . . . You understand . . . as when a man and a woman . . . and I could not . . . could not let others see . . ."

I suddenly knew as surely as if I had done it myself why Mother Filippa had been killed. This was the reason. The dead wolf between her legs was both punishment and accusation, like the sign they used to hang around the necks of people chained in the stocks, proclaiming their sin for all the world to see.

An unclean woman who had lain with animals and had to be put to death for it.

That was how the murderer had seen it.

My senses expanded, and all at once I perceived every rustling in the thicket, every gust of wind, the warmth from the sun against my skin, the chill in my stomach.

The murderer had written these words. And Cecile had been dead for more than a month when someone had tried to cleave Mother Filippa's head and chest in two. Cecile was not the one who had written this. It could be the other of the cabin's temporary inhabitants. It could be Emile. Or . . . it could perhaps also be the man who now had the official right to the cabin and the hunt there. Monsieur Leblanc, who had a dog that attacked horses.

Soft hoofbeats approached along the lane. The carriage rounded the curve by the stand of budding beech trees, and I saw the Commissioner's robust and familiar form on the box.

I was glad to see him.

"M'sieur? There is this gentleman and a young lady as would like to see you ... He says he's a commissioner."

Old Vabonne's maid did not have the polished manners that someone like Madame Montaine, for instance, would have demanded. Very young and clearly a country girl, she spoke with a patois so pronounced that I could barely understand her, and she was probably more at home plucking a hen than announcing visitors. We could hear her clear through the house because she had left all the doors open behind her.

"Well, show them in, then, Marie," said Vabonne with some exasperation.

She came trotting back, almost at a run.

"Mad'moiselle, m'sieur. Come in. Come in. Master's on the terrace."

Old Vabonne sat in a wicker chair similar to the two in the cabin in the woods. A straw hat shaded his lined face, and a checkered blanket had been tucked around his legs. He made no attempt to get up.

"Forgive me," he said. "The legs. They are not what they used to be."

"Good evening, monsieur," said the Commissioner. "And forgive us for disturbing you. This is Mademoiselle Karno, daughter of Doctor Albert Karno. And I am Varbourg's Commissaire des Morts."

"So. Have you come to get me?"

You had to look closely to catch the slight, crooked smile that lifted the right corner of the old man's mouth, half hidden as it was by his thick gray beard. But there was a glint in his dark eyes, and the Commissioner had no trouble recognizing the dry humor behind the comment.

"Not yet, monsieur. But I can reserve a good spot for you."

"Hah." Vabonne gave a brief barking laugh. "Heh. Have a seat, Monsieur le Commissaire, and let us enjoy the wait. Marie! Bring the port. And perhaps a pitcher of lemonade to quench our thirst? Mademoiselle?"

"Thank you," I said. "That would be lovely." I was well aware that I looked like someone who had barely survived a few weeks in the wilderness.

Old Vabonne's property was not a great estate, but not so long ago it had been a large farm with wheat fields, fruit orchards, a small vineyard, and significant incomes from hunting and forestry. But since Vabonne had no sons and his two daughters had both married men from the city with no interest in agriculture, most of the land was leased or sold off, he explained. "And I sit here in my loneliness and am not of much use. But the view is beautiful."

The terrace faced the garden and the vineyards that sloped down toward the river. At this time of the year, the vines were brown and dry and had not yet started their new growth, but the river's shining curve and the soft hills and the woods beyond had a natural symmetry on which the eye could rest without tiring.

"Monsieur, you are perhaps aware that two young people have been using your cabin by the lake as a refuge for several weeks?"

"Yes. I know now. Carreau, that's my gamekeeper . . . but that's right, you have already met him . . . Carreau helped them find the Wolfman the day before yesterday."

"The Wolfman," I said. "Is that what they call him?"

"You have not heard? Terrible story. Raised among wolves, they say, and he never really became a human being even though the nuns did what they could. First he abducted the young girl and kept her imprisoned for weeks, and when she managed to escape, she was so weakened that she died. Except . . . there are now those who claim that she committed suicide out of shame?" He looked questioningly at the Commissioner. "You must know whether that is true, Commissioner?"

"She did not commit suicide," said the Commissioner. "I can assure you of that."

"If you say so. But it is certain that he then raped and killed the convent's abbess. There are even those who claim that he violated her while in the shape of a wolf . . . if the young lady will pardon me."

There was another glint in the dark eyes that were almost hidden by his drooping eyelids, and I had no doubt that he was setting me a challenge.

"You hardly believe all that yourself, monsieur," I said. This was, after all, the same man who had expressed his wonder at God's myriad creations in the margins of his Bible—or so we thought.

"Hah. No. Man does not require such supernatural excuses to behave worse than any animal would. I have always thought it odd that priests claim an immortal soul for man, while they say the animals have none."

"'For that which befalleth the sons of men befalleth beasts; as the one dieth, so dieth the other; yea, they have all one breath,'" I quoted.

"Ah," he said, "you found my Bible. I never had the chance to bring it home. I would be pleased to have it back."

The Commissioner placed it on the table between us.

"And so you shall. But unfortunately, it must remain in our possession yet awhile, since it may prove to be of great import in a homicide case. Monsieur Vabonne, would you tell us if there are among these notes some you did not write?"

"Notes?" He fumbled for his waistcoat pocket and found a pince-nez, which he placed on his prominent nose. "They are just observations . . ." He flipped through the pages. "Hmmm. This is not my writing . . ."

While Marie brought the port and—more appreciated—a large pitcher of pleasantly tart lemonade, he found the various discrepant notes and confirmed that they were written by someone else. All except the page torn from Leviticus. This was now in the Commissioner's pocket, and there it would remain. As the Commissioner had put it, there was "no need to show our full hand."

"Do you recognize the handwriting?" he asked.

"No. No, there is nothing familiar about it."

"Monsieur Vabonne . . ."

"Yes, little mademoiselle?"

"You know Monsieur Leblanc?"

"Yes. His property, Les Merises, borders on mine."

"The cabin lies in the area where he bought the hunting rights, is that correct?" added the Commissioner.

"Yes."

"How would you describe him as a man?"

Old Vabonne observed the Commissioner with his head tilted.

"What has he done?" he said.

"It is merely a general question," said the Commissioner. "We have no reason to accuse him of anything."

"Yet—you mean?"

The Commissioner did not answer.

"Very well. You cannot comment on that. But I can tell you that I have hunted with Antoine Leblanc for most of a lifetime, and he is not a bad man. He can be a bit blustery, and he is not one to wear his heart on his sleeve, but he is a good hunter. Not one of those idiots who blasts away at anything that moves. Always waits until he has a clean shot. No creature is left to suffer when Antoine Leblanc kills it. He cares about the wildlife and treats his dogs with kindness, even though he does not give them silly pet names or invite them to lie on the furniture. He is a good neighbor and a good man. You will not persuade me to say a word against him."

"But you have had certain clashes with him?" I said carefully.

"What are you referring to?"

"His dog attacked a horse, I understand . . ."

He stared sternly at me for a few seconds. "You have also looked in my almanac," he said.

"Yes. Would you explain what occurred?"

It had happened nearly eighteen months ago, at the beginning of November during a wild boar hunt.

"That kind of hunt requires dogs with nerve and guts," explained Old Vabonne. "Particularly if you are working with hunting dogs who are required to come to grips with the boars. That must have been why he brought it. His dog attacks everything he sets it on, and it is afraid of nothing. Iago, he calls it, yes, that's right. Iago. Big, rough-coated hulk of a dog, also useful for hunting wolves, but it has been a long time since we have had the need to do that around here; the Vosges, now, that is different. You can pick up a pelt or two in the mountains there. Anyway, we had had quite a good day; bagged a couple of good-sized young ones and an *überläufer*, and the plan was for us to have a good meal here, and that is when that devil Iago goes straight for the hocks of Mario Ponti's brown gelding. It does not like horses; we have had the problem before, but not as bad as this. The gelding kicked out so that the dog went flying—six or seven meters, you would think that would have frightened it off; but it just went right in again and tried for the groin. Ponti whacked it with a rifle butt and was so angry that he would have shot it, one word followed another, and we had to separate both men and dogs. Leblanc stormed off with the brute and refused to give Ponti his hand in reconciliation, and I, too, got a blast of abuse for my troubles. But he came round that same evening to apologize, and we shared a good bottle of burgundy. He is a widower like me, so there is no one to scold us if we come home late."

"Mario Ponti? Do you mean Ponti the manufacturer?" I asked.

"Yes. Made a fortune on some kind of orange fizz and married a burlesque dancer, I believe. But he is not so bad. He can actually hit what he is aiming at—unlike certain other people."

The Commissioner and I looked at each other. Perhaps it was no coincidence that Father Abigore had turned up at Ponti's? If it was Leblanc who had set his dog on the hearse to steal the corpse, he might have felt a certain schadenfreude by hiding it in the cellar of a man with whom he had had such a clash.

"Can you describe Leblanc's dog?" the Commissioner asked.

"Huge, like I said. Almost the size of a wolfhound, but not a purebred. Gray and rough coated, with ears like a German shepherd or some kind of spitz."

The Commissioner nodded.

"Thank you for your help, monsieur. I will make sure that your Bible and almanac are returned to you when the investigation is concluded."

When we once again sat in the gig we had hired for the day's excursion, the Commissioner held back the horse—similarly hired—while I adjusted the traveling rug so that it covered my ruined skirt.

"Are you tired, Madeleine?"

"Not at all," I lied. "What do you have in mind?"

"Just that we drive by Les Merises and have a look at this Iago, and ask Antoine Leblanc a few polite questions if he happens to be home. Since we are practically just around the corner."

"An excellent plan," I said, unaware of what this lighthearted comment would lead to.

"Hello?"

The Commissioner's shout echoed from wall to wall. There was no reply. No dogs barked, no stable boy came out to see to the horse. All in all there was a sense of abandonment and disrepair about Les Merises. Weeds shot up unchecked between the yard's flagstones, and one stable door hung open, rattling in the wind. Somewhere you could hear a solitary horse neigh, and our hired horse—not much bigger than a pony—raised its head and offered a single shrill whinny in response.

"Stay with the carriage," the Commissioner said. "I'll take a look around."

"Do be careful," I said and thought of Iago, the great devil of a dog that did not like horses, and might not care much for commissioners, either. But if it had been there, then surely we would have heard it bark?

"Don't worry, Madeleine. I shall bring this with me." He swung his powerful black walking stick almost jauntily and headed up the main building's staircase, where he employed it to rap resolutely on the door.

As we had come to expect, no one appeared. The place seemed to be entirely abandoned.

The Commissioner walked around the corner and disappeared. I sat in the gig, waiting. The pony was apparently happy to have the chance to stand still, because it did not move a muscle and did not even bother to answer when the other horse whinnied again. If only I could be so phlegmatic, I thought. I was not at all calm. I wished the stable door would stop rattling. I wished the Commissioner would return. I wished the unseen horse would stop whinnying in such a lonely manner.

I do not know exactly how much time passed, but the shadows certainly lengthened. And finally I could not stand it any longer. I made sure that the carriage brake was on, looped the reins around the back of the seat, and climbed down. The pony stood with its head hanging, one hind leg tucked up beneath it, and barely flicked an ear as I walked away.

"Commissioner?"

I did not call too loudly, affected as I was by conflicting instincts: I wanted *him* to hear me—but not anyone else.

The garden behind the house was just as neglected as the courtyard. Fallen leaves still covered the lawn in a thick blackish-brown carpet, now half rotted. The perennials had not been cut back—the yellow and brown stalks poked up sadly amid delicate green shoots. Behind me the house squatted, an inelegant boxlike structure with dead and empty windows. The Commissioner was nowhere to be seen, but at the bottom of the garden, between some tall chestnut trees, I could see a stone wall and a garden gate, which stood ajar.

"Commissioner?"

I opened the gate all the way and followed the path into something that must once have been an orchard but was now so overgrown that it seemed more like a jungle. Tall yellow grasses, nettle stalks, and blackberry brambles sprawled under crumbling apple and pear trees, and an irregular growth of willow, poplar, and hornbeam shot up between the rows and veiled the symmetry that had once reigned here. Only the path itself revealed that someone still came here—the grass had been cut with a scythe and the blackberry brambles trimmed back to allow passage.

Yet another stone wall and yet another gate. And on the other side of the wall the outline of something that looked like an old chapel, with a corbie-step gable, a small bell tower, and a rusty iron cross that caught the last rays of sun at the top of the tower's pointed profile. Trimmed yew hedges stood like a dark wall against the real forest, which began right behind the chapel.

The door to the chapel was open, but I hesitated to go in. There was something incredibly private about this place. It had been made for solitary worship, not for official demonstrations of piety.

"Commissioner?"

"Madeleine?"

He was there. Some of the uneasiness I had attempted to repress turned into relief. I walked up the worn stone steps and into the small vaulted room.

"It took so long," I said. "I began to . . ."

I stopped midsentence. He was not alone. He was crouched down next to a child, a boy of perhaps seven or eight years, lying much, much too still on the stone floor.

"He is alive," he said, "but I did not dare to move him. I don't know what kind of injuries he has."

The boy was filthy. His near-black hair was matted to his skull in an unhealthy way, and it looked as if he had wet in his pants multiple times. At the edge of his hairline were the remains of dried blood. I knelt next to them both and felt for the boy's pulse. His breathing appeared untroubled, but his pulse was fast and pronounced under my index finger, and the pallor under the filth was alarming. His lips were cracked, and at the corner of his mouth clung a crust of dried-up puss from some kind of infection.

I examined his skull cautiously, first around the wound at the temple, and then proceeded to probe the neck and spine, but I found no clear indication of a fracture.

"The wound is old," I said. "It has started to heal. I don't think that is why he is unconscious. But who is he, and what is he doing here?"

"I can't say with certainty," said the Commissioner. "But I think this is Louis Charles Napoleon Mercier. Named after two kings and an emperor."

It was now completely dark in the chapel except for the play of pale moonlight and leafy shadows on the smooth stone floor. The tall, narrow windows were set so high that it was not possible to look out, but then, there would be nothing to look *at* right now, apart from various degrees of darkness.

Being left here alone with the boy had not been pleasant, but someone had to get help, and the Commissioner could do it more quickly and more effectively than I. He would be back soon, I consoled myself, an hour and a half at the most, he had promised, and by now an hour must surely have passed. I was quite safe in here in any event; no one could get in. I myself had locked the door to the chapel from the inside, and I could feel the outlines of the heavy iron key between my breasts. I had not dared to set it down anywhere for fear of not being able to find it again in the dark.

There was no question of turning on a light. I might as well send a lighthouse signal into the darkness: here—here—here . . . An unnecessary risk, in spite of the locked door.

I had folded two of the blankets from the hunting cabin a few times to create a sort of mattress for the boy to lie on, and covered him with the third. I had the Commissioner's jacket to sit on, but it was not sufficient to prevent the cold from creeping through my body from below. If it had been a summer evening, the stones beneath us might have released the heat that they had absorbed during the course of the day, but at this time of the year the damp of winter still clung to the stone walls, and the temperature in the room dropped dramatically as soon as the sun went down. It was not good for the boy. His hands and feet felt ice-cold, and my attempts to rub life into them were only partially effective.

"What has he done to you?" I murmured, and was spooked to hear my own voice in the darkened space. It was a lonely and sinister prison in which to place a child, I thought. A chamber pot, a tin plate, and a pitcher of water stood by the door, and someone had given him an illustrated edition of Perrault's fairy tales to occupy his time. Otherwise nothing had been done to ease his captivity.

What was most remarkable, however, was not that the boy was hurt, unconscious, and incarcerated—but that he was alive at all. If it *was* Louis Mercier, and that seemed likely, then the unavoidable inference had to be that the man who had given him the false message for Father Abigore was Antoine Leblanc. Which led to the equally inevitable conclusion that he was the man who had later killed Abigore with a single well-aimed blow of a coal shovel. If a man is so corrupt that he does not hesitate to kill a priest in this way, what prevents him from killing an inconvenient witness he has completely in his power?

"Don't be afraid," I whispered to the unconscious boy. "I am here with you, and I won't leave you."

My words echoed hollowly in the dark in spite of their sincerity. Outside I could hear an owl hooting, a shrill and lonely sound, and I caught myself listening, not just to the owl and the wind out there but also to my own heartbeat. I had begun to shiver. It is the cold, I said to myself. It is much too cold in here. In an attempt to keep warm, I wrapped Cecile's faded green dress around my shoulders like a shawl.

The fabric rustled.

Examining the dress once more, I forgot the owl and the cold. Along the hem of the skirt there was one spot where the seam was detectably thicker. The stitches had been partially undone to create a small pocket, and in that pocket my searching fingers found a few folded sheets of paper.

Cecile *had* written something. And hidden it as well as she could.

It was almost unbearable to sit there in the dark with her words on the paper in my hand without being able to read them. There were wax candles by the image of the Madonna, and presumably also matches, but did I dare? I had already made the decision that light would be too dangerous. No, I had to be patient. It could not be long now before the Commissioner returned.

A sound interrupted my deliberations—a faint noise at the door that at first filled me with hope. But instead of the Commissioner's imperturbable voice, there was a snuffle and a short, sharp bark.

"Iago, here!"

It was Leblanc and his dog.

I unconsciously clutched at the key, which lay cold and heavy against my breast. The thought struck me that we had assumed that it was the only one, and that the locked door offered protection against the man out there. But what if that was not the case?

I heard a muffled scraping of stone against stone. Leblanc was in the process of lifting the brick under which the Commissioner had found the key to the chapel. This was the moment when Leblanc would discover that all was not as he had left it. He turned the door handle and found it locked.

"Imogene?" he called. "Is that you?"

For a wild moment I wondered if I should pretend to be Imogene and ask him to go away. But although people often hear what they expect to hear, he knew his daughter's voice too well. I would not be able to mimic it.

Even if I had been able to carry off that deception, I suddenly thought, he would still have been unlikely to leave peacefully. I remembered the fear I had seen in Imogene's eyes when she thought her father had come to take her away from the convent.

I pushed Cecile's papers into my bodice next to the key and waited.

"Imogene! Open the door!" He hit the door with a heavy fist. "I know you are in there!"

He hammered on the door and then rattled its handle as if he thought this would make the lock give.

Where was the Commissioner? Where was the help he was supposed to be bringing? An hour and a half at the most. Surely that had passed?

Bang.

He was using something else to hit the door now. Something harder than a fist.

Bang. Bang. Bang.

Oh, God. Was that an axe?

No, I said to myself. There was no sound of splintering.

"Imogene. I am counting to ten. If the door is not open by then, I will shoot out the lock."

He began to count, slowly but inexorably. I did not know what to do. Would he really use a rifle on the door and risk hitting his own daughter?

"Three. Four. Five . . ."

And the boy. He risked hitting the boy.

"Six. Seven. Eight. Imogene—last chance. Open up or stand aside."

He was going to do it.

"Nine."

"Wait!" I shouted.

"Then open up."

"I do not have the key," I said. "I *cannot* open it."

Would he believe me? And would it change anything?

The only warning I got was the sound of a loading gun. I threw myself down on the floor next to the boy just as the shots rang out. Two shots, so close together that the first had not finished echoing between the stone walls before the last blew door, lock, and handle to smithereens.

"Who the hell are you?"

I raised my head slowly and sat up. A few meters from me stood Antoine Leblanc with a lamp in one hand and the hunting rifle held in the crook of his arm.

A few seconds passed before I could speak.

"Monsieur Leblanc?" I said. "How fortunate that you came. I am afraid this poor boy has been badly hurt. I tried to help him as well as I could, but the door was shut on us, and I could not get it open again, someone must have locked it . . ."

Helpless, innocent, ignorant. It was the only defense I could think of.

It actually made him hesitate for a moment.

"Were you locked in?" he asked.

"Until you freed us."

Behind him stood the dog, large and gray and rough coated as described, growling and with its hackles raised. I tried not to look at it.

"I have seen you before," he said slowly, and set the lamp down on the floor. "You were at the convent. And at the funeral."

The funeral? Was he speaking of Cecile's? That was the only

funeral I had attended recently, but I had not seen him. Or, wait . . . the broad-shouldered man with the carriage, the one who had driven some of Cecile's friends and teachers. Had that been Leblanc and not just a random coachman?

"I don't believe we have been introduced," I said, and forced a smile that was about as natural as the naked grin on a skull. "I am Madeleine Karno. I met your daughter a few times . . ."

This did not help. His face went rigid, and his lips pulled back so I could see his tobacco-stained teeth.

"That doctor," he said. "Doctor Death. You are his daughter."

"Yes." I began to get up, holding out my hand as though we were at a tea party and about to be introduced.

"Stay where you are!"

"But, monsieur . . ."

He raised his rifle and reloaded rapidly.

"Sit down, I said!"

I let myself slide to the floor. It was not difficult; my legs were already shaking so much that they were having a hard time supporting me.

"It is probably best if I stay with the boy while you go for help," I tried, and knew that my little performance was getting more and more labored and less and less credible. I fumbled for the boy's cold hand under the shelter of my petticoat. Not that he could feel anything, it was more to console myself. We wanted to save you, I thought, and now . . .

Now it looked instead as if we had given Monsieur Leblanc the final push.

"He would have died anyway," he said. "The priest. I just saved him a few days of suffering."

Don't tell me such things, I thought urgently. The more he revealed, the more likely it was that he would feel impelled to fire that gun.

"Of course," I squeaked. "I am sure they will understand that if only you . . ."

"May God have mercy on me," he said, and began to take off his left boot.

I did not understand why, just sat completely paralyzed by fear and tried to think of something, anything, that could prevent the unpreventable.

"Down, Iago," he said.

The dog looked up at him, then reluctantly lay down. He took a step backward, on one bare and one booted foot, took aim, and put a bullet through the back of the dog's head. I was still sitting there with my mouth open, trying to comprehend what was happening, when he reloaded, placed the rifle's stock against the floor, placed the barrel under his chin, and used his naked toes to pull the trigger.

He was clearly more used to handling guns than Monsieur Montaine. Most of the back of his head disappeared in a cloud of blood and bone splinters, and he was dead before he hit the floor.

When the Commissioner finally returned about ten minutes later, with a carriage and some men from the convent, I was sitting next to the unconscious Louis Mercier, shaking so badly that my teeth were rattling against each other with a tiny, brittle sound. The cavalry stopped quite abruptly in the doorway, it seemed to me, staring at Leblanc and the mess at the back of his head, at the dead dog, and at me.

"Dear Madeleine," said the Commissioner, "I think you may put down the rifle now."

IV

March 28–30, 1894

Louis Mercier regained consciousness a few hours later on the chaise longue at Carmelite Street. It was easier for my father to examine him there than if we had brought him to Saint Bernardine, and both Inspector Marot and the Commissioner waited impatiently to question him about Antoine Leblanc's deeds and misdeeds.

We now knew with certainty that it *was* Louis Charles Napoleon Mercier, because after one look at the unconscious child, Marie Mercier had thrown herself to her knees at his side and kissed his face again and again, and then—still on her knees—she had seized both of the Commissioner's hands and covered them with just as many kisses while she stuttered her incoherent gratitude for saving her son.

The Commissioner stood with a most peculiar expression on

his face—it had to be his version of disconcerted unease—and repeated, "My dear lady, my dear lady," as if it were the refrain of a song, all the while trying to persuade her to stand up. Apparently, this was what it took to crack the Commissioner's monolithic self-control.

I did not feel cracked, I felt blown to bits and pieces. At first I had been able to hold myself together to some extent. I had cared for Louis Mercier on the trip back to Varbourg, had insisted on warm blankets and great caution in the handling of the unconscious child, and had perhaps clung to that task so insistently because it was better than thinking about Antoine Leblanc and his hunting rifle.

During the trip, the boy came closer to consciousness, though he still did not answer when I tried to rouse or soothe him. His eyes flitted under closed lids, and he moved his lips a little. I moistened them with cold water, and he sucked on the cloth like an infant, still without waking up. Thirst and dehydration were part of the problem, I concluded, and I began systematically wetting the cloth and dripping water into the boy's mouth, only a few drops at a time so it would not end up in his windpipe instead.

But when we got home and my father took over this responsibility, my defenses began to crumble. I sank down into the Commissioner's chair and could not move any farther. I was filthy, and my suit was in a sorry state. I ought to wash myself and change my clothes and do something about my hair. I ought to get up and help my father with the examination and care of Louis Mercier.

But I could not.

I just sat.

I did not say anything, and that was probably one of the reasons no one really noticed me, especially not when Marie Mercier arrived a little later and performed her tearful identification. But I sat with the sensation that my hands were not my own, that my body did not belong to me, and that my head had detached itself from my neck and was floating around like a balloon on a string a few meters above the rest of me.

Then the string broke.

I did not understand myself what happened; I was not asleep, nor was I unconscious, yet what I saw had to be a dream.

Cecile was walking toward me through the salon. She moved among the others, stepped aside in order not to bump into Marot, but no one else saw her, of that I am certain, because no one re-acted. Even though she was naked.

Her black hair fell across her back and shoulders, her lips were moist and vividly colored, precisely the same delicate shade of rose as her nipples. Her eyes were full of life. Her hair was wet, and her naked body also, as if she had just walked through the rain, and glittering trails of water ran down her breasts and across her stomach and thighs. She smiled, but she was not smiling at me. She looked past me, and I turned my head in reflex.

From the other side of the room, by the window, came Emile Oblonski. He, too, was naked, and his member stood unashamedly erect without him making any attempt to cover it. His compact muscular form was whole and free of the injuries I knew he had, and he was just as wet with rain as she was.

They met in the middle of the room. Their bodies slid together, slid into each other without difficulty, without clumsiness. She folded her legs tightly around him and let herself slide down until she engulfed him, and he carried her effortlessly.

At first it seemed that her long black hair enveloped them both. But then I could see that it was not just hair; it was fur. Smooth, shiny black fur broke through the skin along her spine, spread down across her buttocks, covered her legs. They both turned, in a physically impossible way, around the axis that was the joining of their sexes. And with one long smooth jerk it was no longer two people I saw but a black wolf and a golden one, in close coupling.

Infinitely long.

That is how it felt. I could not look away and did not want to, because the sight filled my body with a rush of desire, a pounding pulse I would not have been able to stop. *I* wanted to have fur. I wanted to be an animal. I wanted to surrender myself as they did, without thought, without guilt, without shame. And when they finally parted and trotted off on moist paws, through the salon, past the people, and out the open door, I wanted to follow. Everything in me wanted to follow. But I could not. I sat bound in a chair and a salon and a body, a body that could not be transformed. A body that was not a wolf's.

I fell back into myself with a dull impact, as when an insect hits a window. A small moan of protest escaped me, but I do not think anyone heard me. For at that moment Louis Mercier opened his eyes and looked around him with a blank confusion that was even more fundamental than mine.

Or perhaps not.

I knew *where* I was. I was just no longer certain who or *what*.

Inspector Marot led the boy through his testimony with a gentleness I had not expected. He was soothing, attentive, sympathetic. He waited patiently when the child stopped, prompted him with simple open-ended questions, and of the aggressive walrus there was no trace.

Yes, Louis had been called over by a gentleman who wanted to pay him to run an errand. And though he did not discover the man's name, it was clear from his description, not least of the dog Iago, and from his further explanations, that it was indeed Antoine Leblanc. He had been paid a good sum and promised an even more princely reward to carry a message to the priest's residence at Espérance at precisely a quarter past eleven. He had carried out his end of the bargain and had delivered the note precisely as he had been instructed, but when he showed up to collect the franc he had been promised, the dog had jumped on him and toppled him so he hit his head on the curb, after which the man held him down and "choked him with a rag."

Inspector Marot glanced questioningly at the Commissioner and my father.

"Possibly ether," said my father. "Or chloroform."

When Louis regained consciousness, he was in the chapel. And there he remained, for all three of the weeks he had been missing. Every evening and every morning, someone placed a little food, a pitcher of water, and a clean chamber pot for him, but when he drank the water, he became drowsy and fell asleep. He quickly figured out the connection but did not know what to do; there was nothing else to drink.

The worst part was the cold and the fear of what would happen to him. He was a child of the streets, and he knew that there were people who harmed children for their own pleasure.

Once he had poured the water out of the pitcher without drinking it and only pretended to sleep. It was the man with the dog who came to open the door. Louis had lain completely still and had even attempted to snore a little. He had heard the faint rattling when the man set down the water and a tin plate with food and emptied the chamber pot, but he had not dared to move, because the dog stood over him, sniffing his breath suspiciously.

There was the sound of steps. The man came closer. Louis squeezed his eyes shut and held his breath.

"A child," the man had murmured. "How can one do it when it's just a child."

Then he went back to the door.

"Iago, heel," he said, and the dog left Louis alone. The next day the fairy tale book had appeared next to the pitcher of water when Louis woke up.

"I had thought that I might try to get away, m'sieur," said Louis. "But the dog . . . I was so afraid of the dog. I did not dare. And the rest of the time . . . I just drank the water. It was easier."

"You did the right thing, my boy," said Marot. "Your job was to survive. To find you and free you was the task of the police."

A task the police had not managed particularly well, I thought bitterly. It was pure luck that the Commissioner had found Louis Mercier while he was still alive. But Marot's words comforted the boy and eased the guilt he clearly felt over his own fear.

"Where is the man now?" asked Louis. "Did you catch him?"

"He is dead," said Marot.

"Good," Louis said and did not ask anything else.

Marie Mercier and Louis were sent home in the inspector's own carriage, escorted by a constable. Louis was weak and barely able to stand, but what he needed most of all was rest and safety, and a sufficient amount of food and drink and loving care.

"He will be better off at home," said my father. "A hospital would only make it worse."

Marie Mercier was clearly relieved.

"Thank you," she said again. "Many, many thanks."

The past weeks had left their mark on her. The steely discipline that maintained her beauty regime had slackened. Her face was swollen, and her tears had created grimy tracks in the powder on her face. Her hair had not been washed for a while, and she had probably slept inadequately and eaten too little, but there was still something about her that made the men look at her a little longer and a little more frequently than perhaps they ought to. Even my father was distracted, I noted. And absolutely no one looked at me.

I was unsure whether to feel relieved or deserted. I needed help. I had seen naked people transform themselves into wolves, and I seriously feared for my mental health. But at the same time I knew that I could not speak of what I had seen to anyone and that I would just have to hope this peculiar condition would pass when I was less shaken and exhausted.

Otherwise you will end up in the madhouse.

I pushed the thought away and was able to collect myself enough to stand. Louis and Marie Mercier were just then leaving, Marie with her arm around her son's shoulders. In the doorway, Louis half turned around.

"Thank you, mademoiselle," he said. "I could hear your voice, it was just that I couldn't answer."

Something fell into place inside. A feeling that I had after all managed to save something, that not everything had been in vain.

"Goodbye, Louis. Take good care of yourself and of your mother."

It was my intention to go upstairs to my own bed and my own room. But I did not get that far. The front door had barely closed behind Louis and Marie Mercier before someone with an aggressive fist hammered to be let in.

"Inspector! Commissioner!"

When both these gentlemen were called, in that tone of voice, it could mean only one thing: a crime with a deadly outcome.

And so it was. A few seconds later, an out-of-breath policeman stood in our salon and gave his report.

"I regret to have to tell you that young Adrian Montaine has shot and killed the Wolfman," he said, and then faltered a bit before correcting himself. "Eh . . . I mean . . . Emile Oblonski."

It was clear that he had needed to rack his memory for a few seconds to remember that the Wolfman was human and had a human name.

I was so tired that I was almost incapable of unhooking that miserable corset. Elise had gone to bed long ago, and I did not want to wake her up. I stood in the middle of my own room and wept stupid helpless tears because everything was just too difficult.

Pull yourself together, I admonished myself. Breathe in. Breathe out. Hold your breath. Push the hook out of the eye. You have done it a hundred times.

It helped. The hook and the eye parted company. And when I was finally able to shed my whalebone armor, and my breasts parted and fell more naturally into place, Cecile's folded pages dropped to the floor at my feet.

I had not forgotten about them. But I had also not told anyone that I had them. They were a secret we shared, she and I, and I did not want to let the men into our confidence unless I had to.

I put the pages on my bedside table and poured some water into the basin of the washstand. I undressed completely and washed myself from head to toe, wishing that I could also wash my hair. Unfortunately, that required greater quantities of water and preferably Elise's help, so it would have to wait for morning.

While I washed, the picture of Cecile's naked, wet body kept intruding.

Living, free, and in transformation.

There had been nothing in the way of hymns or soaring angel wings in the vision I had experienced, and rationally I knew very well that it was the peculiar manifestation of an exhausted brain and a shaken mind. That Emile Oblonski had died at about the time I saw him come to meet Cecile . . . was an unsettling coincidence. Nothing more.

I observed my naked body in the wardrobe mirror and thought of the professor. Of August. Who presumably was now sleeping peacefully somewhere in Heidelberg and had no idea that his half-hearted fiancée had reason to fear for her mind. I wondered whether one might be married without being impregnated and conquered. And if so, what I would then do about Papa.

Nothing decisive emerged from these thoughts. At last I put on my nightdress and went to bed. Elise had already turned back the bedspread, and the sheets crackled against my body, clean and soap scented. I turned up the wick of my bedside lamp and sat down to read the last words that Cecile had left behind in this world.

Rodolphe had walked out. He had left her in the cold pavilion, in the murky shadows behind the boards that protected the interior against the snow and damp of winter. She was still breathing in painful gasps and had trouble focusing on anything else.

This was not at all as it was supposed to be.

Yes, he had filled her. For a few floating seconds he had brought her across that red-and-black threshold where she could disappear and lose herself, where only the body mattered.

She could still feel his seed as a greasy stickiness between her thighs.

But everything else. The violence and the anger with which he had used her. The words he had screamed at her then. *Whore, swine. Is that the way you want it?* He had thrust himself into her with such force that her abdomen had been hammered against the bench, and she knew there would be bruises, deep bruises that it would be difficult to explain to the other girls at the convent. Especially Anette, the little uptight snitch, who would no doubt probe and whisper and tattle, and feel so holier-than-thou about it that it was enough to make you throw up.

And his contempt. His coldness. As if only he had the right to feel desire.

She knew it, of course. Knew that when he put his arms around her from behind and tried to force his hand between her legs, he expected her to stop him, expected her to resist. Knew very well that he had supposed that she would say no when he asked if she wanted to sit for a while in the pavilion. But this was the man she was meant to be with for the rest of her life. She had to *know.* If they could . . . If *she* could, with him. And at first it had seemed all right, and she thought maybe it will be fine, maybe he is enough, and then she would be able to give up the other feeling. Give up Emile.

But then.

It was when she understood the magnitude of the gap . . . the infinite gap between what she could have and what she wanted. That was when she began to cry. And then he had become even harsher and had said even worse things. Had called her a hole, a sewer. A public toilet anyone could use.

At that point she knew that they would never be married, and the thought filled her most of all with relief, at least until she thought about what Maman would say. She hoped she would have the chance to tell Papa first. Then he could speak to Maman.

That was not the way it went. When she reached the Descartier family home, she was not let in. Their coachman was there, ready to drive her home, and it turned out that he also brought a letter for her parents that formally ended the engagement. The letter gave no reason, and Cecile was not capable herself of coming up with a plausible explanation. Her thoughts rattled around in her head, and no words emerged, only various sensations—a chill, a sudden cramp, a crawling of the skin that she could not translate into words. But Maman's eagle eye had noted the two unbuttoned hooks on the back of the dress that Cecile had not been able to reach herself.

"Did he get carried away?" she asked. "Did he take advantage of you?"

Cecile was not able to answer. A "yes" was as much a lie as a "no."

"I will go over there," said Maman, and she could not be dissuaded. Perhaps she really believed there was some misunderstanding that she could correct, perhaps she even imagined that she might magnanimously forgive a shy and remorseful young man on her daughter's behalf and allow that these things sometimes happened but that it really only demonstrated that these two young people were made for each other.

When she came home, she was stone. Ice. Iron. The hardest, coldest, most unbending material there was. One nostril had acquired the tic that Cecile recognized from some of her childhood's darkest and most confusing memories, and this time it did not go away. She did not give Cecile more than a single scathing look before she disappeared into Papa's office.

A few minutes later, Papa called her. When Cecile saw his face, something loosened inside her, and the words came tumbling.

"I am sorry, Papa. Sorry. But it was not just me. Rodolphe wanted—he tried—it was both of us . . ."

She sank down at his feet and put her arms around his legs the way she had done when she was little. He understood her so much better than Maman, had always done so, understood that she could not sit still and embroider for hours, understood that she turned black inside if she was not allowed to escape the house and the convent and the *stodginess* at least once in a while.

Today was different.

"Make sure she learns her lesson," said Maman, and placed the cane on the desk before leaving the room.

Cecile got up hesitantly. It had been many years since he had hit her. She must have been nine or ten the last time it happened.

"Papa," she said and was still not quite able to grasp that he intended to punish her in that way. She had done nothing that Rodolphe had not done as well. Didn't he understand that?

He pulled out the chair and set it in front of the desk. Sat down himself and motioned for her to lie across his lap as if she were still a little girl who could be spanked.

"No," she said. "Papa, no."

He looked at her for several seconds.

"You must learn that a daughter of this house cannot behave as you have done," he said, and she recognized her mother's phrase beneath his. *A daughter of this house.* "You have a choice. You can obey me now, as is suitable for a young woman. Or you can leave. And if you leave, you will not come back."

He meant it. It was not just her mother's will that lay behind his words. What she had done was so offensive to him that he literally could not stomach it.

She had never been able to suffer banishment, did not possess the strength to tolerate solitude. Even as a child she had much preferred the cane to the horrible isolation of being locked in her room.

Even now she could not stand it. The threat alone was enough. She took a few uncertain steps and got down on her knees at his side. Bent over his lap.

As he had done when she was little, he pulled down her underwear. She heard his breathing change when he saw the signs of what had happened in the pavilion. She had not dared to ask for a bath, because she did not want Odette to see the bruises and tattle. A quick scrub in cold water was all that she had been able to manage, and she suddenly knew that he would be able to smell it, would recognize the sour-sweet scent of semen and sex.

The first blow made her cry out. She did not remember that it had ever hurt so much when she was small, and surely he had not used all his strength and released all of his despairing anger back then as he did now. The second blow was much less violent, the third really just a smack. But the second before he pushed her away, she felt it.

She was lying across his lap, so she felt it at once.

Felt it. Felt *him.*

A movement that ought not to be there. A nudge, a rising, a momentary excitement.

They stared at each other, two people lost beyond redemption, each in their separate way. He because he would never be able to get past this moment, would never be able to erase it and make himself and her believe that it had not happened. She because she knew in a second's bitter clarity that she no longer *was* a daughter of this house but a stranger who could never return.

She did not run from the room. She carefully straightened her clothes without looking at him. Then she walked out and closed the door behind her. She gave the hansom cab driver her pearl bracelet in exchange for driving her back to school, and two days later she left the convent behind as well. With Emile.

I stared at the creased, slightly damp pages.

Here was the secret that had made the whole family crumble. It was those few moments of unforgivable sin that had sent Cecile into an exodus that she did not return from alive. This was what had troubled her father so deeply that he attempted to blow the memory out of his brain with a pistol. And this was what had made her brother a murderer. Back in the house on Boulevard Saint-Cyr, Madame Montaine was left with a man who might die at any moment and would probably never return to life. And the little sister, the silent child whom no one really saw . . . How I wished that someone or something would watch over that girl.

"Cecile and Emile. We rhyme. We belong together, and now we live like Hansel and Gretel in a gingerbread house. But there is no witch here."

That is what Cecile had written about the first days in the hunting cabin. But later their idyll grew less Eden-like.

"Imo was here with food. It is a long trip for her when the weather is so merciless, but she is a helpful soul, bless her. Emile does not like her and usually leaves when she comes. But what would we do without her? It is so cold here. Constantly so cold, even when the oven door is almost red-hot. I get chilblains on my hands and fear for my health. Imo gave me a little bottle of tonic; it is soothing and allows me to sleep, which is otherwise almost impossible. Today I slept for two hours while she just sat looking at me and held my hand. I was still tired and my head felt heavy when I woke up, so she lay down next to me, and I helped her. But now I am constantly getting nosebleeds; that cannot be healthy. Emile got angry and sad when he saw the marks; he and Imo do not understand each other at all. And my boots have disappeared. Emile says that Imo must have taken them, but why would she do that? I think he did it because I began to talk about returning to the sisters. He fears that we will be punished and that he might be jailed. Imo says that people are saying he abducted me. I ought to write a letter, but I do not dare. Half the time I just want to go home, and the other half I remember why I *cannot* go home, and then I despair again."

A gap. And then, in a hand much less assured:

"We lie together, Emile and I, and then everything is better for a little while. That is the only thing that warms me now, but I start to cough so much from it. He holds me so that I can breathe better, but he cannot make the cough go away. I want to have him inside me all the time so I know that I am not alone. And sometimes he stays in there for hours even if we are just lying still. But he has to go out. Imo does not come anymore. Why, I don't know. We have almost nothing to eat, only what he catches. He eats everything raw—mouse, beetles, worms—but I cannot make myself do that. It is only when he catches a bird or something else that can be plucked and cooked that I can get it down. He *tries* to take care of me, but it is not easy."

And the last words:

"Want to go home. Have pleaded and begged. Emile says he will try. Oh, God. It is enough now. It is enough."

I put down the pages, turned off the lamp, and leaned back on the pillows. Imo. That had to be Imogene Leblanc. Who else could it be? But why had she not said a word? Why had she not revealed where the two young people were? Was it to protect them—or to protect herself? What was it Cecile had written? *She lay down next to me, and I helped her . . . Emile got angry and sad when he saw the marks.* What marks? And what kind of "help"?

The question and the pictures flickered past on the inside of my eyelids, and it took some time to fall asleep in spite of my exhaustion.

The next day I was so stiff and sore all over that Elise finally had to give up fastening my corset. It was as if my bruised body had swollen in the course of the night, and I could not bear the pressure against ribs, lungs, and abdomen.

When I came downstairs, Papa was in the middle of cutting his plaster cast off his arm with a pair of surgery scissors.

"Is that not a little too soon?" I asked.

"Three weeks has to be enough," he said, lips clenched. "I am tired of being helpless."

I did not protest. I could see that it would do no good.

"Next week I should be able to walk again," he said. "Then I will no longer need to impose on you the sort of unreasonable burden you have had to bear recently."

"It has not been a burden."

"How can you say that? Everything you have had to witness, everything you have had to experience . . . that man could have killed you, Maddie!"

There was plaster dust everywhere. The surgery scissors were too small and only nibbled mouselike at the hard plaster crust.

"Let me do that. We need better scissors."

"Madeleine."

"Yes."

"Everything will be fine again."

I did not say anything, just nodded and went down to the laboratory to find a more suitable pair of scissors. What did "fine" really mean? That everything would be as before? I hoped not. I was no longer content to listen with the door ajar, or sit unnoticed while the men debated. It was increasingly clear that I could not let myself be exiled to the back of the gallery—I wanted to be down there on the operating floor, *doing* things.

When I returned to the salon, the Commissioner and Marot had just arrived, one from a few hours of much-needed sleep in his room at the boardinghouse, the other directly from the préfecture. While Elise fetched coffee and extra brioches, I cut off the rest of the Mathijsen cast and tried to sweep the plaster dust off the table without having too much of it form an insoluble bond with the Bokhara carpet's pile.

"Ah, fit again," said the Commissioner. "Or nearly so. That is good to see."

I could tell by the look on my father's face that the sudden lack of support was not comfortable for his healing arm, but he tried to pretend otherwise.

"Yes, it won't be long," he said. "But do sit down. Any news?"

The Commissioner chose his usual chair while Inspector Marot sat down in the brocade chair next to the chaise longue.

"I intend to announce to the préfecture that the murder of Father Abigore has been solved," he said, and smoothed the walrus mustache with index finger and thumb, a gesture that emphasized a certain smug satisfaction. "Though the murderer cannot be brought to earthly justice, having already met his Maker."

"And Mother Filippa?" asked my father. "What about her?"

"The evidence, though circumstantial, is quite strong. We have to obtain a sample of his handwriting to determine if he is the one who wrote the comments in Vabonne's Bible. We know that he was given to rages, and that his own daughter sought refuge behind the convent walls to escape him. That may have been the reason for his anger at the abbess. Mademoiselle Karno observed a confrontation between them . . ."

"Just the conclusion of it," I said for the sake of precision. "It was just one sentence."

"Yes. What was it he said?" The inspector took out his notebook and got ready to take notes.

"He said, 'You are not God's servant, but the devil's.'"

"Exactly. That fits nicely with the disturbed notion that is expressed in the Bible passages. Is it possible to make a cast of his teeth?"

"Unfortunately not," said my father. "The shot entered under his chin and exited at the back of his head. The lower jaw is practically pulverized and the upper jaw greatly damaged. It would not be worthwhile to try."

"Too bad. It would have been a nice definite proof."

"So you have completely given up on the theory that it was Emile Oblonski who killed her?" I could not prevent a certain bitterness from creeping into my voice. Emile lay in the chapel at Saint Bernardine, shot through the chest, waiting for my father and the Commissioner to have time to do the necessary yet pointless autopsy that would formally determine the cause of death. In one of the cells beneath the préfecture, Cecile's brother sat captive, a confessed murderer. The lives of two people wasted with one shot, and all of it so meaningless and misunderstood that my soul ached.

"I consider Leblanc a far more plausible killer," said Marot. "We will ask the daughter for a sample of his handwriting. If it matches—well, then there will no longer be any reason to keep the case open."

Elise arrived with rolls and coffee. No one said anything while she laid the table, but when she had left the salon, the Commissioner straightened himself in his chair with a touch of belligerence.

"But the motive?" he protested. "He might well have felt an anger or a bitterness toward Mother Filippa, who placed herself between him and his daughter. But Father Abigore? Do we know if they even knew each other? And why that whole absurd story with the theft of the corpse?"

"It is not satisfactory," admitted Marot, and reached out distractedly for a brioche, which he tore into pieces with his fingers and began to chew without making the effort to butter it. "We know that he was the one who set the trap for Abigore. We know that he was the one who later set his dog on the hearse horses and stole the body. It is most likely that he deposited it at manufacturer Ponti's as a sort of bizarre revenge for the quarrel they had over the dog. We know it was Leblanc who abducted and incarcerated Louis Mercier, and we know he was strong enough to deliver the blow that brought down the priest. We even have him admitting as much to Madeleine. But *why* did he do all of this? He was a religious man. Might he have confessed something to Abigore and later regretted it? Perhaps he feared Abigore might break the Seal of Confession? These are guesses; I do not know *why*. But I do know that he did these things."

"He said that he was only shortening the priest's suffering," I offered. "Could that be a motive? A sort of mercy killing?"

"Unfortunately that is a justification, not a motive," said Marot.

The Commissioner rubbed the corner of a drooping eye. The bags were even more pronounced than usual, after yet another far too wakeful night.

"We know that he had reason to kill Mother Filippa, but we

don't know that he actually did it, at least not yet. We know that he *did* kill Father Abigore, but not why. Is that how the case may be summarized?" he said, and did not sound all too thrilled at the diagnosis.

"Yes, that is reasonably accurate," admitted Marot. "Luckily the préfecture requires only that I can prove who. It is not necessary to explain why."

The Commissioner looked even more tired, and I understood him. To determine the cause of death was the focus of all his efforts. He most definitely concerned himself with *why*.

"Mademoiselle Karno, I actually came to ask if you would speak with Imogene Leblanc for us," said the inspector. "If possible today? It would be a great help if you could convince her to come out of the enclosure."

I thought of the diary pages that now lay in the drawer of my dressing table up in my room. Oh, yes, I would like to speak with Imogene Leblanc. Very much so.

"I will do what I can," I said virtuously. "Should we go at once?"

Imogene Leblanc's arthritis-twisted hand rested on the head of a large spotted mixed-breed hunting dog.

"I borrowed it from Vabonne's gamekeeper," she said. "Michel Carreau. This is a large house to be alone in, so it is comforting to at least have a dog with me."

She was no longer dressed in the convent's postulant attire but was wearing a high-necked white blouse and an ill-fitting skirt in dark blue serge. A black ribbon around her right upper arm was the only sign of official mourning, but her eyes were red rimmed, and she dabbed them regularly with a handkerchief. The eczema on her face flared red against her pale skin.

At the convent, we had learned that she had gone home as soon as she received word of her father's death, and that they did not know if she was coming back. There were two travel trunks on the parlor floor, which she was apparently in the process of unpacking, one with various items of clothing, the other full of books and papers.

She had let us in herself. There were no longer any servants at Les Merises, it seemed, which was also obvious from the layer of dust on the dark mahogany furniture and the heavy smell of wet dog and old pipe tobacco that hung in the carpets and the drapes. Imogene Leblanc apologized for neither.

"What is it you want?" she said, with a harshness in her voice that teetered on rudeness.

"Allow me to express my condolences for your loss," said Inspector Marot.

Imogene nodded briefly. "Thank you." She pressed the handkerchief against the edges of her nose and sniffed a little.

"And forgive us if we are intruding. But there are certain circumstances that must be clarified before we can close this tragic case."

She did not say anything, just let her free hand slide across the dog's brown-and-white head, only waiting, it seemed, for us to finish and leave. The inspector took out Vabonne's Bible and placed it on the dusty tea table. He opened it to the passage from Revelation, marked with an inexpertly embroidered bookmark that I suspected was a gift from his daughter.

"Mademoiselle Leblanc, is this your father's handwriting?"

She stared at the page for what seemed to me quite a long time. It was the longest comment, the one that contained the despairing cry: HAIL MARY FULL OF GRACE HELP ME PREVAIL NOT SUCCUMB FILL MY MIND WITH WISDOM GIVE ME COURAGE.

"Yes," she said at last. "That is my father's hand."

"Thank you. Can you, for the sake of thoroughness, give me another example of his handwriting?"

"If you insist."

She got up, with a bit of difficulty, and left the parlor with the dog at her heels. Luckily it was not a "devil" like the deceased Iago but a rather more amiable creature. It had barked at us when we arrived but its tail had been wagging at the same time.

"She is not particularly pleasant," I said quietly. My eye had been caught by one of the books that stuck out of the trunk. *On Bacteria: The Theory and Practice of Louis Pasteur.*

"We are here to obtain proof against her dead father," answered Marot. "Why should she be pleasant?"

I took the book and opened it. On the title page was a dedication, written in a confident and easily legible hand: "To Imogene Leblanc, from Louis Pasteur, in hopes of a rapid recovery. Endure. We conquered the Mad Dog, one day we will also conquer the Wolf."

Louis Pasteur *himself*. He was the one who had written this inscription. *Pasteur.*

Imogene Leblanc returned with a few scraps of paper just as I was putting the book back into the trunk.

"I am sorry," I said. "I did not mean to rifle your personal belongings. But did Pasteur really write this?"

Her gaze did not become any warmer, but she nodded briefly.

"When I was fifteen, I was very ill for a time," she said. "My father took me to Paris for a consultation at Pasteur's institute. As you can see, he was very kind."

I was seized by jealousy. It was not very noble of me, and definitely not particularly mature, but I did in fact feel a moment's regret that I had never suffered an illness deemed sufficiently interesting for a consultation with the Great Man.

"But you are better now?"

She held up her free hand so you could see the knots of arthritis. "I still suffer from occasional rheumatism."

She had not mentioned the eczema, and perhaps it did not have anything to do with her more serious illness. Still, I could not help but begin to speculate. If arthritis was only one of the symptoms . . .

She handed the papers to the inspector, whose age luckily rendered him so farsighted that he had to hold them at a certain distance, giving me the opportunity to peek.

"Papa must have thrown away most of his papers," she said. "But I found this."

One was something as prosaic as a shopping list, the other a crumpled and unfinished letter.

Dear Madame Arnaud,

it said.

It is with deep ~~regret~~ sorrow that I must inform you that Lisette ~~is not~~ ~~among gave up the ghost~~ passed away in her sleep Sunday evening after some week's

It stopped in midsentence and showed the effects of having been crumpled up. Presumably Leblanc had started again with a fresh sheet, and the letter, or, perhaps more correctly, the draft, had remained undated and unsigned. It was not written in capitals like the exclamations in Vabonne's Bible, but the angular, clumsy handwriting was still recognizable.

"A sad message, it appears," said Marot.

"We lost our old cook some months ago," Imogene explained. "My father wrote to her sister."

"What was the cause of death?" I asked.

Imogene Leblanc looked at me expressionlessly and still managed to indicate that she found the question inappropriate.

"She was past sixty," she said. "At that age death needs no excuse to come calling."

"Mademoiselle Leblanc, do you know if your father knew the priest at Espérance, Father Abigore?"

"No. I don't think so. Is he the one who was killed?"

"Yes. But you know of no connection between them?"

"My father was a man of faith. He might of course have sought out Father Abigore, but our usual church is Trois Maries down in the village."

"Was he the one who drove you and the students to Espérance for Cecile Montaine's funeral?" I asked.

Once again that expressionless look. She did not care for my interference, I could feel that quite clearly.

"Yes. That is in fact correct."

"Then he might have spoken with Father Abigore on that occasion?" Marot grasped at this straw with a certain eagerness.

"It is possible. I did not notice."

"Mademoiselle Karno observed a confrontation between your father and Mother Filippa," said the inspector. "Do you have any idea what that might have been about?"

"My father did not support my decision to seek admission to the convent. I think he believed Mother Filippa was an ... inappropriate abbess."

"In what way?"

"He understood, of course, that the convent had to keep a wolf pack for historical reasons. But that it was necessary to live with these animals as the abbess did ... even to keep a wolf in her cell at night . . ." A deep blush spread under the eczema, the first sign of human emotions I had seen her express. "It was . . . improper. Unclean. That is what he called it."

"Did you share his opinion?"

She hesitated. Dabbed her eyes and nose and cleared her throat loudly before she continued.

"I . . . I cannot deny that I found it disturbing. One could come up against that animal in the halls at any time. It was . . . wrong."

"Why, then, did you wish to become a nun there?"

"When God calls, one does not question, Inspector."

"But there must be other convents?"

"Not like this one. I attended the school myself as a child and a young woman, and have taught there for three years now. Believe me—that was where my mission lay."

"Mother Filippa told me that your father tried to prevent you from returning to the convent," I said. "Is it true?"

"Yes. He did not understand how important it was. I tried to make him accept my calling and my mission, but I was never successful. It made him terribly upset that I set God's authority above his. Finally he even tried to . . . lock me up. Until I 'got better,' he said. As if my calling was a kind of illness. But that is not how it is, little miss." Her voice suddenly became strangely accusatory. "You arrive with your loupe and your pipettes and think you can tell the healthy from the sick. But not until one is called does one understand that the world is sick, and that one has now been healed."

She had not liked being examined, I remembered. Only Mother Filippa's calm authority had made her submit.

One day we will also conquer the Wolf, Pasteur had written.

"Do you suffer from lupus?" The words flew out of my mouth before I had considered the wisdom of speaking them.

She stared at me with hostile eyes. "I cannot see how that is any business of yours."

I suppose I should have been polite and dropped the subject, but I could not help observing her with a certain clinical interest. Lupus was such a mysterious illness. It crept up on the sufferer in widely different forms—the catalog of symptoms included fever, dermatitis, edemas, hypersensitivity to sun, stomatitis, muscle aches, arthritis, chest pains, cramps, temporary dementia or depression, personality changes, organ failure, hair loss, anemia . . . The list was long and confusing. Some patients had only one symptom, others a whole array, and the illness could lie dormant for years only to reappear with entirely different symptoms. As far back as the 1100s, Rogerius called it *le loup*—the wolf—not only because some of the skin lesions that might occur were reminiscent of wolf bites, but also because of its lurking, inexplicable behavior.

"Do you have symptoms other than the arthritis and your eczema?" I asked.

"Madeleine . . . ," Marot protested. But Imogene Leblanc just continued to look at me with the same cold expression.

"No," she said. "Was that all you wanted to know?"

"It is a difficult condition," I said. "I am sorry."

"Are you? It seems more as if you are curious."

Inspector Marot got up quickly. "I think that is all for now," he said. "We will not disturb you any longer."

"When may I bury my father?"

"Presumably in a few days, mademoiselle. The inquest will take place either tomorrow or the next day. You will, of course, be duly informed. But forgive me—is there no one to support you in this difficult time? A relative or a friend of the family?"

"My uncle is on his way from Bordeaux. I do not have any siblings, so he will inherit Les Merises."

It was probably insensitive of me, but it was actually only now that I felt a stab of compassion. I had had trouble seeing

Leblanc's death as anything but a blessing, even to her. A liberation. But I had not considered that his death also made her homeless and entirely dependent on the whim and mercy of her male relatives.

"Madeleine? We are in a bit of a hurry. I have to be at the préfecture at one, and I would like to be there to present your father's report regarding Emile Oblonski."

I realized that I would need to follow him despite all my unanswered questions. If she was the Imo Cecile was referring to in her diary, then she had visited them. She had spoken with Cecile. They had lain down together, whatever that entailed. I wanted to know why, wanted to know what she thought and felt about Cecile, and about Emile. But I could not ask without revealing that I had the diary pages, and I was not yet prepared to do that. The urge to protect Cecile and her secret confidences was oddly strong.

As I got up, I let my portemonnaie slide down between the backrest and the upholstered seat of my chair so that later, as we were preparing to mount the inspector's carriage, I was able to pretend I had suddenly noticed it was gone.

"I am sorry," I said, and tried to look confused. "I must have dropped my purse. If you would excuse me, I will be right back . . ."

And before he could offer to do it for me, I ran up the stairs and opened the front door without knocking.

Imogene was still standing in the hallway.

"What do you want?" she asked.

"My portemonnaie. I must have dropped it . . ."

She reluctantly escorted me back to the parlor. She walked like someone in pain, I noticed. Lupus was a merciless and often agonizing illness. I should feel more sympathy for her. I really should.

"Oh, there it is."

"I see. Goodbye, Mademoiselle Karno. Again."

But she would not be rid of me that easily.

"Mademoiselle Leblanc, I meant to ask you . . . How well did you know Cecile Montaine?"

"I taught her physics, biology, and chemistry."

"And that was all?"

"What do you mean?"

"I just wonder at the fact that you helped her and Emile Oblonski during their flight. Without saying so to anyone, and without revealing it even after Cecile's death."

Her face once again changed color in a few seconds, from white to red.

"Who gave you that peculiar idea?"

"Cecile did," I said. "She called you Imo, did she not? That is presumably not the way students normally address their teachers at the Bernardine school."

She stood still for so long that the dog began to poke her with its nose.

"I think you should go now," she said. "Have you no respect at all for the dead?"

And that was all I got out of her. The inspector called impatiently from the courtyard, and I barely had time to step out onto the stairs before Imogene shut the door with a sudden and demonstrative shove.

Emile Oblonski lay on a table that was normally used to strap down especially violent criminals. There was of course no need for the sturdy leather restraints, but the jail did not possess proper autopsy facilities, and the préfecture had decreed that he could not be moved, since his soul-less body had become the subject of an unusual legal dispute.

When Inspector Marot and I came in, my father was standing with his back against the wall to relieve his healing leg. His scowl was intense and unmistakable, and it did not take me long to discover why.

He was not the one performing an autopsy on Emile Oblon-ski; the autopsist was an elderly gentleman who, it turned out, was a professor of anthropology by the name of Vespard.

"What is going on?" I asked quietly.

"This is madness," said my father. "Complete madness."

About the cause of death there was no doubt. Adrian Montaine had shot Emile Oblonski straight through the chest, and the shot had ripped a hole in one of the pulmonary arteries. Oblonski had bled to death in a few minutes. It was therefore not the death certificate itself that was the problem, my father eventually explained, but something completely different and considerably more bizarre.

"They want us to test his humanity," said Papa. "They want an attestation of the degree to which Emile Oblonski's physiognomy, heart, and internal organs are different from that of a 'human being.' They have even set a threshold. They will permit deviations of up to ten percent."

"What?" I said. "What kind of nonsense is that?"

"Adrian Montaine's defense lawyer has demanded it. His argument is that murder is the killing of a human being. Ergo this cannot be considered a murder if Emile Oblonski was not . . . sufficiently human."

"Of course he is a human being!"

I had said it a little too loudly. Professor Vespard looked up from the measurements he was in the process of making on Emile's skull. He had cut open the scalp and exposed the cranium and now stood dictating numbers to his assistant, a ginger-haired young man with glasses, all the while letting his caliper touch down on various points that looked as if they had been selected with care.

"Is this your wife, Doctor Karno?" asked the professor.

"No. This is my daughter, Madeleine."

"I see. Would you mind pointing out to the young lady that loud comments are disturbing for a scientist in the process of performing an examination that requires precision?"

I think we all three stared at him with more or less the same expression.

Then my father said, quite calmly, considering the circumstances, "Let me know when you are done. But I must prepare you for the fact that I will personally retest your results."

Vespard raised his caliper in a kind of salute, much like a cavalry officer would have raised his sword.

"Feel free, Doctor. My measurements will stand up to whatever form of test you choose to subject them to."

"It is not your measurements that I doubt," said my father. "It is your conclusions."

I thought of the newspaper that Mother Filippa had saved for so many years. "The Wild Boy from Bois Boulet, Half Beast, Half Human." There was perhaps a certain mercy in the fact that she would not see this.

We ate lunch at a small café close to the préfecture—Marot, the Commissioner, my father, and I.

"Do you really think that the defense will succeed with this tactic, Papa?" I asked.

"It is not impossible. There is already a great deal of compassion for young Montaine and his family, and a jury will be grateful to have a legal excuse to let him go free."

"But . . . How can anyone claim that Emile Oblonski is not human? He had an intellect, could speak, read, and write. What animal can do that?"

"Now he can do none of those things. And it will not be difficult to find witnesses who will declare that he was backward, mute, and uncivilized. His priapism was well known, and that will not help the case, either."

I could see my father's anger at this attack and his frustration at not being able to defend what he considered one of "his" dead. As for me, I sat picking at my coq au vin without much of an appetite.

"Did you get a handwriting sample?" asked the Commissioner.

The inspector nodded and placed the shopping list and the letter draft on the table.

"The daughter identified the handwriting in the Bible as her father's, and even when you take into consideration that this is not printed with capital letters, I believe one can conclude that we are talking about the same hand."

The Commissioner held the letter up to the light and nodded.

"It looks that way."

That gave me an idea.

"Do you remember that particular death?" I asked. "Lisette Arnaud from Les Merises, about sixty years old?"

"The cook. Yes. But her name was not Arnaud; her name was . . . No, I cannot recall."

No, of course. The letter was addressed to *Madame* Arnaud, the two sisters no longer had the same last name.

"Do you remember the cause of death?"

"Pneumonia. The family's own physician had cared for her, and there was no reason for an autopsy, and no wish for it, either."

So why had Imogene Leblanc not just said as much?

Of the three men, it was only Inspector Marot who had actually met her. And none of them had seen the pages from Cecile's diary.

"Inspector, what is your impression of Imogene Leblanc?"

He was in the process of wiping a bit of sauce from his mustache with his napkin and now hesitated in midgesture.

"Why do you ask?" he asked.

"I just thought . . . I have the sense that she had a closer relationship to Cecile than you might think."

"That is possible, but what bearing does that have on the case?"

"I don't know. I just thought I should say so."

He finished wiping.

"Until now there is nothing to suggest that Cecile's tragic but natural death has any connection to the two murders Antoine Leblanc committed," he said. "The only oddity is the peculiar abduction of Father Abigore's body, which may or may not have anything to do with your unappetizing mites. Right now I am leaning toward the theory that Leblanc simply had a bizarre way of handling bodies, and that there was in his disturbed mind just as good a reason for putting the good father on ice as there was for placing the wolf . . . well, you know. Perhaps we just have not found the correct Bible quotation yet."

I refrained from pointing out that the Bible had been created out of a Middle Eastern experience of the world, and that the word "ice" was not likely to be mentioned very often.

"Would it not be an odd coincidence," I insisted, "that Leblanc's madness was constituted precisely so that it made him do exactly what was necessary to prevent the spread of disease?"

"Would it not be even stranger if he knew of the mites' existence? He had barely met the man, and as far as we know, he never met Cecile Montaine, either."

He was right. And still I was left with a frustrated feeling that we were missing something.

"I understand from your father that congratulations are in order," said the Commissioner, possibly to change the subject. I must have looked fairly uncomprehending, because he added, "On your engagement, dear Madeleine."

I had in fact managed to forget all about Professor Dreyfuss for a while. No, about August, I corrected myself. Probably not normal behavior for a newly affianced young woman, but both the engagement itself and days that had passed since then had, of course, been somewhat peculiar.

"Thank you," I mumbled and gazed at Papa. "But . . . nothing is final yet."

Antoine Leblanc's inquest took place in the préfecture's courtroom the following afternoon at two o'clock. Imogene Leblanc showed up dressed in black from head to toe and accompanied by her uncle. He was somewhat older than his brother, a balding, well-dressed man who tipped his hat politely when he and Imogene greeted us on the way up the front steps of the building. He looked oddly untouched by it all, as if he had not yet realized what a cruel story he had become a part of.

The courtroom was from an earlier era when this part of the préfecture had been the town hall of a minor medieval market town. It was no more than twelve meters long by eight meters wide, with tall dark wooden panels and a vaulted ceiling, whose once colorful ornamentation was now faded and cracked so that trellised roses, mythical animals, suns and moons could barely be made out. At one end of the room the judge was seated beneath a carved canopy worthy of a pulpit, while witnesses and lawyers had to make do with the humble wooden chairs that had been set out in front of the empty dock. The usher showed my father, the Commissioner, and myself to seats next to Imogene Leblanc and her uncle. Inspector Marot sat on the other side of the aisle together with Marie Mercier and Louis.

The spectator rows behind us were crowded. The investigating judge had pushed the inquest forward in an attempt to avoid the rumors spreading and attracting too many curious onlookers, but the strategy had been only partially successful. The newspapers had reveled in the murder of Father Abigore and the following hunt for his vanished corpse, and later in as many details about Mother Filippa's death as they had succeeded in extracting from Marot. By shooting himself with a hunting rifle, Antoine Leblanc had cheated the public out of a fascinating and prolonged trial and a suitable climax under the guillotine. A public inquest was, however, unavoidable when it was also the conclusion to the entire murder case, and the public was obviously determined to get as much out of it as possible. Many in the audience were equipped with pen and notebook—clearly gentlemen of the press.

The judge seated under the canopy was the same Claude Renard who had been a dinner guest at Madame Ponti's the night Father Abigore was found, or rather rediscovered, in her ice cellar. There was something wrong with the way his face had been put together, as if all the individual parts—nose, ears, chin, and eyebrows—were too big for his head. It made him look like a caricature by Honoré Daumier, I thought, but his voice was surprisingly beautiful and cut through the murmuring unease in the audience without difficulty.

"Commissioner. Would you please inform this court of the circumstances of Antoine Leblanc's death?"

The Commissioner rose. His position did not come with an elegant black cape like the lawyers wore, but he was wearing what he called his "courtroom" jacket—a somehow official-looking garment in double-breasted black wool, with broad lapels and a double row of silver buttons. He claimed to have had it for thirty years, and while on another man it might have seemed just old-fashioned, it lent the Commissioner's stout figure a heavy dignity.

"I arrived at the residence of the deceased Sunday evening at about seven o'clock," he began. "But initially I did not find him at home. Instead, I and my companion—Mademoiselle Karno—found a young boy, unconscious and locked up inside the property's private chapel . . ."

He continued his account of the chain of events while the journalists hungrily recorded every word. I noticed that Emanuel Leblanc, Imogene's uncle, began to stir uneasily, clearing his throat and looking as if he was considering springing to his feet and interrupting.

". . . and can you describe what you found on your return, Commissioner?"

"The door to the chapel had been hit by several shots from a hunting rifle, fired from the outside against the area around the lock. Inside the chapel, Antoine Leblanc lay dead on the floor, and Mademoiselle Karno was sitting on the floor by the unconscious Louis Mercier. The dog had been shot as well. It was recent, the smell of powder was pronounced, and the corpse was still warm."

"What, in your opinion, had happened?"

"There is not much doubt. Antoine Leblanc forced his way into the chapel—it was sheer luck that no one inside was hit by any of these shots—and then shot first the dog and then himself."

Now Emanuel Leblanc did indeed shoot up out of his chair.

"That is not true," he said so loudly that it had to be called a shout. "My brother was a good Catholic. He would never . . . How do we know that Mademoiselle Karno did not shoot him? What witnesses, what proof beyond her words?"

It was probably naïve, but until then it had not occurred to me that anyone would doubt my explanation. That someone might actually believe that *I* had killed Leblanc was so absurd that I just gaped at his agitated older brother. He was less than a meter away, and as long as the Commissioner was standing in the witness box I did not even have his solid figure between me and Emanuel Leblanc's anger. Suddenly I wished that we had been seated somewhere else.

"Sit down," barked Renard. "May I draw your attention to the fact that you have not been called as witness here and that you are present solely to support Mademoiselle Leblanc? If I wish to hear your opinion, you may be sure that I will ask you. For now it is the Commissioner's testimony that interests us."

Through all this Imogene Leblanc just sat and looked straight ahead, her expression unchangeable. But I noticed that a red, almost circular spot was beginning to appear on her cheek and upper lip, in spite of the thick layer of powder she had applied. I tried to remember if the skin symptoms of lupus worsened due to emotional excitement and stress.

The Commissioner began to list the points of evidence that suggested suicide—the dead man's naked foot, the angle of the shot, the powder residue and burns that indicated that the shot had been fired at close range.

"How was the deceased positioned when the shot went off?"

"He was standing. If he, for example, had been lying down, one would have been able to tell that from the state of the floor." He did not elaborate on the fact that there would have been blood, brain matter, and bone fragments immediately around the head instead of spread out over a much greater expanse around the fallen corpse.

"Where was the rifle when you entered?" asked Judge Renard. "In relation to the body?"

The Commissioner hesitated for only an almost undetectable moment.

"When I entered, Mademoiselle Karno was holding the weapon," he said.

"You see!" exclaimed Emanuel Leblanc.

Judge Renard shot him a sharp look but did not say anything this time. He thanked the Commissioner and let him step down.

Then it was my father's turn to give testimony. He laid out in his usual thorough way the findings of the autopsy, describing the wound and explaining precisely what damage the shot had done, giving the angle.

"When the rifle was fired, it must have been held parallel to the body, with the muzzle close to the chest, pointing up under the chin of the deceased. There was powder residue and small burns from the muzzle flash on the deceased's shirt."

"Is it your opinion that he was able to do this himself?"

"I consider it most likely."

"He is her father!" shouted Emanuel Leblanc. "Of course he has to call it suicide!"

"Monsieur Leblanc. Last warning. If you interrupt again, I will have to ask the court constable to escort you out."

I glanced at the officer in question. He stood by the window and looked reassuringly broad shouldered, in the gendarme's black uniform jacket and kepi, armed with a carbine rifle and both a nightstick and a pistol at the hip.

My father looked at the judge and not at Leblanc when he answered.

"The court is, of course, welcome to ask another doctor to carry out a second examination," he said. "There is no doubt about the angle of the shot. There is no doubt, either, that the deceased was standing when the shot went off. If I may demonstrate?"

Judge Renard nodded, and my father called over the court constable.

"How tall are you?" he asked.

"One meter and seventy-two, m'sieur."

"Good. Leblanc was one meter and eighty-six, so a little taller than you. The hunting rifle, on the other hand, is longer than your carbine, and that evens out the difference to some extent."

While the court officer stood looking exceptionally uncomfortable, my father positioned the carbine so that the butt rested on the floor and the weapon was held close to the body.

"The hunting rifle's muzzle was about forty centimeters from the entry wound. As you can see, a possible killer would need to hold the weapon in *this* way, which is not exactly a natural position, and thereafter bend down to press the trigger *here*—at the level of the victim's shin. Mr. Officer, if someone tried to shoot you in this way, what would you do?"

"Me, m'sieur?"

"Yes."

The court officer looked confused for a moment. Then he slowly pushed the barrel to the side so that it was no longer pointing at his head.

"Like this, m'sieur?"

"Precisely. As you can see, it would be exceedingly easy for Leblanc to avoid the shot entirely."

I could see that his cool presentation of the circumstances made a certain impression even on Emanuel Leblanc. He now looked more tortured than outraged, and I could not help but feel a twinge of pity. He, too, had been raised in the Catholic faith. What my father was in the process of proving, or at least presenting as likely, would make his brother's death even harder to bear because suicide to him equaled damnation. A murderer who had repented and confessed would have a better chance at eternity than he.

"Mademoiselle Karno. Would you approach?"

I was abruptly pulled out of my consideration of the afterlife. This was an inquest and not a trial, so there were no defendants or prosecutors to attack or defend me, but to explain and describe in detail was still worse than I had expected. The darkness of the chapel, its sounds and smells, came crowding back to me. I could almost feel the chill and the hard stone floor, even though I stood here in daylight, in the stuffy and overheated courtroom. When my gaze fell on Louis Mercier for a moment, I could see his eyes grow wider and wider as I described the drama of which he had been an unconscious part.

"Monsieur Leblanc thought that it was his daughter, Imogene, who had locked herself in with Louis. He began to threaten to shoot out the lock if she did not open the door."

"What did you do then?"

"I said that I could not unlock the door, that I did not have a key. But then he realized that I was not Imogene, and he fired. The bullets went through the door. I barely had time to throw myself down on the floor next to Louis."

"And then?"

"I feared for my life and for Louis's. I tried to calm Monsieur Leblanc, to pretend that his crimes had not yet been uncovered, that he did not need to kill us. I did not succeed. He recognized me and presumably understood that discovery was inevitable. He even admitted to me that he had murdered Father Abigore."

"In what way?"

"He said that the priest would have died anyway—that he had just saved him from further suffering."

"But he did not mention Mother Filippa?"

"No. Only Father Abigore."

"We will discuss the two killings more closely later," said the judge. "Let us return to the circumstances surrounding Monsieur

Leblanc's death. You feared for your life, you say. But . . . you were not the one who was killed?"

"No. I think he considered it. But instead he shot first the dog and then himself."

"Why did you take the rifle afterward?"

"I was still afraid."

"But he was dead. You must have known that he could no longer harm you."

"Yes. But . . ."

How could I explain the terror I had felt? The icy fear that it was not over, that there was more. I did not know myself where it had come from. Did I imagine that he would get up again and come at us with half his head missing? All I felt certain of was that there had been no relief, no sense that evil had been conquered, that we could all live safely from now on.

Even standing here at his inquest, surrounded by respectable citizens and armed guards, even now there was no relief.

"I was afraid," I repeated. "I just wanted to be able to defend myself and Louis if . . . someone came."

"Who would that be?"

"I don't know."

My cheeks grew warm. I knew I seemed exactly what I never wished to be: an irrational female who had reacted with her feelings instead of with logic and intellect.

Judge Renard nodded briefly, as if that was also the conclusion he had reached.

"Very well," he said. "You were afraid. You had, of course, been exposed to some violent events. You may return to your seat."

I skulked back to my chair with my head bent, and Marot was called forward in my place.

With practiced ease he related the circumstances of Father

Abigore's murder and presented the evidence against Leblanc. It sounded convincing.

Louis Mercier, too, made a thoroughly good impression—he stood up straight and looked the judge directly in the eye as he told of the message he had brought to Abigore and of his abduction. Marot had been right; not once did the judge ask about Leblanc's motive.

It was only when they came to Mother Filippa's death that the police inspector had to be more circumspect. I was called forward again to describe the disagreement and the words I had heard Leblanc shout at Mother Filippa the day before she was killed: *You are not God's servant. You are the devil's.*

Then with an expressionless face and voice, Imogene repeated that her father considered it highly inappropriate that the abbess allowed herself to be accompanied by a wild animal, one that she even kept with her at night.

The last comment caused a stir among the spectators, and Imogene bent her head so one could not see her eyes.

"Was the wolf dangerous, then?" asked Judge Renard.

"That depends on what the judge means by dangerous," said Imogene.

"Might it attack people?"

"No. It was better behaved than most dogs."

"How then could it be dangerous?"

"I think my father meant . . . He considered it to be . . . *morally* dangerous. He wanted me to leave the convent. But I did not want to. Regardless of what he did!"

There was a passion in that exclamation in sharp contrast to her general lack of expression.

"Mademoiselle, would you describe your father as a violent man?" asked Renard.

She hesitated so long that the judge was about to repeat the question.

"He is dead," she said. "Do you want me to speak ill of him now that he cannot defend himself?"

"Thank you, mademoiselle," said Judge Renard in his gentlest tone yet. "We will not trouble you further."

Inspector Marot now presented the torn-out page from Vabonne's Bible and explained where it came from and who had written the comments. Judge Renard considered it with raised eyebrows.

"How is this relevant?" he asked.

"Your Honor, I must now offend your sense of decency, and I wish to apologize in advance for doing so."

You could almost see how the scribbling journalists straightened up and pricked up their ears. I thought of Sister Marie-Claire and her attempt to save Mother Filippa's dignity in death and felt a stab of discomfort in my chest.

"Please speak, Inspector."

"I think I will instead focus your attention on certain discoveries in the inquest report," said Marot. "Then the judge can determine if it is suitable for public hearing."

The press's representatives drew a collective breath of disappointment. But in their reports in the evening edition they managed to extract quite a bit from Judge Renard's involuntary gesture when he saw the passages the inspector indicated: *Judge Renard became deathly pale as he read. Abhorrence and shock were clearly written on his features, and his right hand flew up to his mouth, as if to prevent an expression of horror and disgust from escaping. The public will never know precisely which horrifying circumstances shook so deeply a man who has sat in judgment of cold-blooded murderers, corpse violators, and rapists with perfect equanimity. We can only speculate. But of his agitation there was no doubt.*

"Thank you," said Renard at last. "I see what you mean, and I acknowledge the connection. But do we have any evidence that connects Antoine Leblanc directly to the misdeed in time or place?"

"No, Your Honor," admitted Marot. He bent forward and explained something to the judge in so quiet a tone that it could not be heard from the witness bench. I guessed that he was saying that the damage to Leblanc's lower jaw made it impossible to show sufficient correspondence between his teeth and the bite marks on the abbess's body. The judge nodded.

"So we have only circumstantial evidence," he said. "And it is no longer possible to question the man and attempt to obtain a confession."

"That is correct, Your Honor."

"Very well, Inspector. While I tend to share your views, I have to set aside the matter of Monsieur Leblanc's role in this disturbing murder as *not proven*. But I do not believe that there is reason to continue the investigation."

Inspector Marot nodded. That was presumably what he had expected, though he had probably hoped for a more definitive result.

Judge Renard continued: "On the other hand, I find the following proved: that Antoine Leblanc murdered Father Joseph Abigore, and that he later took his own life."

"No!" The exclamation came from Emanuel Leblanc, who had again jumped to his feet. "My brother is not a murderer! And he would *never* take his own life!"

You could only feel sorry for the man. But having seen with my own eyes Leblanc shoot off half his head, his error was indisputable.

"I am sorry," I said, without really having considered what effect it might have.

"You!" he said. "You pity me? When it was you . . . When it was your hand . . ."

His one hand flew up and I think he was millimeters away from hitting me. But he did not. The Commissioner took half a step in front of me, but his defense was unnecessary. Emanuel Leblanc had already turned away and taken his niece's arm.

"Come, Imogene. Let us go. I will immediately write to my lawyer and seek redress for this violation of your father's memory!"

"One moment, m'sieur," said the court constable. "The witnesses must sign the protocol."

"That as well!"

"That is the law, m'sieur."

I walked with resolute steps over to the clerk, who was in the process of readying the documents for signature. My intention was to sign and thereafter immediately leave the courtroom so my presence would not upset Imogene and her uncle further. His accusations stung only a little, now that the court had accepted my explanation and found the suicide proved; I could see his behavior for what it was—a last desperate attempt to clear his beloved brother of an unforgivable sin and defend his memory. It had nothing to do with me personally.

But my good intentions could not be carried out. The clerk had his own ideas about the proper order of the ritual, and it was Imogene he waved over first. She had to sign both the inquest verdict as next of kin and the statement that would accompany the summary of her testimony.

The court constable escorted her to the counter. Her uncle had been told to stay where he was, presumably to avoid any further confrontation. Imogene did not look at me when she took the pen the clerk handed her, but I could not help looking over her shoulder. Her face was about as full of expression as one of the death masks my father was occasionally asked to make. Her hands shook a bit, and the writing was awkward, but that might just as plausibly be due to the arthritis that made her thin fingers crooked. Then I noticed it.

The handwriting.

The handwriting . . .

Varbourg, March 30, 1894. Imogene Leblanc.

I suddenly recalled the draft of the letter that was to deliver the upsetting news about Lisette the cook's death:

It is with deep ~~regret~~ sorrow that I must inform you that Lisette ~~is not among gave up the ghost~~ passed away in her sleep Sunday evening after some week's

Antoine Leblanc had not written that letter. Imogene had. It must also have been she who underlined that terrible passage in Leviticus and had written DEATH DEATH in the margin.

I grabbed hold of my father's arm and gave it a discreet tug. But he was tired and probably also a bit distracted, so he just turned toward me and said, "What is it, Maddie?"

Then Imogene lifted her head and met my gaze. And she understood at once. She stumbled, or pretended to stumble, and the court constable grabbed hold of her one arm with both hands to support her. She half turned, leaning against him so that I could not see what happened between them. Then there was the sound of a shot, and the constable tumbled to the floor with both hands pressed against his stomach.

No one truly understood what was happening. My father

took a step toward the wounded man, whose hands were already scarlet with blood.

And I stood like Lot's wife, salt pillared and immovable, until Imogene shoved the barrel of the revolver into my side and cried, "Step back or I will shoot her."

Imogene did not attempt to get to the courthouse exit through the mass of spectators. Instead she hauled me with her out the other door, which led to a hallway with a court office and the judge's dressing rooms. A policeman appeared at one end of the hall, presumably responding to the shot, but he stopped when he saw the revolver next to my ear. She quickly let off a shot in his direction, and he ducked through a doorway and took cover. Imogene backed up, still holding me in front of her, kicked open yet another door with her heel, and began to pull me up a staircase. Up, up, up. At first there were still polished panels and woodblock floors, then the stairwell became more raw and primitive, until it ended in a final narrow stairwell and something that was barely more than a ladder. At the end of the ladder there was a door, and it, too, opened when Imogene shoved it with her heel. She gave a last hard jerk so that I stumbled across the threshold before slamming the door shut after us.

We were met by a turmoil of flapping wings that almost made Imogene fire yet another shot, but it was just a couple of common wood pigeons that flew up, spattering us with gray-white bird droppings before they continued out through a broken window. Imogene looked around and realized that we had reached a dead end. We could hear shouting and running footsteps in the building below us, and it was too late to search for another escape route. She opened the door, grabbed the key that was in the lock on the outside, and locked us in.

We both stood still for a moment, equally out of breath. We were in one of the préfecture's towers, I guessed, a dusty octagonal attic with a multitude of square black archive boxes stacked against the walls, narrow bow windows, and an excellent view of Varbourg and the square in front of the préfecture. Not that the scenery occupied either of us at that particular moment.

There was the sound of steps in the stairwell, and someone turned the door handle.

Imogene stuck the revolver up under my chin.

"Shhh," she hissed.

But if she had hoped to hide, she was quickly disillusioned. You could hear the sound of running and then a hollow thump as someone attempted to break the door down.

The frame began to give, and Imogene reacted instantly. She raised the gun and fired one shot that went straight through the door at chest height.

"Stop," she shouted. "Or the next shot will go through Mademoiselle Karno's head."

I did not know if anyone out there had been hit, but it was quiet, and the attempt to force the door was not repeated.

"Push those in front of the door," Imogene ordered, and pointed at the pile of archive boxes.

I obeyed. There was a glasslike determination about her— she could shatter and be ground into a thousand pieces, but she would never bend. And I thought of the poor court constable and did not doubt for a moment that she would shoot me without hesitation if it came to that.

The boxes were heavy and presumably full of old case files. It took awhile to move them all so they formed a wall in front of the door, and when I was done, the sweat was running down my breastbone, and my corset felt like a steam box.

"Sit down," she said, and tipped the gun in the direction of the floor.

I let myself sink onto the roughly hewn floorboards and leaned my shoulders against the wall. The smell of dust and pigeon droppings was intense, and a strong breeze flowed through the shattered window facing the préfecture square. The octagonal room had windows in seven of its eight walls, the last one being given to the door now hidden behind the boxes.

"How long are you planning to stay here?" I asked, because I could not really see how it benefited her to sit in the préfecture's tower instead of in a cell in the cellar. Except, of course, for the fact that her current position gave her the option of shooting me.

"Be quiet," she said, examining the drum of the revolver. I followed her movements and wished I had enough knowledge of firearms to guess how many shots she had left. All I knew was that the constable's handgun would be of Belgian manufacture, and that was only because I recalled a heated debate about whether that was unpatriotic when there were "excellent weapons of French manufacture" available. The number of cartridge chambers in the cylinder had not come up.

She sat down across from me, with only a slight stiffness to her movements, and pulled her legs up against her chest. If the arthritis had slowed her on the flight up the stairs, I had not noticed. When there was something she wanted, Imogene was apparently more robust than she looked. She let the revolver rest on one knee. It did not point precisely in my direction, but that was not necessary. The room was small; there were barely three meters between us. She would hardly need to aim.

We sat in silence for a while. The warmth I had achieved by

working with the boxes slowly seeped from my body, and the cold came creeping in instead.

"Do you love your father?" she suddenly asked.

"Yes," I said. "Why do you ask?"

"I loved my father above all else," she said. Her thin shoulders drooped a bit, and I suddenly sensed the overwhelming exhaustion that bore down on her. "My mother was a hard and critical woman who thought more of my cousin Ferrand than she did of me. He lived with us, you see. She called him her 'son of the heart' and always took his side. But Papa . . . I was his little girl. He defended me. And when I became ill the first time, he dragged me around to scores of doctors and wise men to find out what was wrong."

"What were the symptoms?"

"I had some attacks . . . fever, headache. And sometimes . . . I just disappeared. As if my body was still there but I was gone."

"Absences."

"Yes. That is what they called it. But they could not say why it happened. Nor why I sometimes had cramps. Some said epilepsy, others brain fever. None of them were right. It was the wolf that came to me, and I could not keep it out no matter how carefully I locked the door in the night."

"Was there no one who guessed it was lupus?" I asked.

She did not answer.

"Why are some people taken ill and others not?" she said instead. "What do you think, mademoiselle? Is it God's will or is it bacteria?"

"I believe more in bacteria than I do in God," I said. "Why would He wish to make us ill?" *God took your mother, chérie.* My relationship with Him had never quite recovered.

"Perhaps God works *through* the bacteria," she said. "Have you ever thought of that? Some bacteria are in the shape of tiny crosses, others like rosaries. Do you think that is an accident?"

"You say that—you who have been examined by the great Louis Pasteur!"

"Precisely because of that. Monsieur Pasteur guessed that it was lupus, but not even he could say where it came from. There are no lupus bacteria with which one can become infected, mademoiselle. Why, then, does God do it?"

"I don't know."

"He does it to teach us something. That is the only thing that makes sense. When I had to struggle against the wolf for seven years, it was so that I might get to know my enemy, so that I might learn how to detect the presence of the beast—in myself and in others. God had a purpose with me. He used seven years to create a perfect tool, and you, mademoiselle, have ruined everything in a few days." The gun jumped in her hand, and I unconsciously pulled my hands up toward my heart, as if I could protect myself against the bullet in that way. But there was no shot.

"I did not know God's plan for you," I said. "Perhaps if you explained . . ."

"Do you think I am a book you may read when you are bored? No, not so, mademoiselle."

She got up abruptly. At the same moment, there was a singing explosion, and the glass in one of the other windows was shattered. Tiny sparkling shards were blown in all directions and fell to the floor with a silvery tinkling.

Imogene Leblanc lay on the floor, but she had not been hit, and she still had the revolver in her right hand. She inched her way across the floor on her stomach until she could shove the barrel into my side.

"Take off your dress."

"What?"

"With or without a bullet hole, Mademoiselle Karno."

I did as she said. My fingertips slipped on the tiny pearl buttons, and I could barely unbutton them, but I managed to at last.

"Lie down on your stomach."

I obeyed that order as well. Bits of broken glass moved beneath me and stuck to the skin of my naked arms. I felt her knee against my corseted back but could neither see nor sense what she was doing before she let me go and allowed me to sit up again.

She had taken off her own dress and put on mine.

"Now it is your turn," she said.

Its fit was looser than mine, with a pleated waist and a high-necked lace-bordered collar. And black, naturally, where mine was a restrained, subdued purple. It did not fit me very well. When I was finished, she smiled.

"Get up," she said.

Only now did I understand her intention. If the sniper in the other préfecture tower got me in his sight, he would pull the trigger. He would shoot the black-clad female figure, not the purple, and would no doubt regret his mistake and perhaps even be tormented by it afterward. But that would not help me very much.

"That is murder, mademoiselle."

"Not at all. It is a test. If God finds you worthy, He will not let a random bullet bring you down."

"You are mad!"

"Get up, mademoiselle. Or I will shoot you this instant."

"I cannot see that it benefits you . . ."

"No? Let me paint you a picture. A clever marksman hits the target he is aiming at. A young woman in black tumbles from the shattered window and falls onto the cobbles of the square below. Where do you think everyone will gather? Where do you think everyone will look?"

"And then what? Even if you get away—what then? Where will you hide? How will you survive?"

"God will not throw away the tool He has spent such a long time creating," she said with rock-solid conviction. "Get up!"

I continued to sit.

She fired. The shot went through the black skirt right by my thigh and hit the floor. I screamed and pulled my leg all the way up to my chest even though I had actually understood that I was not hurt, that she had missed on purpose.

"Damn you!" I cried.

"No, mademoiselle. I belong not to the devil but to God."

I thought that was debatable. With fierce gestures I began to rip the hairpins from my pinned-up hair.

"What are you doing?"

"If you really believe God is on your side, it makes no difference," I said. "I just want to give Him a fair chance to take my side instead." Though we were both dark haired, there was a difference. My hair was more auburn and straight while hers was wavy. I hoped the difference would be enough to at least make the sniper hesitate and take a second look.

She let me do it. I shook the last pin free and then levered myself into a squatting position. I considered for a brief moment whether a small silent prayer would make any difference, but I did not think so. This was not a game of God's devising; the outcome would be determined by human observations and decisions, and cold, raw chance.

I rose slowly to my feet.

A shot screamed by me. I remained standing. Now he had to have seen it, I thought. Seen that it was me and not her.

But Imogene had no intention of waiting. While the echo of the rifle shot was still rolling across the préfecture's roof, she aimed the revolver directly at my chest and pulled the trigger. I sensed it and had time to feel a moment of outrage that she was cheating.

Then I realized that she had not hit me.

I think she was still waiting for me to fall. When she understood that it was not going to happen, she pulled the trigger again.

This time there was just a dry little click. The chamber was empty.

I had absolutely no experience with physical fighting but decided instantly that it was time to change that. I threw myself at her and toppled her backward. She was clinging to the revolver, and I could hear from the repeated clicks that she was still trying to shoot me and apparently did not grasp that she had run out of ammunition. I grabbed her by her wavy hair and started to pound her head against the floor, and I did not stop until she lay perfectly still.

I still believe more in bacteria than in God. But it is a fact that when the Commissioner nine minutes later picked up the Belgian Warrant revolver from the floor, there was still one bullet left in the chamber.

V

November 1887–September 1893

The wolf came to her when she was fifteen.

Until then Imogene had thought that the most important thing in life was whether Ferrand really liked her or just pretended to because it would suit everyone if he could take over Les Merises one day. Beyond that, her greatest concern was whether Sister Beatrice had discovered that she had cheated on her Latin with Veronica and had written some of the difficult words on the inside of her arm. She was looking forward to going home for Christmas, and she hoped Bijou would have her puppies before then so she would have time to see them, even though her father had said that it probably would not be until January.

It was a cold, wet day. The wind came howling in from the northwest, full of rain mixed with tiny sharp hailstones, and it was more or less impossible to go outside. The sisters had allowed the youngest to play in the dining hall and had arranged for the older girls to keep an eye on them.

They played The Wolf Is Coming with the little ones. "The maid goes into the dark forest, picking berries, picking berries . . ." She and Veronica were the forest. It was starting to hurt a bit to stand with her arms raised in this way, especially because that irritating little Camille slowed down the game by trying to sneak to the back of the line so that she would not have to go through the forest.

"Camille," said Imogene, "come on!"

"I don't want to," wailed Camille. "I don't want to play this stupid game!"

"All the others do," said Veronica. "Why are you so special?"

"But I don't want to!" The girl held her arms behind her back so the others in the line could not take her hands.

"She is scared," said the new girl, what was her name? The one with the soft black hair and the big doe eyes. Cecile.

"She is not a baby, is she?"

"Why do I have to play?" whined irritating Camille. "It is just a stupid game and I don't feel like it."

"Camille is afraid of the wolllf, Camille is afraid of the wolllf . . ." A few of the others began singsonging, and the game threatened to dissolve.

"That is enough!" said Imogene. "Cecile, Anette, take Camille by the hand. Then we will start again."

"But if she does not want to?" It was Cecile protesting again.

Imogene had a headache and her neck hurt, and she had just about had it with the stupid girls who would not follow orders.

"We cannot all expect special treatment," she barked. "Get going, or I will tell Sister Beatrice! Do you want to be confined to your room again?"

Cecile bit her lip. Then she whispered something to Camille, and Camille took her hand.

They began again. "Father Wolf, he is in the dark forest, prowling here, prowling there . . ."

Imogene did it on purpose. There was no getting away from that. She had a headache, and her neck hurt, and she was grumpy and annoyed. It was clearly on purpose that she drew out the final lyrics.

"Father Wolf in the dark forest is hungry for little girl pie. When the little maid does not come home, Oh, how her mother must cry, must cryyyyyyyyyyy . . ."

Camille tried to stop, but Anette was not having any of it. With a shriek she threw herself forward and pulled Camille with her.

"Willy-nilly. You're in the wolf's belly. Rip, nip, nip, you're dead!"

Imogene and Veronica transformed themselves from peaceful trees into hungry wolves, and it was Cecile and irritating Camille who were caught. Camille screamed shrilly and loudly as if a real wolf had caught her. Cecile did not make a sound.

Imogene and Veronica threw them on the ground and began to "eat" them. With hard fingers, they pinched and nipped them, and they were quickly aided by the rest of the "wolf pack." The two victims tried to protect themselves by curling up and pushing the pinching hands away, but the superior force was too great.

"Eat them, eat them . . . ," shouted Imogene. "Mmmmm. I think I want to eat a leg!" She grabbed hold of Camille's lower leg with both her hands and pretended to sink her teeth in.

"Stop it! Stop it!"

"Yum, yum, yum . . . Father Wolf is hungry."

She nipped a few more times while Camille writhed and wailed and tried to get away. Then Imogene suddenly received a hard shove in the side.

"Leave her alone!"

Somehow Cecile had got away from the others. She was the one who had shoved Imogene. And Imogene's irritation turned to real anger.

"You are wolf food," she said. "You have nothing to say. Hold her!"

And then the whole pack threw themselves on Cecile. For them it was still a game, though a slightly rougher version of it.

"Come on, Father Wolf," said Veronica, and held out one of the girl's arms to Imogene. "Eat her!"

Imogene stuck her head all the way into the girl's armpit and pretended to tear her to pieces. She snarled and growled for all she was worth. And the rest of the girls screamed and giggled gleefully.

It was only she and Cecile who knew that it was not all in fun. That Imogene had suddenly given way to a desire she did not understand herself and had closed her teeth around fabric and skin and flesh and had bitten as hard as she could.

It had happened at that moment. She could not understand it any differently. Even though weeks passed before the first marks appeared on her own body, that had to be the moment when the wolf entered her for the first time and filled her with a hot, burning sensation in her head, neck, chest, and abdomen.

It was irritating little Camille who tattled, of course. Cecile never said a word.

Sister Beatrice brought them both, Imogene and Camille, to the convent church and made them kneel in front of the Madonna.

"Camille," she said, "show Imogene the marks."

And then Camille had unbuttoned her dress and pulled up

her chemise with a well-practiced martyred expression. Her shoulders, upper arms, and stomach were covered with yellow and blue marks made by the pinching fingers. There must have been thirty or forty.

"Imogene, I am disappointed in you. As a dux, it is your role to correct and care for the others, not to lead the way in a rough game like this. I hereby remove you from your responsibility. And now kiss each other as a sign that you forgive one another as good sisters and friends ought to."

They exchanged cool friendship kisses, one on each cheek. Camille tried to look pious, but her triumph shone through. Imogene burned with shame, outwardly as well as inwardly.

She made an effort to show that she repented and improved. She got up extra early to help the little ones make their beds and get dressed. She tested them in their catechism and comforted the ones who were homesick, and she was especially attentive to Cecile and Camille. She labored so hard over her own schoolwork that even cranky Sister Francine praised her. Still the headache did not go away; it became worse. An odd weakness had invaded her arms and legs, and no matter how much she slept, she was always tired.

At the beginning of February, shortly before Candlemas, she discovered a circular mark on her shoulder. It was red and swollen and very sore. The next day there was yet another, this time on her breast.

Constance, with whom she shared a room, noticed it almost at once. "Who bit you?"

Imogene knew that her face was turning bright red. "No one has bitten me," she said. "It just . . . appeared."

Constance giggled. "Oh, all right. If you say so. But I would not take any more walks alone with that cousin Ferrand if I were you."

"It has nothing to do with that!"

"She is just jealous because she does not have a beau," said Veronica. "Pay no attention to her. But you had better show that thing to one of the hospital sisters."

After what Constance had said? No, thank you. She was not about to do any such thing. Not even when more marks appeared, one on her upper arm, two on her chest, one behind her right ear. She rose early to bathe in cold water before the others got up, and took care never to show herself uncovered. And she prayed and prayed, so intensely that it was noticed, though no one knew what she was praying for.

For it was the wolf that bit her. The wolf that came to her in the night. Its eyes glittered in the moonlight, its fur soft and prickly at the same time, its tongue coarse and warm. When her headache was at its worst, she could see it. Sometimes only as a shadow and other times large as life in the middle of the room, with wide-open jaws and pricked ears, and claws that clicked against the floor. She usually closed her eyes and prayed. She curled up, pressing her knees against the wall; she pulled the blanket tightly around her like a suit of woolly armor. Nothing helped. Its warm breath made her skin flush; its tongue rasped against the inside of her arm, across the round point of her shoulder, behind her ears, and down across her neck and bosom. She could not keep it away. She could not keep it out.

And one day she collapsed in full daylight, right in the middle of the evening meal, where everyone could see. Veronica provided her with a detailed description afterward. How she had suddenly fallen backward and had lain there shuddering with cramps so that her body danced across the floor, with blood around her mouth because she had bitten her tongue and cheek, and spasms so violent that her rhythmically kicking legs had toppled both the bench and the table.

"Poor Imo," said Veronica with eyes that shone with equal parts compassion and fascination. "Was it the devil? Did he come to you? Did he come *into* you? Did it hurt?"

If it was the devil's work, why could he not punish Veronica a little, too? But he did not; she was just as rudely healthy as she had always been, with her shiny hair, her perfect complexion, and her naturally rosy cheeks.

Imogene was no longer able to pretend that nothing was wrong. She was sent to the hospital and examined, first by the sisters and then by the doctors at Saint Bernardine. At first they thought it was a brain infection, but later—when she did not die but in fact got better—they leaned more toward the theory that she had suffered an epileptic attack.

She herself knew exactly what had happened, even though the entire afternoon had become a pitch-black hole in her memory. The wolf had taken her. In front of everyone, in broad daylight, it had overcome her resistance and violated her so deeply that not even the Son of God would be able to forgive her.

When the great Pasteur gave the illness a name, it was only too fitting. Lupus. *Le loup*. What else could it be called?

She suffered for two years. She lost most of her hair, and when it began to grow in again, it was as if it were not really hers. It was lifeless and stiff, like the bristles on an animal—not even the pelt of a wolf but something much less pleasant to touch. Pig bristles, perhaps. Ferrand married the daughter of a landowner from the neighboring town, and shortly thereafter her mother left Les Merises and moved back to her native region.

"All you think about is her!" she had shouted at her husband, so loudly that Imogene could hear it even though she lay in her own room, with the door closed. "Her, that cursed illness, and doctors, doctors, doctors. Throwing good money after bad!"

Two years later Maman died suddenly of a violent stomach

illness, without having spoken another word with her husband or daughter.

Imogene was well aware that it was all her fault.

"Imogene, this is Doctor Fleischer."

He arrived long after she had finally given up. Long after she had come to believe she was the wolf's prey forever and would never be free. The Other Doctor. That was how she always thought of him, even though there had been doctors by the dozen before him. He was the Other, the one who was different. Doctor Wilhelm Fleischer was completely bald and no taller than she was. But he had worked with some of the best doctors and researchers in all of Europe—Fehleisen, Koch, Pasteur—and he had even spent two years in the United States. And he had a cure, he said.

"You have probably heard the expression that you must fight fire with fire?" he asked.

Imogene nodded. Yes, she knew it.

"This is almost the same. We will fight one illness with another. Do you also know what bacteria are?"

"I received top marks in both chemistry and biology," she said a bit indignantly. She was seventeen now and not a child.

"Excellent, then you will understand my explanation better."

He described how he would take a bit of infected tissue and skin from a person suffering from erysipelas—"You may know it better as Saint Anthony's fire"—and place it in a mixture of gelatin and serum, so that the Saint Anthony's fire bacteria multiplied vigorously for a few days. Afterward he would inoculate her with this bacteria. She would become ill . . .

"Very ill. The sicker you become, the better it works!" he said. "High fever, violent headache, skin infections across large parts of your body. You must be brave, but I promise you, once you get a fever, it will help. That is the fire we are going to use to drive out the wolf!"

"Is this not too dangerous?" asked Papa. "With such a high fever, and given that Imogene is already weak . . ."

"There is a risk," said Doctor Fleischer. "But it must be weighed against the chance of a complete cure."

Imogene looked at the small, bald doctor with a calm gaze, and she understood. Fully. She felt how right it was—that the fever fire would burn and cleanse her, exactly as purgatory purified the sinful souls who would otherwise be lost.

"Yes," she said. "Do it. Fire with fire."

They measured her fever at forty-one Celsius at its worst. None of what the wolf had done to her had been half as painful. But purgatory must hurt, she whispered to herself and allowed them to tie her wrists to the bedsides so she could not tear and scratch the infection. It felt as if her skin was burning off, but when she looked down her front, it was still there, just scalded and swollen and full of pus. Her dreams were full of fire. She fought for every breath she took.

But at last the fever fell. The fire burned out and took the wolf with it.

"There, you see," said Doctor Fleischer to her father the day she was examined by him for the last time. "The power of nature is incredible."

"I think we must thank the Lord," said her father. "And you and your bacteria, Doctor."

For five years she was well, and she believed God had forgiven her. She slept peacefully at night and did not need to bar her door and her mind against that which wanted to get in. The fever had been her test, and she had come through it, purified and clean.

That is what she believed. Until the day Mother Filippa sent her down to the wolf stables with a message for Emile, and she found him together with Cecile.

She still did not like visiting the wolf stables very much. She could not free her soul from a final shudder of horror when she saw the gray shadows, the pale eyes, the dark gaping jaws. Luckily all the wolves were outside, she observed. But Emile was not in the little room that served as his home.

She considered turning back with the excuse that she could not find him. But then she heard the sound. It came from the wolf pen, and it sounded as if someone was moaning with pain. She feared that he had been hurt, perhaps had even been attacked by the wolves, and she grabbed a hayfork to protect herself if necessary. When she opened the gate, she saw the wolves at once. It was not the whole pack, just the old pack leader and three of the females. They stood completely still and were staring rigidly at something in the elder bushes, and only one of them turned its head when she came out.

At first she thought that Cecile was merely sitting on his lap, which, of course, was unsuitable enough. But then she realized that the skirt of the school uniform was pushed all the way up to Cecile's waist. That her lower body was bared. And what she was sitting on, what she was raising and lowering herself over in a smooth, slippery rhythm, was not so much his lap as his erect member.

Although they were both facing her, neither of them saw her. Emile's cheek rested on the girl's shoulder and his face was turned away. Cecile's eyes were closed. She had both hands pressed against her own thighs, and her fingers glistened wetly. Imogene stood paralyzed for a moment, as motionless as the observing wolves. Then she threw down the hayfork and fled.

She did not say anything, did not go to Mother Filippa, as she should have. Instead she waited until the next time she had a tutorial with Cecile to bring it up.

If she had expected remorse, if she had expected shame, then she was disappointed. Cecile listened to her without lowering her eyes. She looked attentively at Imogene with soft, dark eyes, and then she took her hand.

"Poor Imo," she said. "Were you very afraid of the wolves?"

"Let me go."

If only she had not touched me, Imogene thought later. But she did. With her unclean hand, the hand Imogene had seen shining wetly, pressed against her penetrated sex.

The headache hit her like a hard, flat blow to the temples. She heard Cecile's voice through a crackling blanket of noise, distorted and barely recognizable.

"Immmmmmmmo. Whaaaat issss wronnnng?"

She disappeared. And when she returned, she was lying with her head in Cecile's lap and a pleat of the skirt's woolly fabric had made a reddened furrow on her cheek.

"I did not dare to leave you," said Cecile. "Imo? Are you feeling better now?"

She still refused to believe it. She had gone through purgatory, she was clean now. It could not be true. But then she saw the damp stains of spittle on Cecile's white blouse, and the pale red blotches where the skin had broken and bled.

"Don't worry about it," said Cecile. "I know you cannot help it. I won't tell anyone."

Then she knew. She could feel it everywhere in her body, from the pulsing temples to the heaviness in her thighs, the burning skin, the odd singing that constantly whined in her ears.

The wolf had returned. And it was stronger than ever.

She wrote to Doctor Fleischer, but he just answered that he no longer used this method of treatment; it was now considered to be too risky. She sent more letters, attempting to explain that she did not care about the risk, that she was afraid, that he had to help her. In the beginning, he was understanding, but gradually his replies became shorter and shorter and finally her letters came back with a scribbled "Return to sender" on the envelopes.

She tried to explain to Mother Filippa, but the abbess did not understand the extent of her terror. "Illness is not necessarily a punishment from God," she said. "Everyone can get ill, even the purest. What exactly is this sin that you imagine He wishes to punish you for?"

"Beastly feelings," she stammered. "Beastly desires."

"Oh, Imogene. We all have those. If God were to punish us just for feeling and thinking something, He would have plenty to do."

Imogene was astonished. Mother Filippa was the convent's most elevated leader, the one who had to be the cleanest, the strongest, the most compassionate. If not even she was free of the beast, then who was?

"Imogene, sickness is not a punishment. Sometimes it just comes to us. If we are lucky, it is a trial from which we can learn. Other times, we must just accept that we humans do not understand everything."

For a long time Imogene considered what she was supposed to learn from her trial. Arthritis tore at her joints, the headaches made it hard to think. She tried to stay as far away from Cecile as possible, but the girl could not be avoided. She wanted to help, she claimed. And her eyes. Her soft dark eyes. They followed every movement Imogene made when she taught Cecile's class, noted every tremble, looked for every sign of weakness. Every time Imogene had to sit down in the middle of a class, or the chalk fell from her bent, arthritic fingers, Cecile was always there, every single time, with the loving concern that she could not brush off.

Including the afternoon that the girl's true intentions came to light.

"Imo, you are my friend, aren't you? You care for me. I can tell."

Imogene had dismissed the class ten minutes early, because she was too dizzy to go on. But Cecile had not gone. She had followed Imogene into the storeroom behind the biology classroom.

"Cecile, stop," said Imogene with all the authority she could muster. "Go join the others. I am your teacher. We cannot be friends."

"Yes we can. I will help you. I can make it stop hurting. And you . . ."

"What about me?" asked Imogene, caught against her will.

"You could perhaps tell Sister Beatrice that I have a private tutorial with you tomorrow. After physics. Could you do that?"

So that she had an excuse. So that she could meet Wolf-Emile and give herself over to *that*, down in the wolf pen, while the animals looked on. Imogene could barely contain her disgust. But the girl continued to stand there looking completely innocent. The gaze was still soft and loving, not at all calculating. Not insolent or challenging. A cramp in her abdomen made Imogene gasp for air.

"Imo, Imo. Come on . . ."

"Go away . . ."

"Are you feeling ill? Sweet Imo, let me . . ."

This time she wasn't even gone. She was still there, still looking out her own eyes, still trapped in her own body, feeling the saliva that dripped down her chin, tasting the blood through the material of the blouse when she bit. Hearing, quite clearly and distinctly, Cecile's cry of pain, and her voice afterward, light, breathless, lighter and younger than it usually was.

"It doesn't matter, it doesn't matter . . . Imo, I will let you. If it helps, I will let you . . ."

There was no one she could talk to. Mother Filippa, the oh, so virtuous Mother Filippa, had taken in a wolf, the old male wolf, because Emile had said it was being harassed by the others. It lay at her feet at mealtimes, it followed her around the convent like a shadow, at night it slept in her room, and who knew . . . who knew what happened behind the closed door? Nausea rose in her throat, and still . . . still she could feel the wolf in her own body every time she thought of it. No help. There was no help to be had. Everything was putrid and unclean, and the beast had penetrated everywhere.

It was her father who saved her. He recognized the signs of the illness and took her to Les Merises, without hesitating, without discussing it with anyone. He did not even allow her to give notice, but merely sent a short note a few days later. And when two of the sisters appeared, full of compassion and questions, he lied and said she was not at home.

The night after the sisters had been there, she had another nightmare about the wolves. She could not stand to be in her bed, she could not stand the house and the night, the darkness, and the moon. Her father found her the next morning in the chapel, still only in her nightgown and with bare feet, stretched out on the floor in front of the Madonna.

He was angry. At her, at the nuns, at the illness that had returned in spite of everything they had done, everything she had gone through to be free. She had never seen him so angry before. He had shaken her so hard that she had finally told him about her fear of the beast, about what had happened at the convent.

His disgust was as violent as his anger.

"You are not going back," he said. "Not to that place."

"I cannot be here, either," she said. "I cannot stand to be with people anymore. Not even with you. Not until it stops, or I die."

"Do not say that!"

"Why not? Better a death in the hope of heaven than a life in sin!"

The moment she said it, she knew that was how it had to be— she had to find her salvation somehow. Alone.

He protested for a long time, but for once she was more stubborn than he was. Finally, he helped her to move out to Vabonne's old hunting cabin, where she was at least certain that the nuns would not find her.

It was the end of September, and the forest around the cabin flamed red against yellow, golden against green. The lake lay like a secret world at her feet when she sat on the veranda and saw the last dragonflies dive toward the surface, greedy, dying, with a hunger that could not be met. Iago lay at her side, the only company she allowed herself beyond her father's short visits.

She was still awaiting her salvation; she had still not understood what God was attempting to teach her. She prayed long and often, mostly to Madonna, because the Mother of God seemed to be more understanding and compassionate than the Almighty Himself.

But she was not without work to occupy her. When Doctor Fleischer refused to help her, she had to try to help herself. She had brought her microscope and her travel laboratory, and in those long autumn days full of transformation, she probed and examined and registered every bit of herself, her blood, the skin flakes of her eczema, her body's temperature and fluids. She even began to compare it with Iago's blood, skin, tissue, and fluids, which initially he allowed her to do, but later liked less and less, until she finally had to anesthetize him with ether in order to take her samples.

It was under anesthesia that she saw them. They came creeping out of the dog's nostrils, tiny pale white specks that revealed their spiderlike nature under the microscope—an eight-legged symmetry that related them to scorpions, ticks, and other arachnids.

At that moment she was seized by an attack that pulled her out of the golden September day, out of the hunting cabin's reality, out of her wrecked body.

All at once she was back in the convent. She even dreamed that she woke up in the small chamber in the teachers' wing where she had lived six days of the week. She woke up, and for the first time in months felt completely light and unburdened by pain. Happy, she dressed and set out for morning prayers. In the hall in front of her walked two young girls hand in hand, dressed in the gray school uniform.

"Good morning," she said, and one of them turned around. It was Christine, and she smiled and curtsied briefly. But when the other figure turned her head, it was not a young girl's profile that appeared but a horrible bubbling mixture of animal teeth, animal drool, animal bristles, and human features. The drool ran from the distorted lips down across the girl's chest, and worms and mites poured out of her nostrils and ears. But the grimacing lips formed human words:

"Good morning, Imo."

Imogene stood as if turned to stone. Other students passed her, curtsied, and hurried on. The lauds bell rang out its last peals.

"Do not to be late, Imogene." Mother Filippa's voice sounded behind her. "That sets a poor example."

But when she turned around, it was not Mother Filippa standing there. It was the wolf. Its eyes were olive green precisely like those of the abbess, and its smile was one no beast ought to have been able to produce.

Suddenly Imogene held a flaming sword in her hands. It stung and burned her palms, but she raised it and swung it at the wolf. The beast stood completely still and did not attempt to evade the stroke of the blade. And the sword cleaved it in two precise halves that fell to the ground like two sides of a cow's carcass in an abattoir. Mother Filippa was standing in front of her, shining and slightly transparent, and laughed and cried with happiness at the same time.

"Thank you, dear Imogene. Thank you. I am free now. You were not too late!"

And when Mother Filippa's soul then rose up and vanished, Imogene finally knew what her calling was. Fire must be fought with fire, not just in Imogene's own body, but in the whole world. She had to find the sword that would do that, the tool that could cleave body and soul, so that animals were purely animals and humans purely human, and not this unclean whorish mixture of one thing and another.

⁂

She came to herself much later in frigid, unforgiving darkness. Overwhelmed by weakness, she lacked any strength to get up, turn on the light, make a fire, or even pull a blanket over herself. Iago had lain down next to her, warming her body with his own, but her hands and feet were numb and senseless from the cold.

Sword. Mites.

Mites. Sword.

She slowly began to understand.

VI

March 31–April 16, 1894

I f Imogene herself had not explained, without concern that she was revealing her own culpability, we might still have proved her guilty of the killing of Mother Filippa but never for the cold-blooded murder of Cecile Montaine.

My father was present during the entire lengthy questioning because it quickly became clear to both the Commissioner and Inspector Marot that his knowledge and medical experience would be necessary.

She sat straight backed and serene on the chair she had been placed in, and even though the préfecture had insisted that she be chained, she managed to make the chains seem irrelevant, like a childish notion she had to endure since it could not be otherwise. My efforts to render her unconscious had left two wide abrasions above one eye and along one cheekbone, but if it caused her pain, she did not reveal it.

Imogene's task had not been at all easy, she explained. The responsibility God had placed on her was this: to test humanity's humanity. She was not an executioner, she was a weapon smith. She just had to create the burning sword, and once that was accomplished, the Lord would direct it Himself.

The mites were the ore the sword was to be made from. They were eminently suitable, precisely because they commonly lived in animals and would not attack a human being who was clean, Imogene believed. But not until old Lisette became ill did Imogene know what was to form the shining sharp edge of the blade.

Lisette's illness was caused by bacteria; Imogene established that herself while she nursed the dying cook. In the mucus Lisette coughed up, she found microorganisms that were related to the erysipelas bacteria that had been her own purgatory five years ago, when she had thought she was cured, and that God had finished testing her. It was a sign that could not be misunderstood.

Lisette thought nothing was amiss when Imogene began to administer nose drops with a pipette. She took it as yet another sign of the young mademoiselle's great knowledge and loving care. Imogene let the mites live for only a few days in Lisette's nasal cavity before she brought some of them back to Iago. Then she waited in breathless anticipation, but Iago did not become ill, and thus she was certain that God's new sword really could distinguish the unclean from the clean. Clean humans and clean animals had nothing to fear; it would strike only at those who corrupted one with the other.

Imogene cried only a little at Lisette's funeral. Her suffering had had a purpose—just like Imogene's own.

The greatest difficulty was how to transfer the mites to the wolf pack at the convent. She was still not able to entirely control her fear of the wolves even though she knew it was an undignified weakness in a servant of God. She had tried to catch one of them in a fox trap, but it was wild and unmanageable and snapped at her so viciously that she could not get near enough.

Then she had the idea with the puppy. It was from old Bijou's last litter, and it was not thriving. It might be because Iago had infected it with the bacterial mites. Once she realized that it was rife with them, she brought it with her back to the convent late one Sunday evening and put it in the wolf pen without anyone the wiser. Later she heard that the new male wolf had killed it, and no one could understand where it had come from.

Now everything was ready—so she believed. The mites would no doubt attack Emile first, since he was closest to the beast. Then it would be Cecile's turn. And then Mother Filippa, who still kept the old male wolf with her most of the time. The rest was in the hands of God. Purgatory would seize them, and cleanse them or kill them.

But months passed. November, December. The nativity of Christ, and still no sign that God's sword was working. Imogene reminded herself that the Lord measured time in eternities, not in brief human weeks, and prepared herself for the fact that it might be necessary to find a new way to transfer the mites. She could not get her father to understand the task that God had set her. He tried to prevent her from returning to the school and the convent, but she defied him—she could not permit herself to be weak now. It was only when Cecile decided to flee with Emile and asked Imogene for help that she began to have real doubts.

If they ran away from the convent, away from the wolves, how would God's sword reach them? And yet their flight was a clear sign that they were in thrall to the beast. She tried to calm Cecile, but she was beside herself and would not listen. As a last resort, she told them about the hunting cabin, so that she might at least know where they were.

She thought about it for three days. Then she knew what she had to do.

"I have not killed anyone," she insisted on the stand, even after she had carefully explained how she had anesthetized Cecile with chloral hydrate and thereafter transferred the mites with a pipette. "I have only made the test possible."

"And Father Abigore? As far as I can see, his only crime was that he prayed for Cecile's soul throughout the night," said my father.

Imogene's gaze wavered a bit. "He must have been corrupted," she said. "Had he been pure, it would not have happened."

"Did you tell your father about . . . God's sword?" asked the Commissioner.

She sighed. "Yes. He was suspicious already after what happened with the puppy. He knew that I must have been the one who brought it to the convent, even though he did not understand the purpose. And then, after Cecile's funeral, when I saw that the priest had also become ill . . . Then I very much needed someone to talk to. But Papa did not understand it. I was very angry at him. He killed the poor priest without giving him the possibility of being freed through the suffering of purgatory. He stood in the way of God's sword and prevented it from testing more people."

"Because he prevented the infection from spreading?"

"It was godless of him, but I could not make him understand that."

"And Mother Filippa? Why did she have to die?"

For the first time Imogene looked affected by her account.

"The old wolves were burned," she said. "It was my idea that I would sedate the new ones and transfer the mites to them. I had Iago with me, and a bottle of ether. But then Mother Filippa came down, and I . . . I used the ether on her instead. But she stopped breathing. She died. Without having confessed, without having cleansed her immortal soul. Without having passed the test. I had to do something to free her."

Only then did my father understand why she had tried to cleave Mother Filippa in two with a wood saw.

"Did you really believe that her soul would rise in front of your eyes?" he asked in astonishment.

"It did in the dream with the sword. And she thanked me! Because she was set free."

"And when this did not happen—what did you think then?"

"That she had sold her soul to the beast, and I had come too late after all."

I had fallen asleep on the chaise longue and woke up confused at an unfamiliar sound—the hollow *clack* every time my father's new plaster boot hit the floor.

"Maddie. Are you still up?"

"I was waiting for you. What time is it?"

"Almost two."

I turned up the wick on the table lamp a little. He stood for a few seconds with his hands resting on the mahogany table and studied his spread-out fingers as if he wanted to reassure himself that they were completely clean.

"Have you heard from your professor?" he asked. "News of the drama at the préfecture must have reached all the way to Heidelberg by now."

"He sent a telegram. I answered."

"Good. He must have been worried about you."

"Papa . . ."

"No, Maddie. I do not think I have the strength now. I know we have a lot to talk about, but . . . it will have to wait."

I got up. Helped him take off his coat and hat. Then I put my arms around him and rested my head against his chest until he began to stroke my hair.

The black widow of the Forchhammer Institute was no more thrilled to see me this time.

"Is he expecting you?" she asked.

"Not yet," I said. "It is a surprise."

I walked past her without allowing myself to be stopped. I liked the sound of my heels on the floor of the corridor. It was a decisive sound that announced a person who had an intention and a goal. I knocked sharply on the door to August's office, and it was only after I had knocked that I noticed what a loud conversation—no, an argument—I was interrupting.

Silence descended abruptly inside the office. Then the door was flung open, not by August but by the same young blond man who had interrupted our first meeting. This time there was no cheerful glint in the blue eyes, and his blond beard looked almost white because the rest of his face flushed darkly with some form of excitation.

"Fräulein," he said when he caught sight of me. "How appropriate." He offered a stiff and ironic salute and marched down the hall with a clacking of heels even more decisive than mine. "The changing of the guards, Frau Gross," he said when he passed the widow.

She stopped and looked from me to August, who had now appeared in the doorway. Her lips were, if possible, even narrower, but she did not say anything.

"Thank you, Frau Gross," said August. "Perhaps I might ask you to bring a fresh pot of tea? And a cup for Mademoiselle

Karno? Thank you for your telegram, Madeleine, but I did not think you were coming until tomorrow."

Already, my resolution had begun to show a few cracks, which was the very reason I had chosen not to wait. I was afraid that I would lose it entirely if I did not act without delay.

"I have come to give you an answer," I said.

"I thought so." He looked at me, not with the intense almost clinical probing I had already been the subject of several times but with a softer and more uncertain look. "I am quite anxious to learn what you have to say."

"I came to discuss the conditions of our marriage."

He nodded. But his gaze was still uncertain. "Come in," he said.

I sat down on the same chair as before. The office looked the same, with its peculiar mixture of jumbled sports equipment and clinical order.

"If we are to be married," I said, "then I have two demands and one question."

"Go ahead."

"First: You must never lie to me."

He did not answer too quickly or too easily.

"That is an unmerciful demand," he said. "Have you considered that the truth is not always the kindest thing two people can say to one another?"

"Yes. Then you will just have to be unkind."

There was a short glint of immaculate teeth. Whether a sneer or a smile, I could not tell for certain.

"You have my word," he finally said.

"And second: In all things you must treat me like a human being. Not like a woman. Do you understand?"

"Do you mean that? I know you are unusual, Madeleine; that is precisely what attracts me. But are you sure that you do not want to be . . . protected . . . just a little?"

"I think I have already answered that."

"Yes. You are right. One thing follows logically from the other. Go on."

"Those are my demands. Now comes the question."

"Yes?"

"Recalling that you have promised never to lie to me: *Why* do you want to marry me?"

He took a long, stumbling breath. Closed his eyes. Opened them again. Made fists. Opened his hands again. I just waited.

"Since I have promised never to lie to you: because I believe that I am in love with you. And because I have an urgent need to be married."

"Why?"

"My dearest Madeleine. And I really mean that. Dearest. The man you saw leave my office a moment ago . . ."

"Yes . . ."

". . . has been my lover for the last three years."

I did not say anything. I sat completely still and let his words sink down into me, all the way into my mind's darkest corners, where they met a dumb knowledge that had lived there for a while.

He observed me. Neither uncertain nor clinical this time, but searching.

"What are you thinking about?" he asked.

"I am thinking . . . that I am happy that you did not lie."

"And?"

"And that I would like you to kiss me."

"Now?"

"Yes. Now."

We both got up. He took my hand and slowly peeled the glove off it. Then he kissed me once on the back of the hand and once on the palm, precisely where my middle finger began. He pulled me close and placed his free hand behind my neck. And he kissed me, not choppily like last time, but for a long time, thoroughly and without reservation. My body gave the same unhesitating yes as last time. If that was animal-like, then I was an animal.

"What are you feeling right now?" I asked, and looked up into his face, a few hand lengths from mine.

"Much the same as you, I believe," he said.

"So you do . . . *like* women?"

"Women—and men."

"If we marry . . ."

". . . will you then be the only one? Will I be faithful to you? Is that what you are asking?"

"Um, actually not. But will you?"

"To the best of my ability. And probably as much as most other married men. I cannot promise more than that."

He was right. The truth was not always the kindest thing you could say. But I nodded. He was still keeping his word.

"If that was not what you wanted to know, what was it, then?"

"If you will let me be myself."

"What does that mean?"

"That you will not place me in a box labeled 'wife.' That you acknowledge that I also have the right to live a life. To make decisions. Grow. Become wiser. According to *my* plan for myself, not yours. And that I may continue to assist my father, even though that is probably not what is expected of the Professor's Wife."

He tipped his head slightly.

"This is not just about my expectations," he protested. "It is also about the expectations forced upon us by culture, society, and religion. Even if I say yes, it would be naïve to believe that all obstacles would then be overcome."

"I know. But I need to know that I will not also be fighting you."

This time it was clearly a smile. "Not over that," he said. "Never that."

When Frau Gross arrived with the tea, we had just let go of each other after yet another examination of man's animal nature. She looked back and forth between us and set down the tea tray with a loud and disapproving bang.

She looks upward, toward the blade. There is not much light; the sky is overcast and the hour early. There is no sun to glisten in the metal. Her face is oddly childish; the cropped hair makes her look like a boy. There are only a few people present in the préfecture's inner courtyard. The priest, whose constant praying is a low rumble that barely makes sense. Her uncle Emanuel, who stands there pale and shaken to his roots, unable to look away and yet equally unable to look at her. The executioner and his assistant, of course. And the Commissioner under whose jurisdiction she will soon belong.

And one more man. It is his face she finally seeks for, his gaze she meets. She knows he is the one who will announce that death has occurred. It is he who will take delivery of her dead body later in the day, and his scalpel, his instruments that will probe her body and her illness. She interrupts the priest.

"Do you think you have solved the riddle?" she asks. "When you have understood my illness, have you understood me?"

The priest believes she is speaking to him, but Doctor Death knows better.

"No," he says. "At that point I will be able to tell the story of your death. Not of your life."

She nods.

They strap her to the board and tip her forward, the executioner and his assistant, and she feels the pressure of the lunette like a cool collar around her neck. She closes her eyes, and does not open them again.

Acknowledgments

A huge thank-you to the patient people who have read, checked, examined, listened, and commented along the way:

Bent Lund
Lone-emilie Rasmussen
Bib Carlson—and all the experts at Memorial Sloan
    Kettering she laid siege to for my sake
Berit Wheler
Lars Ringhof
Anna Grue
Rudo Urban Rasmussen
And not least: Agnete Friis—on whom I cannot place
    the blame this time.